Imagination is more important than knowledge. For knowledge is limited, whereas imagination embraces the entire world.

ALBERT EINSTEIN

Copyright © 2017 by Cressida Cowell
Excerpt from *The Wizards of Once: Twice Magic* copyright © 2018 by Cressida Cowell

Cover art copyright © 2018 by Brandon Dorman. Cover design by Sasha Illingworth and Angela Taldone. Cover copyright © 2018 by Hachette Book Group, Inc.

Little, Brown and Company
Hachette Book Group
1290 Avenue of the Americas, New York, NY 10104
Visit us at LBYR.com

Originally published in 2017 by Hodder Children's Books in Great Britain
First U.S. Hardcover Edition: October 2017
First U.S. Trade Paperback Edition: September 2018

Little, Brown and Company is a division of Hachette Book Group, Inc. The Little, Brown name and logo are trademarks of Hachette Book Group, Inc.

The publisher is not responsible for websites (or their content) that are not owned by the publisher.

The Library of Congress has cataloged the hardcover edition as follows:
Names: Cowell, Cressida, author.
Title: The wizards of once / by Cressida Cowell.
Description: First U.S. edition. | New York: Little, Brown and Company, 2017. |
    "Originally published in 2017 by Hodder Children's Books in Great Britain." |
    Summary: Young wizard prince Xar, who has no magic, and warrior princess Wish, an
    outcast, team up on an adventure that brings them to witches long believed to be extinct.
Identifiers: LCCN 2017029938 | ISBN 9780316508339 (hardcover) |
    ISBN 9780316472159 (ebook) | ISBN 9780316508322 (library edition ebook)
Subjects: | CYAC: Adventure and adventurers—Fiction. | Princes—Fiction. |
    Princesses—Fiction. | Wizards—Fiction. | Witches—Fiction. | Magic—Fiction. |
    Imaginary creatures—Fiction.
Classification: LCC PZ7.C83535 Wiz 2017 | DDC [Fic]—dc23
LC record available at https://lccn.loc.gov/2017029938

ISBNs: 978-0-316-47216-6 (pbk.), 978-0-316-47215-9 (ebook)

Printed in the United States of America

LSC-C

10 9 8 7 6 5

This book is dedicated to my son Xanny, a Hero whose name begins with an "X" (and doesn't).

THE WIZARDS OF ONCE

written and illustrated by

CRESSIDA COWELL

Little, Brown and Company
New York Boston

This is a story with two heroes.

The boy, Xar, is from a Wizard tribe, but he has no Magic, and he will do ANYTHING to get it.

The girl, Wish, is from a
Warrior tribe,

but she owns a banned
Magic object, and she will
do anything to conceal it.

This way to the Warrior Capital
CONQUERED WARRIOR TERRITORIES
...t Mountain
WARRIOR EMPIRE
The Sweet Track
Iron Warrior Fort
The Ghost Wall
The QUEENDOM OF SYCHORAX
Wish's journey
D WOODS
THE BADWOODS
Wizard Fort
Xar's journey
Sinister Little Clearing
...NCANZO's ...INGDOM
Ragged River

Queen Sycorax's
IRON WARRIOR FORT

The Fort has seven ditches and is surrounded by endless forest inhabited by Sprites, Giants, werewolves, Ogrebreaths, and Something Worse than all of these...

Entrance to Queen Sychorax's dungeons

Wish's house

Once
there
was
Magic...

Prologue

Once there was Magic.

It was a long, long time ago, in a British Isles so old it did not know it was the British Isles yet, and the Magic lived in the dark forests.

Perhaps you feel that you know what a dark forest looks like.

Well, I can tell you right now that you don't. These were forests darker than you would believe possible, darker than inkspots, darker than midnight, darker than space itself, and as twisted and as tangled as a Witch's heart. They were what is now known as wildwoods, and they stretched as far in every direction as you can possibly imagine, only stopping when they reached a sea.

There were many types of humans living in the wildwoods.

The Wizards, who were Magic.

And the Warriors, who were not.

The Wizards had lived in the wildwoods for as long as anyone could remember, and they were intending to live there forever, along with all the other Magic things.

Until the Warriors came. The Warriors invaded from across the seas, and though they had no Magic, they brought a new weapon that they called IRON, and *iron was the only thing that Magic could not work on.*

The Warriors had iron swords, and iron shields, and iron armor, and even the horrifying Magic of the Witches was powerless against this metal.

First the Warriors fought the Witches, and drove them into extinction in a long and terrible battle. Nobody cried for the Witches, for Witches were bad Magic, the worst sort of Magic, the kind of Magic that tore wings from larks and killed for fun and could end the world and everyone in it.

But the Warriors did not stop there. The Warriors thought that just because *some* Magic was bad, *that* meant that ALL Magic was bad.

So now the Warriors were trying to get rid of the Wizards too, and the ogres and the werewolves, and the untidy quarreling mess of good sprites and bad sprites, who burned like little stars through the darkness and cast mischievous spells on each other, and the giants, who moved slow and careful through the undergrowth, larger than mammoths and peaceable as babies.

The Warriors had sworn that they would not rest until they had destroyed EVERY LAST BIT OF MAGIC in the whole of that dark forest, which they were chopping down as fast as they could with their iron axes to build their forts and their fields and their new modern world.

You have now entered

THE IRON WARRIOR EMPIRE.

ALL MAGIC IS BANNED

in this territory.

NO SPRITES, NO GIANTS,
NO ROGREBREATHS,
NO SNOWCATS, NO WEREWOLVES,
NO GREENTEETHS
(OR ANY OTHER MAGIC CREATURES).
NO FLYING,
NO ENCHANTED OBJECTS,
NO SPELLING, CURSING, OR CHARMING.
NO MAGIC WHATSOEVER.

And any Wizards entering these lands
may most unfortunately have
their heads removed.

By Order of Her Majesty

Queen Sychorax

QUEEN SYCHORAX, IRON WARRIOR QUEEN

This is the story of a young boy Wizard and a young girl Warrior who have been taught since birth to hate each other like poison.

The story begins with the discovery of

A GIGANTIC BLACK FEATHER.

Could it be that the Wizards and the Warriors have been so busy fighting *each other* that they have not noticed the return of an ancient evil?

Could that feather really be the feather of a Witch?

Could this really be the feather of a Witch?

The Witch feather

I am a character
in this story...
who SEES everyTHING,
Knows everything.
I will not tell you
who I am.

See if you can GUESS.

The story begins here.
(DON'T get lost.
These woods are DANGEROUS.)

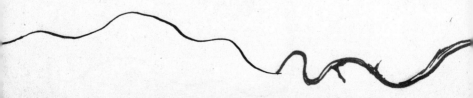

1. A Trap to Catch a Witch

It was a warm night for November, too warm a night for Witches, or so the stories said. Witches were supposed to be extinct, of course, but Xar had heard about the way they stank, and he imagined he could smell that now, in the quietness of the dark forest, a faint but definite stink of burning hair mixed with long-dead mice and a little kick of viper's venom; once smelled, never forgotten.

Xar, pronounced "Zar" (I don't know why, spelling is WEIRD), was a wild young human boy who belonged to the Wizard tribe. He was riding on the back of a giant snowcat in a part of the forest so dark and mangled and tangled that it was known as the Badwoods.

He should not have been there, for the Badwoods were Warrior territory, and if the Warriors were to catch him, well, what everyone *said* was that Xar would be killed on sight. Off with his head! As was the pleasant Warrior custom.

But Xar did not look even remotely worried.

He was a cheerful scruff of a boy, with a tremendous quiff of hair shooting upward from his forehead as if it had accidentally come into contact with some invisible vertical hurricane.

The snowcat he was riding was called Kingcat,

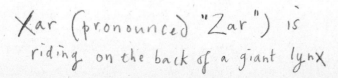

Xar (pronounced "Zar") is riding on the back of a giant lynx a noble creature who was a giant form of lynx, far too dignified for his cheeky master. Kingcat had shining paws so round they looked unreal, fur so deep it was like powder snow and such a rich silver-gray color that it was almost blue. The snowcat ran swiftly but softly through the forest, his black-tipped ears swiveling from side to side as he ran, for he was scared, although too proud to show it.

Only that very morning, Xar's father, Encanzo the Enchanter, King of Wizards, had reminded everyone that it was forbidden for any Wizard to dare set one toe in the Badwoods.

Xar meant well, but he was the kind of kid who acted first and thought later, and that kind of kid is often in trouble. In fact, he was the most disobedient boy in the Wizard kingdom in about four generations, and forbidding things only encouraged him.

In the past week:

Xar had tied the beards of two of the eldest and most respectable Wizards together when they were sleeping at a banquet. He had poured a love potion into the pigs' feeding trough, so the pigs developed mad, passionate crushes on Xar's least favorite teacher and followed him around wherever he went, making loud, enthusiastic squealing and kissing noises.

He had accidentally burned down the western trees in Wizard camp.

Most of these things hadn't been entirely *intentional,*

Spooked Snowcat looking around the perfectly safe clearing

exactly. Xar had just gotten carried away in the heat of the moment.

And yet none of these disobedient things was half as bad as what Xar was doing right now.

There was a large black raven flying above Xar's head.

"This is a very bad idea indeed, Xar," said the raven. The talking raven was called Caliburn, and he would have been a handsome bird, but unfortunately it was his job to keep Xar out of trouble, and the worry of this impossible mission meant his feathers kept falling out. "It isn't really fair to lead your animals and sprites and young fellow Wizards into all this danger..."

As the son of the King Enchanter, and a boy with a great deal of personal charisma, Xar had a lot of followers: a pack of five wolves, three snowcats, a bear, eight sprites, an enormous giant called Crusher, and a small crowd of other Wizard youngsters, all following Xar as if hypnotized, all shivering and scared and pretending not to be.

"Oh, you worry too much, Caliburn," said Xar, pulling Kingcat to a halt and jumping off his back.

"Look at this lovely, pretty little glade here...you see...PERFECTLY safe and exactly the same as the rest of the forest."

Ariel

Squeezjoos →

Xar looked around with breezy satisfaction, as if they had stopped in a delightful woodland dell filled with frolicking bunnies and baby deer, rather than a cold, eerie little clearing where the yews leaned in threateningly and the mistletoe dripped like warlocks' tears.

The other Wizards drew their swords, and the growling snowcats' fur stood up with fear to such an extent that they looked like furry puffballs. The wolves padded restlessly, trying to form a protective circle around their humans.

Bumbleboozle ↓

Only the smaller sprites shared Xar's enthusiasm, but that was because they were too young to know any better.

I don't know if you have ever seen a sprite, so I'd better describe these ones to you.

There were five larger sprites, all faintly resembling a human crossed with a fierce, elegant insect. When irritated, or bored (which was often), they blinked on and off like stars, and purple smoke drifted out of their ears. They were so see-through you could watch their hearts beating.

Then there were three smaller, younger ones, who because they were not yet adult

The Baby ↓

were known as "hairy fairies." Xar's favorite was an eager, slightly stupid little thing called Squeezjoos.

"Ooh, it's lovely! It's lovely!" squeaked Squeezjoos. "It's the tremunglousistly loveliest clearing I's ever seen! What's this fascintresting flower? Let me guess! It's a buttercup! It's a daisy! It's a gerangulum! It's a cauliflower!"

He flew into the upper branches of a particularly gloomy and sinister tree and perched on the edge of one of its fleshy flowers, which had ominous spikes on the ends of its leaves, and was in fact called a sprite-eating hobtrap. The flower snapped shut with the briskness of a mousetrap, capturing poor little Squeezjoos inside.

Caliburn landed on Xar's shoulder and gave a heavy sigh.

"I don't like to say 'I told you so,'" said Caliburn. "But we've only been in this perfectly safe little clearing in the Badwoods for one and a half minutes and you've already lost one of your followers to a carnivorous flower."

"Nonsense," scolded Xar good-naturedly, "I haven't lost him. That's the whole point about being a leader. Whenever my followers get into trouble, I rescue them, because that's what a leader does."

Xar climbed the tree, and two hundred feet up, swaying precariously on a couple of creaking twiglike boughs, he took out his dagger and popped open the sprite-eating hobtrap to release a panting little

Hmm. What's this fascintresting flower?

Squeezjoos
in the nick of time.

"I's fine!" squeaked Squeezjoos. "I's FINE! I
can't feel my left leg, but I's fine!"

"Don't worry, Squeezjoos! That's just
the hobtrap's digestive juices—the feeling will return in
a couple of hours!" Xar called out as he dropped down
from the tree. "You see? I'm a *great* leader! Stick with
me and you'll be fine."

The Wizard youngsters looked very thoughtful
indeed.

At that moment, Xar's older brother, Looter,
came out of the shadows behind them, sitting
astride a great gray wolf and followed by even
more sprites and animals and young Wizard
followers than Xar himself.

Xar stiffened, because he hated his
older brother, Looter.

Looter was a lot bigger than Xar. He was nearly as tall as their father, he was brilliant at Magic, he was good-looking and clever, and my goodness didn't he know it. He was the smuggest smug Wizard you could possibly imagine, and he often snitched on Xar to get Xar into trouble.

"What are *you* doing here, Looter?" stormed Xar suspiciously.

"Oh, I just followed you to see what unbelievably stupid and pointless thing my little baby brother was doing this time," drawled Looter.

"Great leaders like me don't do *pointless expeditions*!" fumed Xar. "We're here for a REASON. It's none of your business, but..."

Looter and Xar

Xar considered telling Looter some elaborate lie about what he was doing—but he couldn't resist showing off.

"...we're going to catch ourselves a *Witch*," boasted Xar proudly.

Ohhhhhhhh dear, oh dear, oh dear, oh dear.

This was the first time that Xar had mentioned to his followers the purpose of their expedition, and it was very unwelcome news indeed.

A *Witch*!

The bear, the snowcats, and the wolves went very still and began to shake. Even Ariel, the wildest and most unafraid of Xar's sprites, shot up into the air and momentarily disappeared.

"There are Witches in this part of the Badwoods now—I know it," whispered Xar excitedly, as if a Witch were a delightful sort of present that he was offering everyone.

There was a long silence, and then Looter and his Wizard followers began to laugh.

They laughed and they laughed and they laughed.

"Oh, come on, Xar," Looter said at last, once he'd gotten his breath back. "Even *you* must know that Witches have been extinct for centuries."

"Ah yes," said Xar, "but what if some of them survived and have been hiding all this time? Look!"

Here's what I found in this very clearing only yesterday!"

Out of his rucksack he carefully took an absolutely gigantic black feather.

It was huge, like the feather of a crow but much, much larger. A soft black, fading at the end to a glowing, shiny, dark green, the color of a mallard's head.

"It's a Witch feather…" whispered Xar.

Looter smiled his most superior smile.

"That's just the feather of some big old bird," scoffed Looter. "Some giant crow—you get some weird things living in the Badwoods."

Xar frowned and hung the feather from his belt.

"I've never seen a bird as big as this one must be," said Xar grumpily.

"It's all nonsense," smiled Looter. "Only a brainless fool like you wouldn't know that. Witches were destroyed forever."

Caliburn flapped downward and landed on Kingcat's head.

"'Forever' is a long word," said the raven.

We're going to catch ourselves a WITCH.

"You see!" said Xar triumphantly. "Caliburn is a bird of omen, who can see into the future and into the past, and *he* doesn't think that Witches are gone forever!"

"All I know is, if Witches were *not* to be extinct for some reason, you wouldn't want to go meeting one in a dark place," said Caliburn, shivering. "What do you want a Witch for, Xar?"

"I'm going to catch the Witch," said Xar, "and remove its Magic and use it for myself."

There was another horrified silence.

Eventually, Looter spoke. "*That*, little brother, is the worst plan I have ever heard in the whole history of plan-making."

"You're just jealous YOU didn't think of it," said Xar.

"I have a few questions," said Looter. "How are you going to catch the Witch in the first place?"

"That's what the net's for," said Xar, taking a net out of his rucksack and holding it up.

uh
`oh
,

uh
`oh,

uh
`oh...

You couldn't fault his *enthusiasm*, at least. "One of us will volunteer to be wounded ever so slightly, and then the blood will attract the Witch…"

"Oh great," smiled Looter. "Now you're going to wound one of your sad little followers? In a forest stuffed with raving werewolves and Blood-Sniffing Ogrebreaths? Come on, you're completely crazy…This plan is as pathetic as you are…"

Xar ignored him. "And then I'll entangle the Witch in this net when it attacks. Next question."

"Okay. Question two," said Looter. "No living Wizard has ever seen a Witch, so how do you know what one looks like?"

Xar opened his rucksack and took out a book the size of a large atlas entitled *The Spelling Book*.

Every Wizard is equipped with a Spelling Book, given to them at birth. Xar's was looking extremely worse for wear. One part of it was invisible (it accidentally got dropped in invisibility potion). Another bit was burned so black you could barely read it (this happened when Xar set Wizard camp on fire), and many of the pages were loose and dropping out all over the place (too many adventures to go into here).

Xar opened the book to the contents page, which had the twenty-six letters of the alphabet written on it in very large gold script. Xar spelled out "Witches" by tapping on each letter in turn, and *whirrrrrrrrr*, the book turned its own pages, which seemed to go on forever and ever and ever, the chapters in front turning invisible as the book riffled through the rest of them like an endless pack of cards, until eventually they stopped at the right place.

"That's weird...It doesn't say what they look like...but they're green...I *think*..." said Xar.

Someone else thought Witches could turn invisible and that they had acid blood. Another thought that they squirted blood through their eyes.

"I'm sure we'll recognize one when we see it," said Xar, impatiently shutting the Spelling Book. "They're supposed to be pretty horrible, aren't they?"

"Awesomely horrible," said Caliburn gravely. "The most terrifying creatures that ever walked this earth..."

"So even if you *do* catch this Witch, how will you persuade it to part with its Magic?" asked Looter. "I'm imagining that invisible, green-acid-blood-squirting Witches, the most terrifying creatures that ever walked this earth, will not give up their Magic if you ask them pretty please..."

"A*ha*," said Xar craftily. "I've thought of that."

With a grand flourish he put on some gloves, reached into his rucksack, and took out...a small saucepan.

Silence again.

"You do realize that's a *saucepan*?" said Looter.

"This is no ordinary saucepan," said Xar cunningly.

And then he took a deep breath before he made his shocking announcement.

"This particular saucepan is made out of IRON…"

Most of the Wizards took a horrified step backward. The sprites let out shrieks of alarm. Looter alone refused to be impressed.

In fact, he laughed so hard Xar thought he might fall over. "This is too good… You're going to fight a Witch with a *saucepan*!" sneered Looter. "You're no 'great leader,' Xar. You're a liar and a loser; our father is ashamed of you—and now I know why you're so keen to steal Magic from a Witch. There's a Spelling Competition at the Winter Celebration tonight and *YOU* can't do Magic…XAR CAN'T DO

This saucepan is made out of IRON.

MAGIC..." taunted Looter.

Xar turned red with embarrassment, then white with anger.

The fact that he couldn't do Magic yet was one of those hidden sores that you didn't want anyone else to see. Wizard children were not born Magic; their Magic came in when they were about twelve. Xar was *thirteen*, and his Magic still had not come in.

Xar had tried doing Magic. For countless hours he had tried. Really simple things, like moving stuff with his mind. But it was as if it were a muscle he didn't really have. "Relax," everyone said. "Relax, and it will happen." But it was like trying to move something with arms that weren't there.

And recently he had begun to worry...what if it NEVER happened? It was an unlikely calamity, but what a disgrace to the whole family it would be if a child born to the King Enchanter HAD NO MAGIC.

The thought of it made him feel a little sick.

"Poor little baby Xar..." crooned Looter cruelly.

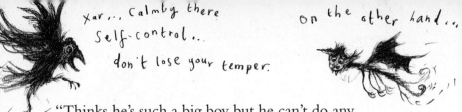

Xar... calmly there
Self-control..
don't lose your temper.

On the other hand...

"Thinks he's such a big boy but he can't do any Magic whatsoever…"

"My Magic WILL come in," hissed Xar. "But in the meantime, I swear," he spat, eyes so *small* with

or yous coulds hit him with the saucepan..

anger that he could barely see out of them, "I SWEAR I'm going to catch a Witch, and I will squeeze so much Magic out of that Witch, Looter, that I will BLAST you out of existence..."

"Oh yeah?" grinned Looter. He reached into his rucksack and took out one of his staffs. A Wizard's staff was about the size of a walking stick and Wizards concentrated Magic through them.

"Your spelling won't work on me when I am carrying IRON!" roared Xar, rushing forward to hit Looter with the saucepan.

Which was perfectly true, but most unfortunately, in his charge forward, Xar tripped over a long tangle of bramble and his gloved hands lost their grip on the saucepan and it went sailing over Looter's head and into the undergrowth.

Looter pointed his staff at Xar and whispered the word of a spell under his breath. Looter's body trembled as the Magic quivered through him and channeled out of his hand and into the staff, which concentrated it into one quick, fierce, hot bolt of Magic that blasted out of the end of the staff, hitting Xar on the legs.

Xar stopped, mid charge, his feet stuck to the ground by Looter's spell.

"HA! HA! HA! HA! HA!" laughed Looter's followers.

"*REMOVE THE SPELL!*" shouted Xar, struggling to shift his feet, but it was as if they had turned to lead.

"No, I don't think I will..." smiled Looter.

Xar lost his temper.

He snapped his fingers.

REEOOOWWW!

Before anyone could blink or think, Kingcat launched himself at Looter, huge jaws agape, eight hundred forty pounds of silvery-gray killing machine. Screaming in terror, Looter was pinned up against a tree trunk, looking aghast at the great cat's nightmare face, inches away from his own, and what felt like four kitchen knives sinking into his shoulder. They had already drawn blood.

None of Looter's own sprites or animals had time to move or protect him.

"One more click of my fingers," spat Xar, "and Kingcat will take off your head."

"Cheat!" panted Looter. "You cheated! You're not supposed to use your animals to attack a fellow Wizard!"

"*REMOVE THE SPELL!*" shouted Xar.

Looter was now every bit as angry as Xar himself. But what could he do?

He pointed his staff at Xar and removed the spell so that Xar's feet could move, and then Xar made a signal to Kingcat to let Looter go. "You're mad…a lunatic…" raged Looter as Kingcat dropped him, and Looter gazed in astonishment at the four neat, bleeding puncture wounds in his shoulder. "Your animal has BITTEN me…if you DARE to enter that Spelling Competition, I am going to ANNIHILATE you…"

Looter turned to Xar's followers.

"Who wants to come with ME rather than staying here with this silly little madman and his stupid Witch-trap?" shouted Looter.

One by one, Xar's followers backed away from Xar and toward Looter, and climbed on board their wolves or snowcats, muttering things like, "Sorry, Xar...this is a bit too crazy, even for you," and, "If Witches aren't extinct, they are bad Magic, Xar...We shouldn't be here..."

"You see?" crowed Looter triumphantly. "A great leader has to have someone to lead, and no one wants to follow a Magic-less lunatic. Good luck with meeting your *Witch*, loser-boy."

And then Looter rode away on the back of his wolf, followed by most of the other Wizards.

"Cowards!" roared Xar, nearly *crying* he was so angry. He ran into the undergrowth to retrieve the saucepan and then shook his fist at their departing backs.

"WE'LL SHOW YOU! WE'LL CATCH A WITCH, WE'LL TAKE MAGIC FROM IT, AND THEN WE'LL BE SO MAGIC *WE'LL FLY WITHOUT WINGS!*"

Xar turned with a sigh to the bedraggled remains of his followers.

Why did Looter always have to spoil everything?

Xar had hardly anyone left now, only three young Wizards whose Magic hadn't come in either: a girl called Heliotrope and two boys, Rush and Darkish, a large lad with even larger ears who had reached the age of seventeen without showing any signs of Magic whatsoever and who was slightly on the dim side.

Good luck with meeting your WITCH, loser-boy...

"Bother, he's left me with the losers," tutted Xar.

"Hear I say, Xar, that's a bit unfair," protested Rush.

"Will we really fly without wings?" said Darkish, flapping his big arms up and down.

"Of course we will," promised Xar, rubbing his hands together excitedly, for Xar could never stay down for long. "Those cowards are going to be *so sorry* they left…

"Darkish, you're the biggest, so you need to do the most digging," ordered Xar. "Rush, I'm afraid we're going to have to *wound* you a little to tempt the Witch into the trap…And if anything goes wrong…"

"I thought you said this mission was completely safe?" said Rush suspiciously.

"Well, nothing is ENTIRELY safe…" Xar backtracked quickly. "Life is dangerous, isn't it? After all, you could get killed just climbing a tree like I nearly was just now."

"This is not just climbing a tree!" spluttered Caliburn from above as the three young Wizards began to obey Xar's orders. "This is intentionally trespassing on Warrior territory, trying to set a trap for the scariest life-form that has ever walked this planet!"

Caliburn sighed.

Nobody was going to listen to *him*.

Caliburn perched rigid on the tree branch, with his head under his wing, as if—for as long as he buried his head under there, if *he* couldn't see the future—the future would not happen.

But, of course, the old bird knew that would not work.

Nighteye

Xar's Sprites

Timeloss

Tiffinstorm

Squeezjoos

Mustardthought

Bumbleboozle

Hinkypunk

Ariel

2. A Warrior Called Wish

Meanwhile, a stout and terrified Warrior pony with two young Warriors sitting on his back had set out secretly from iron Warrior fort under cover of darkness.

Warriors were not supposed to leave the fort after nightfall, for the Warriors were petrified of the Magic that was out in the forest.

Iron Warrior fort was the largest hill-fort you could possibly imagine, with thirteen watchtowers and encircled by seven great ditches cut into the hill. How scared these Warriors must be of everything that is Magic to have built such a mighty fort, white as bone, with little slit windows like the blink of a malevolent cat!

But nonetheless, this particular Warrior pony had managed to sneak out without being spotted by the nervous sentries who clanked their way along the fort walls. And perhaps, just perhaps, those sentries were *right* to be anxiously straining their eyes into the endless green wilderness that surrounded and engulfed them, watching, peering, struggling to see what might be out there.

For something BAD was watching the pony from high up in the treetops.

It is too early to tell what that *something* was.

Something BAD was watching the pony... from high in the treetops...

Many bad things live in the Badwoods. It could have been a cat-monster. It could have been a werewolf. It could have been a rogre. (Rogres are a bit like ogres, but a lot more scary.)

Time will tell what it was.

But it wasn't surprising that the pony had caught the *something's* attention.

For the pony was cantering far too noisily through the undergrowth, and bumping along on his back were a skinny little Warrior princess and her Assistant Bodyguard, Bodkin. They were wearing red cloaks over their armor, which made them shine out like stars in the dark green forest.

Short of wearing a big archery target on the top of their heads or a sign saying EAT ME, O HUNGRY MONSTERS OF THE BADWOODS, nothing could really have made them stand out more.

The princess had a very long and regal name, but everybody called her Wish.

Warrior princesses, of course, ought to be impressively tall and absolutely terrifying, like Wish's mother, Queen Sychorax.

But Wish was neither scary nor large.

She had a curious little face that was rather too interested in the world around her and hair that stuck out too wispily, as if she'd accidentally hit some unnoticed bit of static electricity.

A black patch covered her left eye. She seemed to be searching for something with the other.

"We're not supposed to come out here on our own in the *day*, let alone in the nighttime!" said Bodkin the Assistant Bodyguard, looking nervously over his shoulder. Bodkin wasn't the regular bodyguard of this weird little princess. Her proper bodyguard had fallen ill with a nasty autumn cold.

Bodkin had landed the highly sought-after role as understudy for a royal bodyguard, even though he was only thirteen years old, because he was very studious, and he had come out top of his class in the Advanced Arts of Bodyguarding exams.

However, this was the first time he had done the actual *job*, and he was finding it a good deal harder than he had thought it would be.

The princess wouldn't do what she was told, for starters.

And although he studied very hard, to be honest, Bodkin didn't really like fighting very much, and the thought that he might actually be in a real situation where there was a possibility of violence was making him feel a little sick.

"There could be werewolves or cat-monsters or giants out here," said Bodkin, "and then there's the bears and the jaguars and the Wizards and the Rogrebreaths…and even dwarves can get nasty when they're hunting in packs."

"Oh, don't be so gloomy, Bodkin!" replied the princess. "We'll go back as soon as we find my pet. This is all your fault anyway. You frightened him when you said you'd report him to my mother, and so he completely panicked and ran away."

"I was only trying to stop you from getting into any more trouble!" said Bodkin. "You're not allowed pets! They're against the Warrior rules!"

Bodkin was a boy who really *believed* in the rules. He was hoping to work his way up from being an Assistant Bodyguard to a Household Defender, and you didn't do THAT by breaking any rules.

"And you're most particularly not allowed this *kind* of pet…"

"He must be terrified," worried Wish. "We couldn't possibly leave him running away all on his own in the terrors of the Badwoods—all alone and scared, and raving fangmouths might be chasing him or something…

"AHA!" she said with triumphant relief. "THERE HE IS!"

AHA!
There he is!

She hauled on
the pony's reins to
bring him to a halt,
and picked up something
that was scurrying through
the undergrowth. "Thank
goodness!" She stroked whatever-
it-was gently and made soothing
noises as if to say: "Don't worry, it's fine,
you're safe now, you're with me"—the sort of
noises that might calm a petrified dog or cat or rabbit
that had been running scared and all alone through the
Badwoods after the setting of the autumn sun.

The pet was not a dog or a cat or even a rabbit.

"That pet of yours is a SPOON!" objected Bodkin.

The Assistant Bodyguard was right.

The pet was, indeed, a large iron dinner spoon.

"So he is," said Wish, as if she'd only just noticed,
getting back up on the pony and drying off the spoon
with the end of her sleeve.

"And that spoon is ALIVE, Princess, he's *alive!*"
said Bodkin, giving a little shiver of horror as he looked
at the spoon. "Which means that he is an
entirely banned Magic enchanted object.
Haven't you seen the signs all over Warrior
fort? Absolutely no Magic! No enchanted

That pet of yours is a SPOON.

objects! No animals indoors! All Magic must be reported to a higher authority so that reports can be made and the Magic gotten rid of!"

"I'm not sure he's Magic, exactly…" said Wish hopefully. "He's just a little *bendy*…"

"Of course he's Magic!" snapped Bodkin. "*Ordinary* spoons do not jump up and down to get you to stroke them; *ordinary* spoons just lie quietly and feed you your dinner! Look at this one! He's *bowing* to me!"

"So he is," said Wish proudly. "Isn't that clever?"

Bodkin breathed very heavily indeed. "This is not clever. This is breaking so many rules it is difficult to know where to begin. Where did you find this spoon?"

"He just turned up in my room one day, like a wild mouse or something, so I fed him some milk, and he's been hanging out with me ever since…which was nice because before he came, I was a bit lonely. Haven't you ever been lonely, Bodkin?"

"Well, I have, actually," admitted Bodkin. "Ever since I did so well on the exams and

Before he came, I was a bit lonely …

got appointed your personal Assistant Bodyguard, all the other Assistant Bodyguards said I had gotten above myself and now they're not talking to me and—*Hang on a second!* That's not the point!

"The point is," said Bodkin, "if an enchanted object turns up unexpectedly in Warrior fort, you really ought to tell your mother, Queen Sychorax, immediately, so she can remove its Magic, NOT adopt it as your pet."

At the mention of Queen Sychorax's name, the spoon swayed from side to side as if terror-stricken and then hopped into Wish's waistcoat, hiding behind her body armor, so that only the bowl that was his face was staring out, lit up with a strange, glowing Magic light.

"Look, you've scared him again!" Wish replied. "The thing is, I don't think he wants his Magic removed."

"It's a completely painless process," said Bodkin.

"But he doesn't want to do it," said Wish.

"All right, then," said Bodkin, folding his arms determinedly. "In which case you have to let the spoon go, back into the wild. He belongs out here in this scary jungle with all the other monsters and Magic things. These are his people. I am putting my foot down, Princess. You absolutely cannot take him back to the iron fort with you. You cannot keep this spoon as your pet. It's against the rules, and you will get in the most terrible trouble if anyone finds out."

Wish looked very sad indeed. "But I kind of identify with the spoon because he's like me and he doesn't fit in with all the other spoons—"

"He doesn't fit in with the other spoons because he's *alive*, Princess, he's *alive*!" interrupted Bodkin.

"And all the other Warriors ignore me," Wish carried on. "You and this spoon are my only two friends. If I lose the spoon, that just leaves you."

"Well, technically speaking, *I* can't be your friend either, because *you* are a princess and *I* am a servant, and those are the rules," explained Bodkin.

"In which case, if I let the spoon go, I will be losing my only friend!" said Wish.

"Okay, Wish." (Bodkin was so upset that he forgot to call her "Princess.")

It was time for some stern words.

"I like you, I know you mean well, but let's face it. The reason you haven't got any friends is you're a bit weird, and weird doesn't go down well in Warrior fort. You need to try to be more normal. And the first step to being normal is to get *rid of the Enchanted Spoon*."

Wish tried one last, desperate argument.

"But my mother has enchanted objects *herself*!" said Wish. "What about this, then?"

To Bodkin's horror, Wish drew a large ornamental sword from her scabbard.

It wasn't like an ordinary sword. It had a very dirty, old-fashioned hilt, and even beneath the greenish grime that covered it, you could see that it was beautifully designed, with intertwining leaves and mistletoe and the leaves of other sacred trees twisting all over it.

On one side of the blade was carved these words, in very fancy curly old-fashioned script:

Once there were Witches...

And when Wish turned the blade over, the other side was engraved with:

...but I killed them.

"*Where did you get that sword?*" said Bodkin in awed tones.

"Well, it was quite odd, actually. I found it lying in the main courtyard yesterday afternoon, and it didn't seem to belong to anyone, so I picked it up."

"*Didn't you hear the announcement at breakfast this morning about how a very valuable sword had gone missing from your mother's dungeons?*" Bodkin gasped. "*Didn't you guess it might be THIS sword? Didn't you wonder if picking things up that don't belong to you might be STEALING?*"

"Yes, I did," admitted Wish, stroking the sword longingly. "But I was just going to hang on to it for a while longer, pretending it was mine. I'm so ordinary, and it's so special, and it would be lovely to own something so special, don't you think?"

"*No, I don't think! Thinking is DANGEROUS! The Defenders of the Royal Household are turning the fort upside down looking for this sword, and you've STOLEN it!*" goggled Bodkin.

"I haven't stolen it, I've only *borrowed* it. I was just about to give it back, but then you frightened the spoon and I thought we might need something special to protect us if we were going into the Badwoods on our own. I have a very strong feeling that it might be an *Enchanted* Sword," ended Wish triumphantly. "Even my mother has enchanted objects, which means they must be all right!"

"Your scary mother isn't keeping that sword as a PET!" cried Bodkin, waving his long, thin arms around. "You don't keep pets in DUNGEONS! She's locked it up in the dungeons to keep it safe!"

Wish looked at the sword in a slightly worried way, as if this was only just occurring to her. "Ohhhh... yeeeessss ...Now that I come to think of it, you could be right about that. It did seem kind of out of character for my mother...She doesn't really like anything Magic, does she?"

"Where have you been living for the past thirteen years?" cried Bodkin. "There are whopping great signs up all over the fort—you can't have missed them! Your mother LOATHES the Magic! She HATES the Magic! She has sworn never to rest till she has rid THE ENTIRE

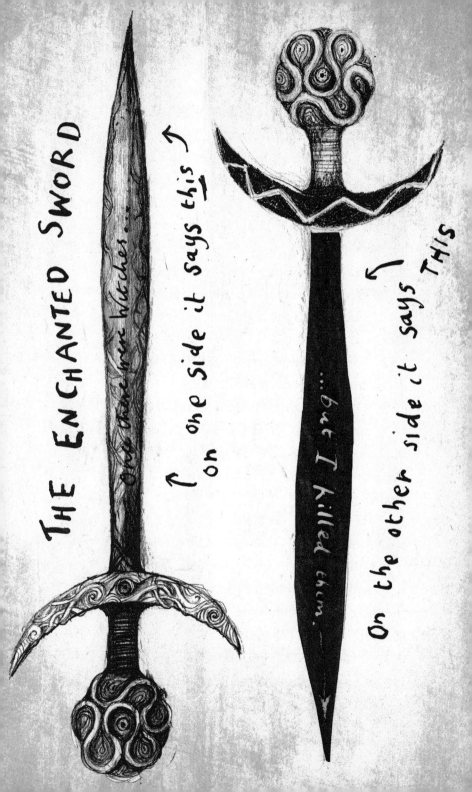

THE ENCHANTED SWORD

Once there were witches...

On one side it says this

...but I killed them.

On the other side it says THIS

FOREST OF ANYTHING MAGIC AT ALL!"

Wish furrowed her brow. "Yes, I have to say I don't really understand that. Surely, just because SOME Magic is bad, it doesn't mean that ALL Magic is bad?"

"You're not supposed to understand!" screeched Bodkin. "You're a WARRIOR; you're not supposed to be asking questions! It's very, very simple—you're just supposed to be obeying the Warrior rules!"

Wish suddenly looked very dejected.

The spoon now standing on top of her head drooped.

"Bother, you're right," said Wish sadly. "I've messed up again, haven't I, Bodkin?"

"You most certainly have," said Bodkin.

And then he added hurriedly, "Your Highness," for in the excitement of the situation he had forgotten the Warrior rules about "How to Correctly Address Royalty."

This was the problem with Wish.

Whenever you spent any time with her, you found yourself breaking rules without even realizing it.

"If my mother ever finds out about this, she's going to be

BOTHER. I've mess- up again, haven't I Bodkin?

hopping mad, isn't she?" said Wish, even sadder still.

"Absolutely hopping," agreed Bodkin, giving a little shiver at the thought of it.

"I wish I was NORMAL like everyone else," said Wish. "What can I do to make everything right again?"

Bodkin gave a sigh of relief, for it looked like at last, the princess was seeing sense.

"Okay, don't be sad, all is not lost," he said, giving Wish a little pat on the shoulder to cheer her up. "You didn't mean to do the wrong thing. But you need to release this spoon into the wild RIGHT NOW and take this sword back to the fort immediately, and you have to stop doing things like this and start behaving like a normal Warrior princess and—Hang on—What was that?"

There was a sudden noise above them, like the snapping of a twig when *something* brushes up against it.

They had been so busy arguing they had forgotten that they were not in the safety of iron Warrior fort, about to dig into a splendid dinner (for Warriors were very keen on their food).

They were all alone in the Badwoods, after dark.

And for the first time, they realized they were being watched.

I mentioned, did I not, at the beginning of this chapter, that something bad was watching them, quiet and dangerous, up in the treetops?

A cold feeling came over the back of Wish's neck, where the hairs pricked up like the spines on a hedgehog. She looked all around, at the silent black trees, their branches twisting, gnarled like the knobbliest of goblins' fingers.

She looked up, and she could not see anything, only perhaps a certain darkening and a shimmering thickening of the air above them as if that air was choked with something awful, as indeed it was. And the coldness radiating out of the heart of that shining density was a coldness you have never felt before.

Colder than the coldest depths of the northern ocean, colder than icicles, colder than polar caps, colder even than death itself.

The freezing mist of the wildwoods' ancient past crept under Wish's armor and sank like death into her bones.

Was it Wish's imagination, or did the very air above them seem to be GRINNING?

The spoon stood straight up on top of Wish's head and sniffed the air around them.

Suddenly he went rigid as if sensing something terrible…and dived down into Wish's armor to hide.

Wish put on her helmet.

"Run, pony, run!" squealed Wish, and the exhausted little pony started violently and broke into a shambling, terrified, wobbling gallop.

Bodkin
the
Assistant
Bodyguard

Anybody watching would have thought that they were mad, for it looked like they were running away from nothing at all.

But there was definitely something very odd going on.

Wish and Bodkin could see nothing above them
except for the dark night sky, stars, and trees, but
something about the way the tree branches were moving
suggested that an invisible presence was hurtling against
them.

And the air rushing above them was so cold that
it burned the top of Wish's forehead, and as the pony
galloped faster and faster, the wind blowing directly
behind them began to make an odd noise, like no wind
that Wish had ever heard before.

"Now, you see, Bodkin, aren't you glad I brought
the sword with me? I thought we might need it," panted
Wish, trying not to panic.

"Glad? Glad? We could be sitting right now in front
of our dinner safely in the dining room in Warrior fort—
and I think today it was going to be deerburgers, which
is my favorite—and this pony is going in the wrong
direction!" flapped Bodkin. "The fort is the other way!"

But whatever-it-was that was chasing them didn't
want them to go back to the fort, so it was chasing them
farther and farther and farther into the Badwoods.

"Does anyone know we're out here?" cried
Bodkin, who had drawn his bow and was shooting
desperate arrows upward even though he was a terrible
shot and he couldn't see what he was shooting at. "Will
they send out search parties?"

"I'm afraid not," said Wish, squinting up, trying to work out what was pursuing them, "or not till the morning, anyway. I told my mother I was going to bed early with a headache."

"Brilliant," said Bodkin, "brilliant. As it happens, I think I can feel a bit of a headache coming on myself... Don't worry, Princess... You mustn't worry... I'm here to protect you..."

Wish shook the spoon at whatever-was-following-them.

She may have been a somewhat weird Warrior princess, but she certainly had courage.

"YOU BETTER NOT FOLLOW US, WHATEVER-YOU-ARE!" shouted Wish at the terrifying, screeching nothingness. "For WE are armed with an *ENCHANTED SPOON*!"

"The *sword*, Princess," murmured Bodkin through white lips. "The sword sounds more scary..."

"*AND* A SWORD!" shouted Wish, waving the sword in her right hand and the spoon in her left. "A sword so dangerous it was LOCKED IN MY MOTHER'S DUNGEONS!"

But that, if anything, seemed to encourage whatever-was-following-them even more, for the wind above them gave a hungry whine and rushed after them even faster.

"Never fear, Princess!" cried Bodkin, shaking so much with anxiety that he could barely load his bow. "This is a bad situation, but *I* will save you, for as a personal Assistant Bodyguard to the princess *I* have been trained in the most Advanced Arts of Bodyguarding!"

Unfortunately Bodkin discovered in those desperate moments that he had a terrible disadvantage as a potential bodyguard.

He had a medical condition that caused him to fall asleep in situations of extreme danger.

He had barely said the last words of that brave speech before he collapsed on the princess's shoulder, snoring loudly.

"Bodkin!" shrieked the princess. "What are you doing????"

Snore, snore.

"Bodkin!" shrieked Wish. "Wake up NOW!"

Bodkin woke up with a start, mumbling, "Where? What? How?"

"Badwoods…" panted the princess. "Being chased…something terrible…Advanced Arts of Bodyguarding…"

"Oh yes! I've been carefully trained for exactly these sorts of life-or-death emergencies!" cried Bodkin, fitting another arrow into his bow, and unfortunately falling asleep again at the moment of aiming it, so that

You better not follow us!
For WE are armed with an
Enchanted SPOON!

he tipped forward, and accidentally shot the poor pony at the hindquarters.

The pony squealed protestingly as the arrow grazed his bottom, and then ran on in wild desperation through the pitch-dark forest.

Wish's heart was beating fast like a rabbit's, and she didn't even notice when the brambles shredded her clothes to ribbons and tore long, painful scratches into her legs.

The pony came upon an ice-cold stream and forced his way through the briars and splashed down into it—though the cold of the water burned them all like fire—in the hope that whatever-was-following-them would be put off the scent.

The pony clambered out the other side and galloped through the darkness.

Oh murmuring mistletoe... thought Wish in terror.

I should never have done this.

Magic is banned for a reason.

Warriors are not allowed out after dark for a reason.

Iron Warrior fort is built like it is for a reason.

She could feel her heart beating so hard it felt like any moment it would break out of her chest.

"Faster! Faster!" urged Wish, so choked with panic she could barely breathe. The pony galloped into a sudden clearing in the forest.

The whining of this strange wind had an edge to it now, like the painful scritch of chalk on stone—a sound that grew louder as if building up to attack.

Louder and louder the noise grew…

SCRRITTCCHHHHHH!!!

There was an extraordinary noise as if the very air itself were being torn apart like a giant piece of paper.

Terrified, Wish turned her face upward to confront the attack with her drawn sword…

There was a shout from a human voice somewhere behind her and…

Suddenly everything happened very quickly.

3. The Witch Feather Begins to Glow...

O kay, I'm getting a little fed up now," said Rush, who was lying, pretending to be wounded, in front of a concealed net that was Xar's Witch-trap. "We've been here for hours."

"Make your 'helps' a bit more pathetic," Xar called out bossily from his hiding place behind a nearby tree.

"I could wound Rush if you like," grinned Tiffinstorm, showing little fangs. "He looks quite tasty."

"I'm fine, thank you," said Rush hastily. "Face it, Xar, maybe Witches really are extinct like everyone says...and it's getting really late. Frankly, I'm more worried about Warriors than I am Witches."

"Don't worry," said Xar breezily. "CRUSHER WOULD TELL US IF THERE WERE ANY PROBLEMS, WOULDN'T YOU, CRUSHER?"

Crusher's job was hanging on to the rope to pull the net tight when the Witch came upon them, and keeping lookout. The giant was a long way up, so Xar had to shout to get his attention.

"Hmmm..." said Crusher thoughtfully. "There IS a bit of a problem, actually," he

admitted, but Xar could not hear him because the giant was so far away and he spoke so ve-e-ry, ve-ry slowly. (Giants operate in a slightly different timescale from everyone else.)

However, it didn't really matter, because Xar wasn't listening anyway and the problem that Crusher was thinking about was slightly different from Xar's idea of a problem.

Some people think that because giants talk slowly, they must be stupid. But they could not be more wrong. Giants are big, and they tend to have BIG thoughts, and Crusher was a Longstepper High-Walker giant, one of the deepest thinkers of all.

So the problem, thought Crusher, *is this: Is there a limit to the expanding universe, or will it go on expanding forever?*

(I told you it was a BIG problem.)

If space is infinite, and stars are infinite, thought Crusher, *doesn't that mean that there must also be infinite numbers of Crushers out there? How is that possible and what are the implications of that?*

Which was all very interesting, but unfortunately it did mean that although Crusher was vaguely holding on to the rope, his mind was wandering among the stars and therefore he was entirely unaware of any approaching danger.

A Longstepper High-Walker giant does not make the ideal lookout.

"Just a little longer, Rush..." whispered Xar, eyes bright. "There are Witches about—I'm sure I can smell them..."

Xar closed his eyes and sniffed the air.
Please...thought Xar, *please, gods of the trees and the water... You don't know how hard it is, growing up in a world full of Magic when you have no Magic of your own. Everybody laughing at you, pitying you... Let that be a Witch because I need to be Magic. I want to make my father proud of me.*

At that very moment, Xar's sprites sprang out of the darkness to rotate around Xar's head in a glowing spritely halo, eyes blazing red suddenly, hissing like a nest of wasps: *"Witchessss... Witchessss... Witchessss..."*

"I knew it!" said Xar in excitement. "Draw your wands, sprites! Get your bows ready. We're about to be attacked!"

"No, we're not..." sighed Heliotrope, who was now thoroughly fed up with Xar and his mad schemes and wanted to go home. "Witches are extinct— everyone knows that..."

But Rush, lying on the ground, felt the air all around him grow suddenly so cold that he shivered.

Xar called down encouragingly, "Don't move,

Rush! You're doing brilliantly...You look very victim-like...The Witches are really going to be fooled.

"Crusher! Get ready now!"

Silence from above.

"CRUSHER!!!!"

"Yes? I think I've made a breakthrough!" announced Crusher, thrusting his head down through the tree canopy, with snailish slowness in human time but surprising quickness in giant time, because Crusher was excited. "I'm leaning toward the idea that space might be FINITE..."

"Crusher! That's not important right now! And I told you not to think deep thoughts!" snapped Xar, for the process of deep thought made a giant's head smoke and smolder like a forest fire, and this meant that their exact location could be pinpointed from a considerable distance by, say, enemy Warriors or Rogrebreaths or, indeed, Witches.

"We're being attacked!" shouted Xar in exasperation.

"Oh!" Crusher broke off from his giant daydreams, remembered where he was, and got a good hold on the rope.

What nobody noticed, in the anxiety of the moment, was the great black feather swinging from Xar's belt.

If anyone had been looking at the feather at that moment, they might have noticed that it had begun to GLOW, dully but ominously, in the darkness.

I'm sure there's some sort of reasonable and scientific explanation for it ...

But a crow's feather would not do that, however large the crow.

4. The Witch-Trap Catches Something

From Xar's point of view, here is what happened. Xar was waiting, hiding behind the tree, trembling with excitement.

The sprites hummed louder and louder, whirling around his head, screeching, *"Witcheswitcheswitcheswitches!!!!!!!!!"*

Xar heard the sound of hoofbeats, and *something* galloped into the moonlit clearing, too fast to stop, something that if Xar could have seen it properly had the legs of a pony below, and human bodies in the middle, and a great indistinct cloud above it.

What strange monster was this?

Rush was frozen with terror, he could not move, he would be run down…

SCRRITTCCHHHHHH!!!

There was a tearing noise, as if the atmosphere were being ripped apart like paper.

And then Xar's senses were assaulted all at once by the worst smell you could possibly imagine: rotting corpse and moldy eggs and dead-man-six-weeks-gone with unwashed-feet-and-underarm-reek, while a splintering scream like the death agony of five hundred foxes buried itself in Xar's brain and reverberated inside his head till he felt like he might go crazy.

What is going on????? thought Xar, with the tiny part of his mind that could still think.

Rush curled up like a little hedgehog, rather pathetically putting his hands over his head, as if that would protect him from whatever horror was making THAT noise and THAT smell.

Xar yelled up to Crusher.

And then everything happened all at once.

The cloud or wind howled louder. Who knew what it was? Maybe Xar was right, and it really was a Witch...But *whatever-it-was*, it screamed downward, and at exactly the same time seven of the sprites whacked their spells with their wands, sending the spells whipping toward the center of the clearing, with white-hot heat, like speeding fireflies, and Crusher hauled like crazy on the net and there was a gigantic explosion...

THWACK!

BANNNNNNGGG!

Xar threw himself flat on his stomach behind the tree to get out of the way.

There was a great screeching noise.

Something was ricocheting around the clearing, something unusually huge and dark and feathery, and then exiting with a dreadful piercing wail.

Clouds of black and green smoke filled the glade, and Xar got to his feet, coughing.

Hanging in the center of the clearing was his dangling Witch-trap, Crusher holding on to the other end for dear life.

Something was struggling wildly inside, and all around the net was a force field of air, red as blood, red as fiery flame.

What on earth just happened? thought Rush, coughing and choking with the remnants of that smell, and unable to believe that he was still alive.

"It worked..." Xar gasped, staggering to his feet, thanking his lucky stars. "Oh my goodness...it WORKED! We've done it...We've really caught a Witch...That's its force field...Stop attacking it, sprites, it's pointless..."

Sure enough, the sprites' spells, shooting out sparks, were trying to push their way through the bright red air. But the air turned redder still, and spiky, like living, breathing, flaming thorns.

Rush looked at the struggling net and gulped, openmouthed. "Oh by mistletoe and all things ivy, maybe Xar really has done it... Maybe he's caught a Witch!!! Let's get out of here..."

Rush scrambled to his feet, jumped on the back of his snowcat, and ran away, as did Heliotrope and Darkish.

They assumed that Xar was going to follow them.

But Xar was about the only boy in the entire world who really was crazy enough to stay in a clearing with an actual live Witch.

"You's BRILLIANT! You's MARVELOUS! You's the best leader in the WORLD! Er... what's do we's do now, Boss?" asked Squeezjoos nervously.

Even Xar was now terrified, but he would rather die than admit this to his sprites and his animals.

"Surround the Witch!" ordered Xar.

Complaining loudly, the sprites nonetheless surrounded the net in a burning circle, and Xar forced himself to put one foot in front of the other and approach the net, his hands so sweaty with fear he nearly dropped the very small saucepan.

The smell in the clearing was so chokingly bad it was like swimming through a disgusting sulfurous soup.

Xar stood
underneath the net,
staring up at it as it slowly swung
above them, back and forth, back and
forth...

Rather unexpectedly, the four distinctive
legs of a HORSE were dangling down from the
holes in the net.

"Wow..." breathed Xar. "Who would have
thought it? Witches aren't like birds, they're more like
centaurs.

"Okay, Witch!" shouted Xar, trying to make his
voice sound scary and waving the saucepan threateningly
in one trembling hand. "Don't try anything stupid! We
have you completely surrounded, and I am armed with
a weapon made of IRON!"

There was a short silence, and then a small, shaky
voice from inside the net said:

"*I'm* not a Witch...Witches are extinct!
Everyone knows that...Why are you attacking
us? What do you want?"

"Well, of course, a Witch isn't going to
ADMIT it's a Witch, is it?" said Xar. "Don't
you try to trick me, Witch!"

"I'm not trying to trick you," said the
voice, less shaky now and more indignant.

"My name is Wish, not Witch.
Even if Witches *did* exist, they're supposed to be
green, aren't they? With acid blood and feathers and
everything..."

There was another pause. "Well, what kind of
monster ARE you, then?" demanded Xar. "Are you
some kind of centaur?"

"No, no," said the voice. "That's just my pony.
I think he may have fainted. My friend Bodkin and I
were going through the forest, and something suddenly
started chasing us...LET US GO!"

Botheration. It wasn't a Witch after all. It had all been for nothing. His horrible, superior older brother had been right all along, and the entire evening had been a waste of time.

"Let whatever-it-is down, Crusher," sighed Xar, flattened by pulverizing disappointment.

Slowly, Crusher let down the net. The pony had not fainted, poor thing—he had been hit by one of Tiffinstorm's sleep-inducing curses and he lay on the ground, snoring loudly.

But Xar saw that there were humans in the net too, a small human dressed head-to-toe in armor, who scrambled up from the snoring pony and stepped out of the net, waving a large ornamental sword, and behind the teeny little human, a slightly larger human, skinny as a rake and also encased entirely in armor, who was stumbling to his feet as if he was just waking up.

We know that these two humans were Wish and Bodkin. (Bodkin was the taller one, and Wish was the little one with the sword.)

But Xar had never met a Warrior before.

And he could never imagine that Wish and Bodkin might be heroes of this story, just like he was himself.

All *Xar* saw was that these were two humans wearing iron breastplates and carrying iron swords, which meant they must be Warriors, and Xar had been brought up to hate the Warriors like poison, because they were the enemy.

Excellent.

After lurching this way and that from fear to excitement to disappointment, Xar was spoiling for a nice, straightforward FIGHT.

If he couldn't catch a Witch, at least he could kill an enemy.

"*WARRIORS!*" cried Xar fiercely, narrowing his gaze, getting a good grip on his saucepan, and drawing a heavy oak staff from his rucksack.

"Warriorsss... Warriorss... Warriorsss..." hissed the sprites, burning red with anger. "Kill them... kill them... kill them..."

"It's a *WIZARD and its creatures!*" cried Bodkin in alarm, pointing at Xar and leaping protectively in front of Wish. "And they look aggressive!"

They certainly did, and Wish stared around, petrified, at the burning sprites, on fire with fury, flames licking off their long limbs, sparks spitting all over the place; the growling wolves, bear, and snowcats showing their teeth; and way, way above them, the gigantic figure of the giant in the background.

They were hopelessly outnumbered, and giants were supposed to eat people. Sprites could Magic you

into a slow death, and one look at those
snowcats told you they could tear you
to pieces. Wish had an Enchanted
Sword, but she knew she wasn't a
very good swordfighter, and let's
face it, Bodkin hadn't been much
help as a bodyguard so far.

They didn't have a chance.

"Don't worry, Princess!" shouted
Bodkin bravely. "I'll deal with them!"

Bodkin drew his spear and shook
his sword.

He advanced in a menacing
manner.

He caught sight of the giant.

He stopped dead in his furiously
warlike pose.

He blinked twice.

And then his eyes closed, his
head flopped forward, and he
slo-o-owly toppled over like a
falling tree, accidentally chopping his spear
in half with his sword as he fell.

And he lay there with his mouth open.

Xar looked down at the fallen Bodkin in
astonishment. Was this a trick?

"Snowcats! Wolves! Cover me!" ordered Xar. Their fur bristling, the animals circled around Xar, ready to pounce. "Bear! Cover the guy on the ground! He may be faking!"

The bear put a big bear paw on Bodkin's chest and sat on him.

"Sprites! Leave this to me! I'll show these wicked Warriors that we Wizards know how to fight!" cried Xar, and he launched himself at Wish, saucepan in one hand, staff in the other.

Wish parried Xar's thrust with the Enchanted
Sword, and the fight began.

Wish found that fighting with an Enchanted
Sword made things a lot easier than fighting with a
normal sword. The Enchanted Sword could anticipate
where the next saucepan-thrust or lunge from Xar's staff
was coming from and throw itself in the way of that
attack, dragging Wish with it.

The sword jerked her this way and that, with

Wish gripping it with both hands, looking for all the world as if she were hanging on to the tail of a wild bull.

Caliburn was in a frenzy of worry, and he flapped about the fighters' heads, squeaking: "The Enchanted Sword! Be really careful with that Enchanted Sword! Don't let it touch you! There's something wrong with it!"

"An Enchanted Sword!" breathed Xar. "Impossible!"

How could a *Warrior* be fighting with an Enchanted Sword? Warriors didn't use Magic.

The Enchanted Sword made a sweeping lunge forward, and this thrust finally disarmed Xar. His staff went spinning into the undergrowth, followed by the saucepan.

"Do you surrender?" said Wish, holding the Enchanted Sword above Xar's head.

"I surrender," said Xar from between gritted teeth.

"Don't trust him! Wizards are tricksters!" shouted Bodkin, who had woken up from his faint but was still trapped beneath the bear.

Wish ignored this instruction, and instead relaxed, stepped back, and lowered the sword.

Which was a mistake. Bodkin was right. Xar was not to be trusted.

"Kingcat! Nighteye! Attack!" shouted Xar as soon as the sword was lowered.

Kingcat leaped in and smashed Wish down to the ground. The force of the blow knocked the Enchanted Sword out of Wish's hand, and as soon as it left her grip the enchantment left it—the sword went dead and fell to the forest floor, as cold and lifeless as a normal sword.

Xar picked it up, and eight hundred and forty pounds of powder-blue giant lynx in the form of Kingcat leaned on Wish's chest and cracked open her helmet with his jaws, like a nutcracker cracking a nut.

The two halves of the helmet fell away, and Xar was looking straight into the face of an odd-looking little girl with a patch over one eye.

"It's a girl!" said Xar in surprise.

The sprites laughed uproariously at this. "Xar was being beaten by a girl…"

Wish was looking straight into the face of a snarling snowcat and a Wizard boy, who was holding the Enchanted Sword over her head in a purposeful fashion.

"And now," said the Wizard boy, "do *you* surrender?"

5. When Bad Stars Cross and Worlds Collide...

I most certainly will *not* surrender!" said Wish.

"You CHEATED!"

"Wizards don't play by Warrior rules," said Xar.

"Cheat of a Wizard!"

"Wickedness of a Warrior!"

"Curse-maker!"

"Forest-poisoner!"

"Child-eater!"

"Magic-destroyer! May you be ground by the teeth of the Great Gray ogre into pieces that are smaller than the eyes of lice on a fly!" cursed Xar.

Both Xar and Wish were cold and tired and had just had a terrible fright. Fear had turned to anger, as it so often will, and they settled easily into shouting the kind of insults and nasty language at each other that have been exchanged between Wizards and Warriors since the Warriors first invaded from across the seas and the two sets of humans met in battle in the wildwoods centuries before.

Xar's face was flushed with temper, and he held the sword over Wish's head in such a purposeful fashion that Bodkin shouted out:

"DON'T KILL HER! SHE'S THE DAUGHTER OF QUEEN SYCHORAX, AND IF YOU KILL HER, QUEEN SYCHORAX'S REVENGE WILL BE TERRIBLE!"

Xar stared at Wish in astonishment. "A daughter of Queen Sychorax...? But you can't be!"

Queen Sychorax was a legend in the forest, known for her cruelty and height and her pitiless Warrior strength. How could this tiny matchstick of a girl be scary Queen Sychorax's daughter?

"A daughter of Queen Sychorax! Killher, killher, killher, killher..." hissed the sprites, creeping through the air toward Wish, their bows loaded with the most deadly of their curses. One word from Xar, and they would let them fly.

Xar had always boasted that if he ever met an enemy he would kill them instantly.

But boasts are one thing.

And actually *killing* a real live girl your own age who is right in front of you and clearly terrified though trying not to be, with a sword you have just cheated her out of…well…that's quite another, and Xar found he could not do it.

My ancestors *would have done it*, thought Xar guiltily. Looter *would not have hesitated*.

But Xar paused uncertainly.

And then to his further surprise, he found himself being attacked by what appeared to be *a spoon*, making ferocious lunges and rapping him painfully on the head.

"I'll call off my spoon if you call off your bear…" panted Wish.

To the disappointment of the sprites, who were hissing like hornets, Xar lowered the Enchanted Sword and gave a sign to his bear, who let Bodkin go with a grunt. The Enchanted Spoon stopped rapping Xar on the head, gave him a small, apologetic bow, and hopped back down to Wish.

The Wizard and the Warriors stared at each other in amazement, still hostile and suspicious, but also curious.

"I am Wish, daughter of Sychorax, Queen of

I am Xar the Magnificent, son of Encanzo, King of Wizards.

the Warriors," said Wish, "and this is my Assistant Bodyguard, Bodkin. Who are you?"

"I am Xar the Magnificent, son of Encanzo, King of Wizards," said Xar. "These are my companions. My wolves, my bear, my snowcats: Kingcat, Nighteye, Forestheart. My bird, Caliburn. My giant, Crusher. And my sprites: Ariel, Mustardthought, Tiffinstorm, Hinkypunk, Timeloss."

The sprites weaved viciously around the Warriors' heads, sparking and burning menacingly.

"Don't forget usssss," squeaked Squeezjoos.

"Oh yes, these are sprites too, but they're so young we call them hairy fairies," said Xar. "Bumbleboozle and the baby and—"

"Squeezjoos," whispered Squeezjoos into Bodkin's ear, suddenly and alarmingly. The long trail of his antennae sent goose bumps all over Bodkin's scalp, as Bodkin flapped him desperately away.

Wish gave a sigh of jealousy as she looked at Xar's companions, particularly the sprites.

She reached out a hand to the one Xar called Squeezjoos, which was a funny-looking little thing, furry as a bumblebee.

I'm afraid that Squeezjoos bit her.

"Wow!" said Wish, sucking her finger. "Sprites are tougher than I expected. They're kind of violent...and they don't seem to like me very much..."

"Of course they don't like you, you stupid Warrior," said Xar. "Your wicked mother captures our giants and dwarves and sprites in her terrible traps and then we NEVER SEE THEM AGAIN."

"But my mother doesn't *kill* the sprites she captures," said Wish. "She just has this Stone-That-Takes-Away-Magic that she keeps in her dungeons and all she does is mercifully remove their Magic by placing them upon the stone..."

Wish's voice trailed off as she remembered how much she didn't want the spoon to have his Magic removed.

"In a completely painless process..." Bodkin prompted her.

"And you think *that* does not kill them?" hissed Tiffinstorm. "Why not just remove their hearts entirely? A sprite without its Magic is a sprite who has lost its soul…"

Oh dear… Wish did not know what to think now—this all sounded so sad.

"But the Magic is bad for them," she said falteringly, "and they use it to curse us… and giants eat people… That's why my mother traps them… She told me so."

Xar and the sprites laughed at such ignorance. "Giants don't eat people!"

Wish looked up at the giant in wonder.

And then to Bodkin's horror, the giant leaned down, and ve-ry gently picked Wish up in his giant fingers, and lifted her into the air. It should have been frightening. But the giant moved so slowly, and his fingers around her were so comfortingly huge, that all Wish felt as she rose up, up, UP into the treetops was excitement at the new experience.

"Look around you and look down," said the giant. "What seems important from up here?"

Wish looked over the edge of the giant's fingers and caught her breath with the surprise of seeing the world from an entirely different viewpoint. The forest canopy stretched out for miles in every direction, and the night sky above was crammed with stars that went on forever. Down below, the humans were as small as sprites, and the sprites were just glowing flecks of dust. One of the humans—Bodkin—was shouting something—"PUT—HER—DOWN!"—but it was such a long way away Wish had trouble hearing him, and his anxiety seemed, from this vantage, mistaken and missing the point.

"The forest is important," said Wish, "and the stars…"

"Correct," smiled the giant. "Look into my eyes. Do I look like the kind of person who would eat human beings?"

The giant's face was covered with a network of

wrinkles and laughter lines like the wandering paths on an old map, and his eyes were kind and wise.

"No," said Wish. "You don't."

"Correct again," said the giant. "Unlike ogres, giants are vegetarian."

Crusher grinned and pulled up a small tree. He gave a huge smile at Wish as the entire tree disappeared into his enormous mouth, crunching whole branches as if they were mere twigs. "Be-t-ter for the dig-e-estion," he said dreamily.

The first seeds of doubt about all that she had been told about Magic creatures were sown in Wish's mind when she looked up at the giant's kind face, laughing so loudly at his own bad joke.

"Crusher doesn't seem like a good name for you," said Wish.

"It's short for Problem-Crusher," said Crusher.

"Are you all right?" cried Bodkin anxiously.

"Of course I'm all right," said Wish as the giant gently put her back down. "That giant really is NOT dangerous…"

Was it possible that Warriors had been mistaken in their view of Magic all along? Could there be another way of looking at things, other than the Warrior way?

Wish's worldview was spinning upside down, and that is always a difficult moment.

"Don't listen to them, Princess!" said Bodkin. *"They're putting a spell on us! They're trying to make us see things from their point of view!"*

Xar was looking equally thoughtful.

"Warriors want to destroy all Magic." He frowned, gazing at the Enchanted Sword he was holding in his hand. "Surely a Warrior princess shouldn't have Magic objects?"

"No, she shouldn't," said Bodkin. "I have been saying that for some time."

"Be careful with that Enchanted Sword, Xar," urged Caliburn. "There's something wrong with it...I can feel it in my feathers..."

Staring at the blade, Xar suddenly realized Caliburn was right, there was indeed something odd about the sword, something so strange and out of the ordinary and downright UNCANNY that he nearly dropped it in his excitement.

"Oh my goodness, Caliburn!" Xar gasped. "I don't believe this! This is incredible! I'll tell you what's wrong with this sword! It's made out of iron! And so is the Enchanted Spoon! They are *iron and Magic MIXED TOGETHER!*"

Unbelievable!

Inconceivable!

"Impossible!" Caliburn gasped.

"Where did you get this sword?" breathed Xar, turning it over and over in his hands.

"I found it in the corridor, but it's an Enchanted Sword so I think it made its way out of my mother's dungeons on its own," said Wish, her heart sinking. "That's not your sword, Xar. It belongs to my mother! Give it back RIGHT NOW!"

Wish made a grab for the sword and Xar whisked it out of her reach, Nighteye stepping between them and growling warningly, so she couldn't get any closer.

"Hang on a second..." said Xar. "What's *that*?"

Xar noticed, for the first time, the words written on the blade:

Once there were Witches...

The hairs stood up on the back of his neck.

Xar turned the sword over and read the words on the other side:

...but I killed them.

After the word *them* there was an arrow that pointed to the tip of the sword, where *something* was now glistening.

A single drop of green blood.

The three humans looked at the green stain, slightly smoking.

"Don't touch it!" screeched Caliburn.

6. Be Careful What You Wish For

The three youngsters, the bird, the sprites, and the animals stared at that single drop of green blood with growing horror and, in Xar's case, excitement.

"Witchblood!" said Xar in delight.

"What do you mean, '*Witchblood*'?" protested Bodkin. "Witches are extinct!"

But he did not scoff as convincingly as he might have done had he been tucked snugly behind the seven ditches of the Warrior hill-fort. There was something about the Badwoods after dark, when the hair-ice* was prickling and growing all over each twisting twig of dead wood, that made one fear that possibly, just possibly, Witches might not be so extinct after all...

"This is a *Witch-killing* sword," said Xar. "Look! It says so on the blade. And it found its way out of your Warrior dungeons because it sensed that the Witches were walking once more in the wood."

"That's not possible..." said Bodkin.

"Although it IS true," said Wish slowly, "that just before Xar caught us in that trap, we were being

*Sprite word for: fine strands of ice that form on dead wood in freezing conditions.

attacked by *something*, and I think I may have wounded the something with the sword."

"You were being attacked by a Witch and that is Witchblood." Xar smiled.

"No, it isn't! Lots of things have green blood," said Bodkin. "Cat-monsters! Rogrebreaths! Greenteeth goblins! Greenteeth ogres! It can't be a Witch, because Witches are extinct."

"*Probably* extinct," corrected Caliburn.

"Definitely NOT extinct," said Xar, pointing to the center of the clearing.

There, right beside Xar's Witch-trap, was another black feather, a feather like a crow's but significantly larger.

Xar picked it up.

As the feather came close to the feather that was hanging around Xar's belt, both feathers began to glow a dull greeny glow, a glow of ominous Magic. And as Xar held the feather up to the tip of the sword, the stain glowed too, like the luminescence of a firefly but with a spookier green tinge to it.

"*Witches!*" Xar grinned.

There was a terrible silence.

Witches might have returned to the Badwoods.

The most dreadful creatures ever to have walked the earth, alive once more.

The two enemy groups, animals, and sprites stepped a little closer to one another, looking out at the dark forest all around them, joining in mutual horror at what might possibly be *out there*...

"If that really IS Witchblood—it probably isn't, but if it is—even that single drop is very, very dangerous," shivered Caliburn. "Wipe it off on that tree bark, Xar, before it hurts anyone..."

"Oh, I'm not going to waste it..." said Xar. "There must have been a *reason* that I caught someone called 'Wish' in my Witch-trap...What are the chances of that happening? I wished to be Magic and the universe is trying to tell me that it's granted me my wish!"

"It could be telling you something else! The universe is very complicated!" shrieked Caliburn. "It could be testing you! It could be warning you not to make wishes as foolish as that one!"

But Xar was not listening to Caliburn.

Here was fate, showing him the way to get Magic out of a Witch.

"DON'T TOUCH THAT, XAR!" shouted Caliburn, so anxious that the feathers dropped out of him like black rain.

"Don't touch it...don't touch it...don't touch it..." hissed the sprites.

But Xar reached out the palm of his hand and

pressed it hard against the tip of the sword, where the green drop of blood was glistening.

He scratched it once, twice, in the shape of the first letter of his name: X.

And from that moment, Xar's story took a different path, a path that would be very difficult to come back from.

"Noooooooooooo!!!!!!!" begged Caliburn.

It was too late.

Too late…too late.

The tip of the Enchanted Sword pierced Xar's hand…

…and he screamed and doubled over in pain, holding his hand to his stomach.

Caliburn took his wings away from his eyes. "Oh, Xar…What have you done????"

Xar straightened up.

His eyes were alight with excitement, although the pain of it was making him shiver and shake his hand like it had been burned.

"Too late." Xar grinned, holding up his hand, and

oh Xar…

I can't look…

Too late. X marks the spot.

there, in the center of it, was the Witchblood mixed with *his* blood in the shape of an X.

When bad stars cross…and worlds collide…X marks the spot.

"What did he do that for?" asked Wish.

"I'm going to use the Witchblood to perform Magic," said Xar confidently.

"Will it work?" asked Wish.

"He has absolutely *no idea!*" said Caliburn. "Do you think that Xar is the sort of person who *thinks things through*??? We don't know what that green stuff IS! You better hope it isn't Witchblood, Xar, because Witchblood is supposed to be exceptionally dangerous! You may be able to use it to perform Magic, but it could turn you over to the dark side…You might become one of the Witches' creatures…Your father would lose his kingship…"

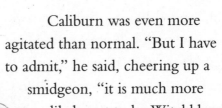

Caliburn was even more agitated than normal. "But I have to admit," he said, cheering up a smidgeon, "it is much more likely not to be Witchblood after all. There are plenty of things with green blood in the Badwoods...It could be werewolf blood—and that would just turn you into a werewolf..."

"Bother," said Xar, shaking his hand a little more uncomfortably. "I never thought of that."

"...which would be inconvenient," said Caliburn. "All that not going out after midnight and howling at the moon and extra body hair and everything, but it wouldn't be the end of the world."

"It would's be GREAT!" squealed Squeezjoos. "You'ds be all furry like ME! Oh please! Turn into a werewolf, Xar! Turn into a werewolf!"

But Xar didn't look that happy about the idea of turning into a werewolf.

And Wish and Bodkin took a step backward, just in case.

"And it may just be Rogrebreath blood...That doesn't have any effect at all...*as far as we know*...You're right," said Caliburn. "I shall look on the positive side. Let's hope it's just Rogrebreath blood. In which case we shouldn't really be hanging around here, because don't forget, Rogrebreaths *do* try to follow you if they've wounded you, to get their blood back."

"How do they do that?" asked Bodkin, in horror.

"You don't want to know," said Caliburn. "Let's just say they're kind of attached to their blood, so their methods of recovering it aren't pretty."

"Well, whatever you say, *I'm* still hoping it's Witchblood," said Xar obstinately. "But even if it isn't, I still have the sword, don't I?" Xar hung the sword from his belt.*

"That's not your sword!" said Wish. "Give us back our sword!"

"Sword?" said Xar, innocently opening his eyes wide. "What sword?"

"The Enchanted Sword that belongs to my mother and is presently shoved into your belt," said Wish.

"Oh *that* sword," said Xar, vaulting onto Kingcat's back. "*That* sword has been given to me by fate, so I can be the boy of destiny and lead my people to fight back against you Warriors. You can't argue with fate."

"It hasn't been given to you by fate!" yelled Wish. "You're STEALING it! Give us back our sword, you burglar!"

---

*Not to be recommended. A sword should always be put safely away in a scabbard, but Xar was not someone who worried much about health and safety.

Xar ignored her and turned to the others, saying, "Come on, everyone! We need to get back so I can beat Looter in the Spelling Competition."

"Hang on a second, what about us?" asked Wish. "*We* can't go home, can we! Your sprites' spells have sent my pony to sleep."

The pony was, indeed, still snoring peacefully in the center of the clearing.

"Well, you really shouldn't have gone out in the Badwoods after dark if you didn't want anything bad to happen…" advised Xar with sheer, unbelievable, Xar-like cheek.

At that moment there was a distant sound of stamping horse-feet and a cry of dogs, and the sprites hissed in alarm: *"WARRIORS!"*

Queen Sychorax's iron Warriors had spotted the giant in their Badwoods territory (Xar had been right about the deep thoughts, the smoke) and were galloping out of iron Warrior fort to investigate.

"There you are; your problem is solved," said Xar to Wish. "Your people are coming and they can take you home."

"But we'll be in big trouble because we sneaked out of the fort without permission!" said Wish. "Please, will you help us get back to our own fort without them finding us?"

93

"I haven't got time to do that before the Competition starts," said Xar, "but I'll very kindly let you come with me, and you can stay the night in my room in Wizard camp."

"That's BURGLARY *and* KIDNAPPING!" said Wish furiously. "Take us back to iron Warrior fort and give me back my sword, you horrible Wizard!"

"Well, I really don't see what that's got to do with *me*?" said Xar in surprise. "Why should I care about the problems of a couple of enemy Warriors? I'm doing my best, but you're being very difficult."

If Wish had been doubting that Wizards were as bad as everybody said they were, she instantly changed her mind.

"My mother was right about you Magic people!" stormed Wish. "You're cheats, and you're treacherous, and you have no morals, and you're completely out of control, and—"

"She's right, Xar!" squawked Caliburn. "You get *back* from the universe what you *give* to the universe. And kidnapping this girl and stealing her sword means you can expect something truly dreadful from the universe in return: Do As You Would Be Done By, or You Will Be Well and Truly Done..."

"Well, the universe ought to be very pleased that I'm not leaving them here to be attacked by Witches.

I can't understand why you're not all happy for me." Xar frowned. "It's terribly selfish of you. I AM THE BOY OF DESTINY! I AM THE CHOSEN ONE!"

He turned to his animals and the giant.

"Nighteye! Forestheart! Crusher! Bring these stupid Warriors and their pony to the fort after me!"

"I's'll fly with the Warriors too!" squeaked Squeezjoos. "I's'll stay with them and look out for jagulars!!!"

"Don't feel you have to, Squeezjoos," said Xar, rather offended.

"I's WANTS to!" sang Squeezjoos, ever enthusiastic. "I *likes* her! She's a bit funny-looking…and she's only got one eye…but she smells more like an apricot than a humungular being…and I likes her hair!"

Squeezjoos flew into Wish's hair and fluffed up the back of it so it made a fuzzy little bird's nest for him to hide in.

"Well, there's no accounting for tastes," huffed Xar crossly. "I'd have thought you'd want to hang out with

The Spoon was jealous. This was his territory.

the boy of destiny, but if you feel sorry for these poor weirdos, it's up to you, Squeezjoos...

"Come on, everyone!" yelled Xar. "Race you back to the fort!"

Kingcat leaped forward in a silvery-gray bound, and the animals followed in a wild, crazy pack, the sprites zooming ahead.

Turning back time is impossible.

Probably.

But...

IF Xar could have seen Wish after he left her in the clearing, and...

IF he could have seen the look on her face as she suddenly realized she couldn't make things right by putting back the sword, and that her mother would inevitably now discover her disobedience in that uncanny way that mothers do, and...

IF he could have known that Wish's mother wasn't the kind of mother who had given her daughter the impression that she would forgive her daughter for anything...

IF he could have seen Wish crying, with a spoon who couldn't talk trying to comfort her with no words, and the Assistant Bodyguard, also sad, patting her on the back, and Squeezjoos pulling faces and turning cartwheels to try to cheer her up...

with a Spoon who couldn't talk trying to comfort her...

IF he could have seen all that, would Xar have wanted to turn back time, even though that is impossible?

Possibly.

But...

Looking into other people's lives when they are not right in front of you is also impossible...

Probably.

I say "probably" because turning back time and looking into other people's lives when they are not right in front of you are both things that require the kind of Magic we call "imagination." Xar had not developed that kind of Magic yet, any more than he could move objects with the sheer power of his mind or fly without the helpful addition of wings.

So as soon as Wish was out of his sight, Xar promptly forgot about her, and carried on with the much more important task of congratulating himself on how clever he'd been as he rode on Kingcat's back to Wizard camp.

Meanwhile, back in the clearing, Wish had stopped crying because Wish was a practical person, and crying wasn't going to help.

"What are we going to do now?" said Bodkin, with round, goggling eyes, bulging with dismay at the way the situation had developed.

"We're just going to have to follow that cheating burglar of a Xar-boy to his Wizard camp, and steal that Enchanted Sword back off him, and then we can sneak back into our own fort before morning," said Wish. "That sword is Magic-mixed-with-iron, and we mustn't let it fall into the hands of the Wizards."

"Oh, is that all we have to do?" said Bodkin hollowly. "And here I was thinking we had a problem..."

"On the plus side, we DO get to ride these snowcats," said Wish.

Warriors don't quit, Bodkin!

"That's a *plus* side?" said Bodkin, looking in horror at the gigantic wild beasts standing uncomfortably close to them. "But they're banned animals! It's against the rules!"

Timidly, Wish put out her hand, and touched the unbelievable softness of Forestheart's head. She had been absolutely dying to ride on one of the snowcats from the moment she set eyes on them.

Gingerly, Wish climbed onto his back.

"Will you be following us, Crusher?" Wish called up to the giant.

Crusher looked delighted to have his feelings consulted. "I'm a bit slo-o-ower than those snowcats," he said, giving a great smile like a cracked pumpkin. "But I'll be right behind you. I'll be fine. I'm a giant!"

Of course, what was she thinking? A giant could take care of itself. He was probably a terrifying fighter, even if he *was* a vegetarian.

"Follow Xar, please, snowcat," said Wish.

Forestheart leaped up and bounded forward with velvet suddenness. *I'm actually riding a snowcat, IN REAL LIFE* ... thought Wish with disbelieving excitement as the lynx weaved smoothly through the trees, the night wind blowing back Wish's hair. Wish forgot the peril of the moment and whooped in joy.

By holly and mistletoe and Witches' toenails and the

stinky breath of the Goggle-Eyed Goblinhopper! thought Bodkin, all alone in the clearing. *That little princess was more like her mother than she looked. Stubborn! Reckless! Pigheaded! And the Wizard boy was even worse! What was it with royalty? Maybe all the rich food they ate went to their heads.*

But what could poor Bodkin do? He couldn't stay here all alone in the possibly werewolf-infested wood, enjoying the cool night air and playing spot-the-Rogrebreath.

And besides, he ought to be protecting and controlling the uncontrollable little princess—that was his job. So, reluctantly, he climbed on top of the second banned animal, who equally reluctantly allowed himself to be climbed on, and leaped forward after Wish.

The giant Crusher leaned down and gently picked up the sleeping pony in one giant hand. He smoothed the pony's mane with one giant finger, like a human might pet a mouse, before very gently putting the pony in one of his pockets, and ve-ery slowly lumbering after Bodkin and Wish and the snowcats.

"Don't worry!" shouted Wish across to Bodkin as Nighteye caught up with Forestheart. "It's going to be fine!"

"Don't worry?" said Bodkin sarcastically. "*It's going to be fine?* So far tonight we have: broken out of Warrior

fort without permission…taken an Enchanted Spoon as a pet…stolen your mother's extremely precious and, as it turns out, exceptionally dangerous sword…let that same sword fall into Wizard hands, thus putting into peril the entire War Against the Magic…and NOW we are traveling into the heart of enemy territory on the back of a whole load of banned animals, having been kidnapped by a lunatic Wizard boy, who may or may not be about to turn into a werewolf…

"Why would I worry?"

Bodkin's stomach gave a loud rumble.

"AND we've missed supper. Deerburgers. My favorite."

Squeezjoos zipped ahead like a little streak of white lightning, screeching, "*I's* the lookout! *I's* the

lookout! AAAAAAGHHHH! There's a *jagular! There's a jagular!* . . . Ohhhh . . . No, *sorrys*, my mistake, is a tree trunk. SORRYS, everybody . . ."

Silence fell as they followed Xar farther and farther into the dark wilderness of the wildwoods, deeper and deeper into the unknown, where strange eyes seemed to glare from behind trees and terrifying shrieks of the nighttime screamed all around them, that could be jaguars or could be werewolves or could be worse than all of these . . .

Luckily, Bodkin did not see two things that happened after they left the clearing, or he would have been even more worried than he was already.

Firstly, the giant Crusher was captured by Sychorax's iron Warriors.

Wish had been right to be concerned about him. Giants are deep thinkers, but unfortunately the fact that they operate in a slower time zone puts them at a severe disadvantage when faced with much smaller enemies. Crusher just about had time to think: "W-H-A-T O-N E-A-R-T-H I-S G-O-O-I-N-G—" before the Warriors on their plunging horses exploded into the clearing and wound iron chains around and around his legs. The Warriors warned him that if he made a sound they would kill the pony, so the giant was silent as he was dragged away toward iron Warrior fort, making the treetops sway as he stumbled and blundered after the angry antlike Warriors. (What were they so CROSS about? Giants didn't understand crossness; it seemed like such an obvious waste of time.)

And then there was silence. But the air in the clearing seemed to chill a few degrees colder than it had been before, and the snow moved and swelled, like a white sea turning stormy. Was it that something was descending into the clearing? Had something been watching? Could it be that something was looking for the Enchanted Sword?

Ah yes, *that* would have made Bodkin worry.

But if that something was a Witch, however unlikely that may seem, Bodkin was going to need very advanced bodyguard skills indeed…

Witches' feet make no footprint.
Witches' bodies make no shadows.
But they make the trees, the land, the moss
a little colder as they pass.

CURSE SONG of the SPRITES

We're not there, that's just air, that glimpse of wing you
saw right there
That dying cow, that wasn't us, so don't you cuss, and
don't you *dare*
Cross-the-sprites-and-curse-their-spite-and-make-your-
hand-a-stony-fist
You can't punch us, we don't exist, we're only mist,
And that was just the wind that hissed.
We don't care, and we weren't there, and for a dare, we
would *never* snap that chair
And-leave-it-looking-like-it-was-perfectly-all-right-and-
wait-for-someone-big-and-fat-and-old-to-put-their-
lardy-fat-behind-on-it-and-SMOOSH-BANG-
HA-HA-HA!-SMASH!!!!!-the-entire-thing-shatters-
into-tiny-smithereens-and-then-they-land-upon-the-
stony-floor-and-break-their-jaw-and-fuss-and-roar-
and-cry-until-they-cry-no-more...
And that was not the eerie sound of fairy laughter when
they cried. And if they said it was, they *lied*.
That dying child, that wasn't us, so don't you cuss and
don't you *dare*
Cross-the-sprites-and-curse-their-spite-and-make-your-
hand-a-stony-fist.
You can't punch us,
We don't exist,
We're only mist,
And that was just the wind that hissed.

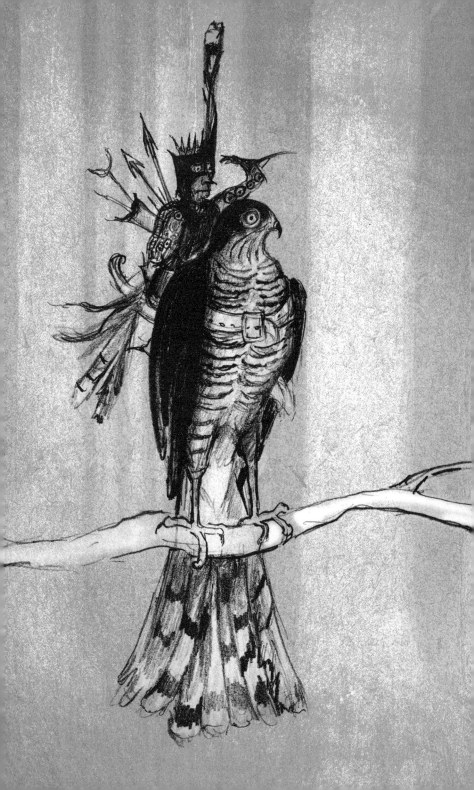

7. Wizard Encampment

The animals flitted through the maze of the dark forest for what seemed like hours. Wish, Xar, and Bodkin crossed the frozen river and the broken Ghost Wall that marked the end of Warrior territory and the beginning of the land of the Wizards, and eventually they reached a part of the wood that was so tangled and mangled with briars and fallen trees and vines that it was impossible to carry on.

The moon came out from the clouds, and Xar got Ariel to point at the barbed mountain of choking vegetation in front of them. In front of Wish's and Bodkin's astonished eyes, the brambles and branches slid out and through and over each other as if invisible fingers were unraveling a complicated knot from a fishing line. With a creak like the bending of ancient knees, the trees swayed and bent left and right, and the vegetation flattened so that a clearing lay in front of them.

The hairs stood up on the back of Wish's and Bodkin's necks, as the spines might rise on a thorny hedgehog, when they saw what lay inside the clearing. A truly gigantic circle of ancient trees, most of them giants. Yew, birch, rowan, alder, willow, ash, hawthorn, elder, apple, poplar—every species you could imagine—the most important being the oak, of course. No sign of any human habitation, but a sound of music and a smell of chimney smoke.

Now that they were so far away from home, and so deep in enemy territory, Wish was beginning to feel very, very frightened. What if Xar held them for ransom? Xar had said he would let them go the next morning, but Xar didn't seem very trustworthy.

"Where's your fort?" asked Wish shakily.

"Underground," said Xar.

Imagine a camp that had been sunk underground. Each one of those gigantic trees was hollow, and drew light down into the rooms hidden underneath. Xar led them to the tree-tower that housed his room, a great ancient yew so wound around on itself that it looked as though in the tree's youth, a giant had taken it gently by the topmost branches and twisted the trunk around in his hands as if the yew were a piece of clay. They climbed a series of ladders and platforms and in through the window of Xar's room.

Wish's heart sank even further. There was no way out now. They were stuck here, surrounded by enemies. What if Xar told the other Wizards about her? What if there were Wizards worse than Xar who really could Magic you into a slow death?

She felt a little sick.

There was no ceiling in Xar's room, so above them was the night sky and the stars. The floor had such huge cracks in it that you could see right down into the main hall forty feet below. "Don't worry," said Caliburn reassuringly to the astonished Bodkin and Wish, watching Xar strolling across a floor that seemed to be made partly of air. "The floor is held together by Magic."

Xar opened his rucksack and took out the Spelling Book, to find the spell about turning people into worms. It was right beside the page that told you how to turn people into cats (easy) and cats back into people (trickier).

First, Xar thought, he would punish Looter by turning him into a worm using the Witch Magic. Then, in a dramatic climax, he would draw the sword and show everyone how he could use Magic-that-works-on-iron. And then, of course, they would all start clapping and cheering him, chanting his name, and his own father would bow down before him, saying: "Xar, I am so sorry I ever doubted you...I always knew you were something special. I know we have had our misunderstandings in the past, but you are the hero we have all been waiting for."

It was all going to be SO satisfactory.

Xar memorized the spell and slammed the book shut.

"Come on, sprites!" said Xar briskly. "The Competition is going to start in a couple of minutes and we need to get down there so I can HUMILIATE Looter. Everyone follow me...except you, Forestheart, Nighteye, Kingcat, the bear, and Squeezjoos..."

"Oh why does I's have to stay behind?" said Squeezjoos.

"Well, YOU seemed to like the Warriors so much," said Xar pointedly, for he had been feeling a little jealous. "So you can stay here and guard them."

"Don't you worry, Boss...I'S'LL protect them..."

"I didn't say PROTECT them, Squeezjoos, I said GUARD them; they're enemy prisoners..."

"But I DID's wants to comes with you and sees you turn into a werewolf!" said Squeezjoos, very disappointed.

"I'm sssure I can seeee a few more hairs on his armsss already," hissed Tiffinstorm, eyes bright with malicious pleasure.

"Oh, shut up, both of you!" snapped Xar. "I'm not going to turn into a werewolf! This is Witchblood and I'm going to use it to perform Magic!"

"But you don't know if it will work yet," Caliburn pointed out. "And shouldn't you find out what that stain is before you go in front of a whole load of other people and possibly turn into a werewolf in front of their eyes?"

Xar looked at him as if he were completely crazy.

"But that would mean WAITING," Xar replied. "And the Spelling Competition is happening RIGHT NOW. Anyway, even if the Witchblood doesn't work, I know the sword works."

"You're not allowed to take swords into Spelling Competitions, Xar, let alone IRON ones," said Caliburn.

"And it's our sword!" protested Wish.

"I wish you'd stop saying that. This a Magic sword," said Xar. "So it belongs to *me*, and all your gloomy, what-you-give-to-the-universe-the-universe-will-give-back-to-you stuff, Caliburn, well, all I can say is, by bringing this sword to me, the universe clearly thinks I'm pretty special…"

"And the universe is RIGHT!" squealed Squeezjoos.

There was no talking to Xar when he was in this kind of mood.

"The universe is really tipping it down now," said Caliburn gloomily as big splatters of rain came down on their shoulders.

Downstairs in the main hall, the jubilant sound of dancing giants and happy voices could be heard. Upstairs in the little room tangled with jungle vines, swaying in the wind, rocking like a boat on the sea, a heavy drenching rain was now falling in Xar's room.

"Why on earth would you design a room with no ceiling?" wondered Bodkin. "It's not very practical."

"Tiffinstorm!" said Xar. "Do us a weather spell before we all drown. And you'll have to stay here to keep the spell up so the prisoners don't get wet..."

Tiffinstorm huffed crossly, "WhyisitalwaysME-whohastodoeverything? I wanted to see the Spelling Competition!" before sulkily looking in her wandbag and getting out a number four. She picked out a spell and batted it up into the air with the wand, and a nice little invisible umbrella of wind sprang out the end of the spell, hovering some three or four feet above them, so that the rain poured over the edges in a waterfall.

"Oh my goodness," marveled Wish. "That's incredible!"

"Don't be impressed!" warned Bodkin. "Remember, Magic may look attractive on the outside, but it is danger, it is chaos..."

"You have to admit, it's extremely useful if you don't want to get wet, though," said Xar.

"A *ceiling* works quite well too," said Bodkin.

Xar slammed the door and locked it.

"He's taken the sword with him," said Wish, very disappointed. "We'll just have to wait till he comes back,

and then we can steal the sword off him when he's
asleep."

"Okay, so say we do successfully manage to steal
the sword off Xar," said Bodkin. "How do we get back
to our fort? We can't WALK back—it's miles away."

"Oh dear, Xar was right. We're prisoners!" said
Wish, peering out the window into the blackness
of the night. It was a long way down to the bottom of
the tower, and there was absolutely no sign of the
giant or the pony. "And I'm worried that poor
Crusher might have been captured by my mother's
Warriors..."

"Poor Crusher? He's a GIANT, Wish!" said
Bodkin, very shocked. "Whose side
are you on?"

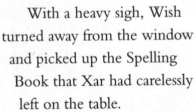

With a heavy sigh, Wish
turned away from the window
and picked up the Spelling
Book that Xar had carelessly
left on the table.

"Bodkin, you HAVE
to see this book. This is
unbelievable!" said Wish,
forgetting her fear and her
anxiety and nearly dropping
the book in her excitement.

116

The Spelling Book

A Complete Guide to the Entire Magical World

This book iss the propperty of

Xar the Maggnifisent

Boy of Dessting

The Spelling Book

Hello! Welcome to the Spelling Book.

To use, simply tap out your question
on the letters below.

Your personally selected question is:

How Do You Escape From A Magic Tree
In A Wizard's Fort And Make Your Way Through
The Badwoods When You Have No Transport, No Map,
And No Means Of Knowing Where You Are?

Please note: If the Spelling Book malfunctions, you will
unfortunately have to turn all 6,304,560 pages YOURSELF.
Sorry about that.

The Spelling Book

JUMBO FRILLY-EARED DREAMER GIANT

There are many different species of Giants: Frost Giants, Colossal clumpers, Dreamers, Monumentors... Despite their name, Giants actually come in various sizes: This is an embarrassed Mammoth Gargantopper Lumper Giant, who has just accidentally trodden on somebody's house

whoops! I'm so...

JUMBO FRILLY-EARED DREAMER GIANT

having a thought...

Short-legged Giants like this one have very long arms so they are excellent climbers

Most Giants are herbivores, and about the size of the treetops, they can hide from Raptorgriff flocks flying above wildwoods. (see page 2,000,041)

A Short-Legged Frilly-Eared Dreamer Giant leaping through the marshland, using his arms for propulsion.

page 1,230,493

The Spelling Book

LONGSTEPPER-HIGH-WALKER GIANT

Longstepper High-Walker giants make huge holloways (sprite word for "paths") as they wander through the wildwoods, thinking great thoughts about life on earth and the mysteries of the universe.

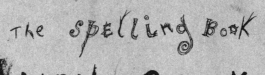

The Spelling Book
HAIRY – BACKED ROGRE

The Spelling Book

GRUNTLEOGRE ROGREBREATH

ROGREBREATHS I HAVE KNOWN:

THE STINKY ARMPIT GRUNTLEOGRE ROGREBREATH
(Hairy-backed version)

The Gruntleogre puts cow poo under his armpits as a charming perfume to attract female Gruntleogres. YUCKY But true.

WARNING: DO NOT ATTEMPT TO REASON WITH THIS MAN. HE ISN'T VERY REASONABLE.

The Spelling Book

SPELLING

Your Handy Magic Guide
to How It Works

Most sprites are too small for their Magic to have any
effect on larger creatures than themselves all on its own.
Their Magic must therefore be concentrated in small
"spells" like little balls or "bombs" that the sprite keeps
in a spell bag around its waist.

The sprite also
has a quiver of wands,
and when a Spell needs to
be launched, the Sprite
chooses the correct
wand for the Spell,
and WHACKS it toward
the victim.

Spell bag with
Spells inside

page 1,233,495 (and a quarter)

The Spelling Book

DIFFERENT TYPES of SPELLS

- Flying Spell
- Water Spell
- Fire spell
- Love Spell
- Growing spell
- Spell of Forgetting
- Invisibility Spell
- Thunder Spell

IMPOSSIBLE NOTIONS
No. 34721: SPELLING

Hvae you ntoiecd taht it deos not ralely matetr the odrer you put the ltteres in as lnog as you hvae the frist and lsat ltteres in the rghit plcae?

The Spelling Book

LOST WORDS

As the Longstepper High–Walker giants crisscross the forests of Albion, their heads smoking, they are also collecting LOST and ENDANGERED words. The giants' view is, if you lose the words to DESCRIBE things, how can you THINK about them?

Here are some sprite words for things that are in danger of becoming lost:

FIZMER: Rustling noise in grasses

DRAGONCOLD: Weather so freezing it makes the breath smoke so that people look like dragons

HAAREIS: Frost growing like fungus on dead wood

WILL–O'–THE–WISP: Trails of light following afte sprites as they fly through woods in the darkness

HOLLOWAY: Paths made through wildwoods by wandering giants

COWBELLY: Word for mud at the bottom of the river

page 2,143,204

The Spelling Book

ELF-LOCKS: The tangled hair of sleepers

GHOST TRALES: The light trails made by sprites at nighttime (see also, will-o'-the-wisp).

SNAILY SLUDGE: The revolting booger-trail left by a Rogrebreath

FLITTERS: To move house, *go walkabout*

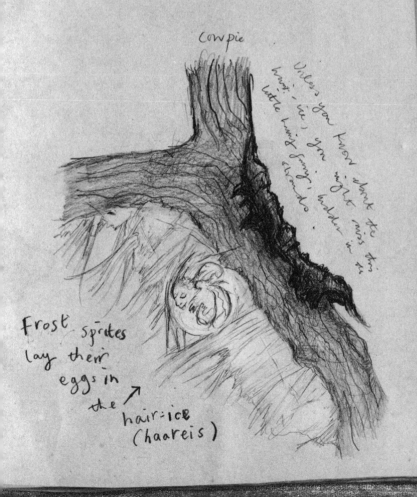

cowpie

Unless you know about the hair-ice, you might miss the little hair-sprites' cradles

Frost sprites lay their eggs in the hair-ice (haareis)

THE SPELLING BOOK

SPRITE CURSES

In the world of MAGIC, words have POWER, so CURSING is a very powerful weapon. The Droods (Druids) have made quite an art of it.

"May yoo get a cold that makes your nose drip like a snotty streem of booger-sludge for FIVE HOLE WEEKS and may yore armpits itch like they are being bitten by wererats…"

"May yoo be swallowed by a cow, that is eaten by a whale, that is on its way down to the dreeriest depths of the sandiest wastes of the endless and bottomless ocean…"

(PLEASE NOTE: Sprites have an ARTISTIC approach to spelling—they think it doesn't matter what ORDER the letters are in, as long as you understand what they have written.)

The Spelling Book

WITCHES

Witches are extinct, so here at the Spelling Book we cannot show you a picture of a Witch, because nobody alive has ever seen one.

What to Do if Witches Were by Some Awful Chance NOT to Be Extinct:

1. We have no idea.

2. Don't try running. They'll catch you.

3. You could use iron — but Magic people are allergic to iron.

4. See point 1, above. Oh, and don't look at them. Just looking at a Witch can scare a person to death.

page 1,391,604

The Spelling Book Thanks You For Reading,
And Would Gently Remind You That
Things Generally Turn Out All Right

IN THE END.

DIE!

Niteye eating Looter

Snocats FoREVER

When my MAGIC
comes in I will bee
the MOST MAGIC ~~pursonn~~
purson
in the UNIVERSE

"We really shouldn't have anything to do with these things, Wish..." said Bodkin uneasily. "They're Magic...We shouldn't be looking...We shouldn't be listening...We shouldn't be holding them..."

"But this book says it has six million pages in it!"

"That's impossible," said Bodkin, peering over her shoulder despite himself, for Bodkin loved books and a book with six million pages in it was something he had to see.

"Look!" said Wish. "It says it's a complete guide to absolutely everything you need to know about your Magic world. Maps, recipes, Magic species, Wizards, Witches, dwarves, goblins, lynxes, sprites...and then there's a breakdown of all the different types...and then there's a section on lost words...That sounds interesting ...Languages: Dwarvish, Elvish, Giantish, Doorish— what's *Doorish*? I didn't know doors spoke..."

The book was very confusing to read because lots of the pages were falling out, and when they floated back in again they were in a different order, and whoever had written it was very disorganized and kept going off on tangents that might lead somewhere or might be dead ends.

"And some of the spelling in this book is nearly as bad as mine!" said Wish triumphantly.

"That's not a good thing, Wish," Bodkin said. "You know your mother would say there's only ONE way to spell things, and that is the RIGHT way. Anything else is chaos...disorder...anarchy..."

But Wish wasn't listening.

"Oh my goodness! Look! I'M in this book!" said Wish in astonishment, turning to a picture in the giants section. "AND Crusher! How is that possible?"

Bodkin squinted over her shoulder. "Well, that's just a picture of a girl, isn't it? It doesn't have to be you..."

"The girl has a spoon on her head!" Wish pointed out.

"So she does..." Bodkin sighed. "I suppose it could be you because this book is Magic..." Bodkin shivered because it was really quite an eerie thought that a book could be Magic enough to write you into it without you knowing. "Which is why we REALLY, REALLY should not be reading it..."

"I'm only looking at it to see if it can help us escape."

Squeezjoos and Tiffinstorm and the snowcats were not doing a very good job of guarding Xar's prisoners. It had been a long, tiring day, and they had

SPOON MOODS

Anxious

Sad

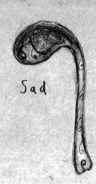

Excited

Scared

Cross

Sleepy

page 2,531,294

all fallen asleep, so maybe they COULD escape, thought Bodkin, his heart lifting.

Wish frowned. "Now, how did Xar make it work? He tapped on each letter on the contents page, and the pages magically turned to the right place...Bother, my spelling isn't that good. Bodkin, could you help?"

Bodkin leaned over Wish's shoulder and tapped "How do you escape from a Magic tree in a Wizard's fort and make your way through the Badwoods when you have no transport, no map, and no means of knowing where you are?" into the Spelling Book.

However, all the answers seemed to involve some sort of specialist equipment, like flying carpets or shoes with wings, and a lot of them pointed out all the *dangers* of the Badwoods in horribly realistic and ghoulish detail, such as giant cats and werewolves and mushrooms with teeth, and Bodkin didn't particularly want to be reminded of these.

The two of them jumped nervously at an unbelievably loud noise coming from below Xar's locked room—a noise like about twenty thunderclaps going off at the same time, which was the sound of some of the Wizards in the main hall fighting one another.

"Good gracious, what was that?" exclaimed Bodkin.

Wish peered between the cracks in Xar's walls, and she could see right down into the main hall.

The Spelling Competition was beginning.

Bag of
Wizard
Staffs

SPELLING STAFFS

A beginner Wizard, like Xar, can only use a staff made out of birch. Oak is a good all-around choice, while willow is used for healing. Ash is used for spells of transformation and enchantment, but it can be hard to control. Blackthorn is a dangerous wood, used for spellfights and dark Magic. Only the very greatest Wizards can use a staff made out of yew.

YEW

BIRCH   OAK   WILLOW   THORN   ASH

page 4,905,632

8 · The Spelling Competition

This was a feast of FIRE, so bonfires leaped high in all corners of the main hall and a great leaping circle of fire marked out the spelling ring, right in the buzzing center of the rowdy banquet.

The hall was jam-packed with Wizards of all ages and sizes; happy, sleepy giants dancing or snoozing ponderously on the edges of the room; and howling wolves, lumbering bears, and snowcats watching carefully in the shadows from the branches above, their tails swinging. Fiddles and horns danced through the air playing themselves quite independently, with no visible musician in sight.

In one corner of the room, Encanzo the Enchanter was deep in political conversation with the other adult Wizards. Swivelli, a Wizard from a rival tribe, was arguing that the Wizards needed to fight back against the Warriors just as their ancestors had in the past. "The time has come for BATTLE," said Swivelli, "and for a new leader—ME—to be king, rather than you, Encanzo…"

The Young Wizards' Spelling Competition was taking place in another corner, and Looter had been beating everybody until Xar swaggered in, followed by the bear and the wolves and the sprites zooming overhead, stealing hats and pinching noses, and generally showing off. And within two seconds:

Ariel had zoomed underneath all the banqueting tables, tying people's shoelaces together so that when they stood up and tried to move away, they fell face-first onto the table, hopefully into something squishy and messy like STEW.

Timeloss turned patches of the floor into ice.

And all the other sprites were making nuisances of themselves in an equally naughty manner...

"What are *you* doing here, Xar?" sneered Looter. "Your Magic hasn't come in yet."

"I'm here to challenge *you*," said Xar grandly.

"What with?" grinned Looter. "Don't tell me you caught your WITCH, did you, baby brother?" he said lightly. He turned to his laughing friends and jerked a thumb at Xar. "This loser thought he was going to catch himself a Witch and steal some of its Magic..."

"HA HA HA HA HA!" laughed the young Wizards.

Xar shrugged carelessly. "Maybe I *did* catch that Witch, Looter," he said. "Why don't you try some of your spelling on me, and we'll see what happens? Or are you AFRAID?"

"Watch out, Looter!" warned Darkish. "He did catch *something*...I don't know what it was..."

"Of course you didn't catch a Witch," jeered Looter. "And you can't do Magic, little baby boy. I warned you, if you dared to enter this Competition I would ANNIHILATE you, and I *will...*"

Xar walked into the chalk circle, and as he stepped in, there was a short, sharp humming noise, and a force field of Magic leaped over both himself and Looter in a thin, see-through dome, hissing with power.

Everyone was quiet with that quiet where you know something is going to happen. Timeloss drew one of his wands, as did Bumbleboozle. But they couldn't help Xar now that he had stepped inside the circle.

Xar was on his own.

Xar held out his hands toward Looter.

"Oh, you're going to do Magic without a staff, are you, Xar?" scoffed Looter, and his friends all laughed loudly at this. Magic without a staff was advanced Wizard work, and only Great Enchanters like Xar's father could do that.

"Be afraid, Looter, be very afraid," warned Xar. "For I have not only the Magic of the Witch, but my Magic has the power to work on *iron...*"

"HA HA HA HA HA HA HA!" jeered all the young Wizards.

"Oh really?" smiled Looter.

He was going to enjoy this sooooo much.

"That's right," said Xar. "*I* am the boy that
destiny has chosen."

Confidently, Xar held his hand with the Witch-
stain on it out in front of him.

Feel the power… thought Xar. *Feel the power…*

"Imagine in your head… Feel the power in your
fingers…" That was what the teachers always said.

But Xar got redder and redder in the face, and more and more angry, and it was just like every other time he had tried to do Magic and failed...

Nothing, *nothing* happened.

Looter had been creeping warily around the edge of the circle, in case that lunatic brother of his really HAD caught himself some extinct life-form. Impossible though that was, you never knew with Xar. He had a way of making impossible things happen.

But now Looter's eyes lit up.

"Ohhh dear," crooned Looter, holding his staff lovingly in his hands, "ohh dear...so, boy of destiny, chosen one...where is your scary Witch Magic now, then?"

"The boy of destiny!" laughed the young Wizards outside the circle.

"I don't understand," said Xar, bewildered and furious. "I AM the boy of destiny. I CAN do it...I know I can do Magic..."

Botheration! thought Xar. He had been so sure, what with the Witch-killing motto on the sword and everything, that this must all be a sign from fate. But maybe he had been wrong...and if this wasn't Witchblood, then what was it?

Please, please, let me not turn into a werewolf in front of everybody, thought Xar. *That would be embarrassing.*

Not for the first time, Xar wished he had taken Caliburn's advice. He could feel his skin prickling all over as if hairs were about to sprout out of it at any moment.

"You can't do Magic," said Looter. "But *I* can. Let me show you how I do it. I wonder, what I shall do first? Maybe I'll do...*this!*" He pointed his staff at Xar—there was a flash of sheet lightning and the white-hot heat of Magic light shot out of it, hitting Xar full in the chest so hard that he was thrown up into the edge of the invisible circle of the Magic force field.

Oh bother, thought Xar dully, picking himself up. *This isn't going to plan...*

"I'm going to turn you green," grinned Looter, shooting blasts of Magic at Xar, who turned brilliantly green as he was shot to the other side of the ring, trying not to scream as the blasts hit him like punches in the stomach. "And red...and yellow...and pink..."

As Xar was blasted across the spelling ring, turning violently different colors, he felt more and more nauseated, and he struggled not to be sick in front of everyone.

"HA! HA! HA! HA! HA!" roared the cronies of Looter and the Wizard children who Xar had played tricks on and bossed about in the past.

"You need to be taught a lesson." Looter smiled. "And I am going to teach you a lesson you will never, ever forget."

He advanced closer to Xar, who was now doubled over in pain, groaning.

"You're small *now*," said Looter. "But I shall make you smaller..."

He pointed his staff at Xar and muttered a spell under his breath. "S–H–R–I–N–K..." was the spell. "Shrink..."

Oh dear...not a shrinking spell, thought Xar. *That's really painful. And I'm already kind of on the small side. I'd better bring out the sword.*

But he didn't have time before the Magic screamed out the end of Looter's staff and hit the doubled-over Xar and lit him up at the edges as if he were a Xar made out of stars.

Xar stifled a howl of pain as those stars set into a viselike grip, and a pinch that began in his forehead spread across his entire body as the Magic tightened and pinched and compressed and crushed him, as though he were wearing a suit of armor that was slowly squeezing shut like the closing of a fist.

"Say I've won!" shouted Looter, backing off to give Xar a moment to give up the fight. "Surrender!"

Xar's mouth was squashed out of shape by the

shrinking process, but he managed to shout, "No! I won't!"

It came out weirdly, squeakily through the shrinking, squirming O of his lips.

"All right, then," said Looter. "You'll have to go smaller still..."

This time Xar did let out a yell as the spell hit him in a trembling shriek of pinches and pressure, shrinking his bones down a size smaller than they were. Bother. This wasn't giving him time to draw the beastly sword.

"Do you give up?" said Looter.

"Of course not!!!" yelled Xar. "Now you have *really* annoyed me, Looter!"

Luckily this made Looter stop doing Magic for a second, because he was laughing so hard he nearly dropped his staff. "Oh, I've REALLY annoyed you, have I? I'm so scared, I'm so scared..."

So, while Looter was busy laughing, Xar was able to draw the sword. In the nick of time. For if his hands had gone any smaller, he wouldn't have been able to hold it.

But he could just about get his palm around the handle and get enough grip to pull it out of his belt.

And it was a moment of triumph.

Xar drew the Enchanted Sword, with that satisfying swishing sound that swords make, and as they heard it, the gaze of the onlookers turned from scorn into surprise and horror as they realized what that sword was made of. Iron...

Looter took a step backward.

"You can't bring an IRON SWORD in here..." spluttered Looter. "Where did you get that from, you lunatic?"

"I broke into Warrior fort," lied Xar boastfully, "and stole it from right under the Warriors' snooty little noses...And I *can* bring it in, because it's a Magic Witch-killing sword. And, as you will see, *my* Magic, which HAS come in, can control it and enchant it..."

Looter shot an anxious bolt of Magic at the approaching Xar, and with one satisfying slice of the sword, Xar cut it in half before it reached him.

"Was that another shrinking spell, Looter?" jeered Xar. "Better try another one, for I am coming closer..."

Then the fight began in earnest, with Looter shooting hot, quick Magic bolts from his staff, and Xar intercepting them and breaking them in half so they fell uselessly to the ground as fast as Looter could direct them toward Xar.

The sword felt as if it were coming alive like a freshly caught salmon in Xar's hand, and it was anticipating Looter's next move before he made it.

Xar wasn't as light as Wish, so it wasn't quite as

clear that it was the sword doing the fighting rather than Xar himself. He just looked like he had suddenly and miraculously turned into the Best Swordfighter in the World.

The crowd was now pointing in an admiring rather than mocking way as Xar ran around the spelling ring carving up Looter's spellbolts and slicing his staff, shouting, "What have you to say about my Magic NOW, Looter?" and generally showing off.

It's working! thought Xar joyfully.

And it was every bit as exciting as he had dreamed it would be.

He could hear Heliotrope saying to Leafsong, "Wow, fighting with a sword is kind of cooler than with a staff, isn't it?"

And Leafsong replying, "Do you think Xar really *is* the boy of destiny?"

I'm a star! thought Xar exultantly. *I knew I was a star all along! And now everybody else will know it too.*

And then everything went wrong.

Suddenly, mysteriously, the Enchanted Sword began to drag Xar rather too violently to the left and to the right.

What's going on? thought Xar.

One moment it was as if he and the sword were one and the same, and he was in triumphant control of it, the next it felt worryingly as if the sword were trying to escape from him.

Xar was having to hang on to the sword with both hands, until, with a great plunging leap that pulled him three feet up in the air, the sword dragged itself out of his grasp and rocketed up through the dome circle of the Magic surrounding them, which caused the entire circle to explode.

BOOOOOOOOOOMMMM!!

The force of the explosion sent Magic ricocheting around the main hall in huge, violent blasts, ripping holes in the ceiling, and fireballs the size of pumpkins flew across the room.

The Enchanted Sword, after exploding out of the Magic circle, sailed up into the rafters of the ceiling of the main hall and disappeared in the direction of Xar's room...

When the smoke cleared, Xar and Looter had been thrown onto their backs and were lying on the floor, choking and coughing.

A great crack had opened up beneath Xar's feet and had split right across the floor of the room.

"WHAT IS GOING ON HERE?"

The King Enchanter's voice was cold as ice.

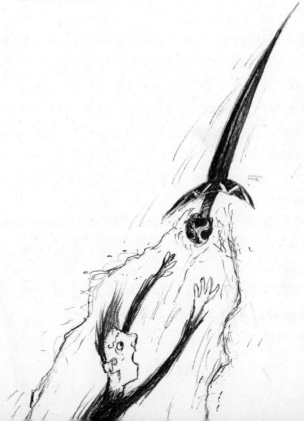

9. Encanzo the King Enchanter

The King Enchanter was a tall man, and Magic had made him taller still. It was curiously difficult to look at him, for he always seemed to be very slightly changing shape, blurring in and out at the edges. But underneath the constantly changing outline of his face, where Magic came and went like waves on a coastline, he was stern and unbending as a cliff.

He was such a very powerful Wizard that there was something very scary about him, even when he was just standing there quietly. He had one black fingernail on his right hand, and there was a story of how the fingernail had turned that color, but no one dared ask the Enchanter what the story was.

Two very large, very old snowcats settled themselves on either side of the Enchanter as if they were statues framing a door.

Xar and Looter staggered to their feet like a couple of carbon scarecrows.

"Xar!" snapped the Enchanter. "What has happened here? And what are you doing competing in the Spelling Competition?"

The cold anger dropped from the Enchanter's voice for a second as he asked, "Has your Magic come in at last?"

The Enchanter's voice was eager. *Too* eager, for
it told his son how much the Enchanter wanted that
Magic to come in.

"It has," said Xar.

"It has not!" said Looter.

"Well, Xar?" said the Enchanter sternly, and this
time you could hear his disappointment. "Has it come
in, or has it not?"

"Maybe not," admitted Xar sulkily.

"Then why are you competing in this spell—" began the Enchanter, but Looter was so angry he rudely interrupted his father.

"He cheated! He's completely out of control!" roared Looter. "He went into the Badwoods this evening with some mad plan that he was going to catch a *Witch* and use its Magic for himself—and then he tried to attack me with this ir—"

Looter was going to tell the Enchanter about the sword, but unfortunately the Enchanter punished him for his rudeness by sewing Looter's lips tight with Magic before he got to the end of this sentence. One flick of the Enchanter's little finger, and Looter's mouth shot together like he had lockjaw.

Ranter, Xar's tutor of Wizardry and Advanced Spellwork, now rushed forward. Ranter was a huge pomposity of a man, with a nose like a dignified lobster and various quivering outraged chins. His air of dignity and calm was disrupted by the fact that he was being closely followed not only by some very grand and ancient sprites, but also six small piglets, oinking lovingly up at him.

"I have tried to speak to you about this on many, MANY occasions, Enchanter!" cried Ranter. "And you have chosen not to listen! This is only the latest in a long line of disobediences! In the past week your son has: ridden his snowcat up the fort flagpole...removed the flag of the Wizard tribe and replaced it with a pair of Your Excellency's underpants...he has burned down the west part of the camp—"

"That was an accident!" objected Xar, interrupting. "I was just teasing the chimney sprites and they couldn't take a joke...Besides," he added hurriedly, "it wasn't me and I wasn't there..."

And with the last complaint, Ranter's voice dropped to a thrilling, furious quiver that made his chins shiver from side to side, banging against one another. "And worst of all, he has poured a 'Love-Never-Lies' potion into the pigs' feeding trough, so the pigs are behaving in a most OUTRAGEOUS fashion..."

Despite his intense annoyance with his younger son, the Enchanter's lips twitched with amusement. He looked down at the pigs, gazing up at Ranter adoringly. "Ah yes, I did wonder why you had taken to having pigs as followers, Ranter...Not very dignified for a senior Wizard of your standing, I thought..."

"The pigs," spat Ranter, "are not my idea! Your son has inflicted them on me! And you should not find this amusing, Enchanter. Your son's disobedience and lack of Magic brings dishonor on our whole tribe."

"What do you have to say for yourself, Xar?" said the Enchanter.

"You have no evidence!" shouted Xar, furiously

LOVE-Never-Lies Potion

If you drink a Love-Never-Lies potion, you will
fall in love with the next person you see. It is also
a truth drug. The liquid turns from red to blue
when the person holding it is telling a lie.

ABSOLUTE
WHOPPER
OF A LIE

LIE

TRUTH

punching the air. "I am Xar the Magnificent and I demand a fair trial!"

"Of course," said Encanzo the Magnificent. "Could you show me what you have there, Xar?"

He pointed to a package that was poking out of one of the pockets hanging around Xar's waist.

Ve-ry reluctantly, Xar took the package out of his pocket, and Encanzo insisted he unwrap it.

The package turned out to be a burned flag of the Wizard tribe tied around a half-full bottle of "Love-Never-Lies" potion.

Encanzo shook out the flag. "Ye-e-e-es...I would call this evidence, wouldn't you? And I pronounce you...GUILTY."

"I've never seen that flag before in my life!" proclaimed Xar.

Unfortunately, Xar was still holding on to the bottle of "Love-Never-Lies" potion.

And a "Love-Never-Lies" potion has two properties. One is that if you eat it or smell it, you fall in love with the next person or animal you see. The other is that it turns from red to blue when the person who is holding it tells a lie.

Encanzo watched the "Love-Never-Lies" potion as slowly the liquid turned from maroon to a sort of smoky indigo.

"Someone must have put that flag and that 'Love-Never-Lies' potion into my pocket because they certainly don't belong to ME!" said Xar, carrying on lying in a hopeful sort of way.

The indigo of the "Love-Never-Lies" potion darkened to black at the magnitude of this untruth. The bottle filled with smoke and shook in Xar's hand, the cork shot off, and Xar hurriedly recorked it. But not before a fine mist of "Love-Never-Lies" potion had drenched the little piglets sitting in a quiet but loving circle at Ranter's feet, and this fresh sprinkling made them jump to their feet again, oinking madly and making ruder and ever ruder noises as they tried to get Ranter's attention.

"AAAARGHH!" roared Ranter, batting at the piglets. "GET OFF ME! SHOO! YOU BEASTLY CREATURES, SHOO!"

Only Xar dared laugh at this entertaining sight, because the Enchanter had stopped being amused. He was staring down at his younger son, with thunderous eyebrows descending over his fierce hawk eyes.

"You are not only guilty of everything Ranter and Looter have accused you of, Xar, you are also a liar and a thief," said the Enchanter grimly.

Curse his beastly father! Why did he always have to make Xar feel so small?

"And now you must give up these silly little tricks of yours and GROW UP," said the Enchanter. "While all these other things are just stupid and babyish, trying to obtain a source of bad Magic is a serious crime that Wizards have been expelled for in the past—"

"And he SHOULD be expelled!" said Ranter, breaking in with excitement. "The last son of Encanzo the Magnificent, King of Wizards, not to have Magic! It's shaming! It's terrible! WHAT IF THE MAGIC NEVER COMES IN? We would be the laughingstock of the woods."

Xar's stomach did an uncomfortable flip.

"You are only saved from expulsion by the sheer stupidity of your idea, Xar," said the Enchanter with withering coldness. "Even a thirteen-year-old should know that Witches are extinct. And if there really *was* such a thing as a Witch out there, only a madman would try to get within a hundred yards of it."

Encanzo pointed his finger at Xar. Encanzo did not need a staff to concentrate his Magic. It blasted out with such pure intensity it was not even visible.

Xar's blackened clothes closed around him so tightly that he could barely breathe.

There was a writhing snake pattern on the broken dust of the mud floor where Xar was standing.

The patterned snakes on the floor began to move around one another, and then they grew solid, slid up and off the floor, and twined their way around Xar's legs, and his now-living clothes carried him up in the air like he was swinging from the branches of a tree, and the hissing snakes turned into liquid mercury that curled around him, solidified, and turned into chains, so that he was hanging suspended in the air, twisted around with bonds.

"LET ME DOWN!" cried Xar, furious with temper.

"You have gone into the Badwoods, against my express instruction," said the Enchanter. "You sought to take Magic from a dark source and bring it into this fort to cheat your way into winning a Spelling Competition. I will keep you up there until I decide your punishment."

"I don't see why I should be punished at all!" fumed Xar, struggling in the chains, his legs kicking wildly in the air. "It's not fair! I don't see why you always pick on *me*!"

"I always pick on you because it is always *you* who has done everything," replied the Enchanter in exasperation.

Caliburn spread his wings and whispered in the Enchanter's ear.

"I would suggest patience," said the raven. "It's very important that you are patient with children, and try to see things from their point of view."

"I have *been* very patient with the boy," said the Enchanter from between gritted teeth, "but I am running out of patience. The boy must learn to obey me, and if he does not, he must be punished."

"The more strongly you punish him, the more he will rebel," warned Caliburn.

Demendor, the Ambassador to the Court from Drood High Command, stroked his beard and put his finger high in the air. "A boy without magic is a sign the gods are most displeased!"

"That's true," said Swivelli, for he was always trying to overthrow Encanzo (this is another story I'll tell you about later). "And maybe your failure to punish and control your son effectively is a sign you are not fit to be the ruler of this tribe..."

Ah, being a father and a king is harder than it looks.

And everyone thinks they could do a better job than whoever happens to be the parent or the monarch at the time.

"BE QUIET, THE LOT OF YOU!" cried Encanzo the King Enchanter. "When I need your advice I will ask for it. Xar is merely being childishly disobedient and showing off in front of his friends because his Magic hasn't come in yet."

Xar lost his temper.

"Well, at least I'm trying to DO something!" shouted Xar. "At least I'm trying to ACT! Whereas you, Father, *you* do nothing at all!"

The hall full of Wizards drew in their breaths simultaneously. The outline of the Enchanter hummed with fury. Great shooting sparks came off him, and above, the clouds drifting across the high ceiling of the room grew darker and darker, and great rumbling bursts of thunder echoed throughout.

Caliburn put his wings over his eyes. Was Xar actually *trying* to get himself expelled?

"Why aren't we going out there to fight the Warrior army?" shouted Xar.

"That was just the point that *I* was making," purred Swivelli, eyes alight with pleasure. "Even Encanzo's *own son* thinks his father is not doing a good job as king..."

Swivelli broke off, because the Enchanter's finger had given a little flick and the torque around Swivelli's neck tightened inexplicably, and it was quite a while before Swivelli could breathe again.

"Confronting the Warriors would only be a good thing if it was a fight that we could *win*," said the Enchanter, trying to keep his temper.

"Why do you think we cannot win it?" shouted Xar. "Maybe the Warriors are wiping us out anyway while we hide here in our slowly shrinking forest, twiddling our thumbs, and thumbing our fiddles and doing our silly little Magic spells and love potions, while they burn up our forest and kill our giants and destroy our entire way of life!"

Encanzo the King Enchanter's eyes blazed.

"We are hiding from the Warriors like cowards," Xar shouted back. "Why are you teaching us to be such cowards, Father? Maybe *you* are a coward..."

"Silence!" stormed the Enchanter. "Or I will MAKE you silent! I will sew your lips tight with Magic!"

"Do it, then," said Xar. "I do not care."

"Enough!" shouted the Enchanter. "I have decided your punishment. You and your sprites and your animals shall be locked in your room for the next three days."

"It's not enough," muttered Ranter furiously.

Xar looked stricken. "No! Father!"

"Then you should not be disobedient, should you?" said his father the Enchanter in his sternest voice. "Now, be silent."

"I was the one who was disobedient! Don't punish THEM! Punish ME!" said Xar angrily.

"Three days," said the Enchanter, even more

coldly and white with temper. "Every time you speak I will add on one more day."

Xar opened his mouth to speak…and shut it again.

"Four days," said the Enchanter. "You shall not leave your room for four days. And if you do not listen to me and disobey me further, I will take your animals and sprites away from you FOREVER!"

Xar *did* care about that. Oh my goodness, he cared about that.

He was silent.

"*I* am the king here…" said the Enchanter. "ALL of you in this room need to remember that. And Xar needs a reminder of *who we are*…"

His father continued, "You have a very fine opinion of yourself, Xar, but the truth is, you are conceited, you are willfully disobedient, you are astonishingly selfish, and the fact that you tried to obtain bad Magic from a Witch shows you do not understand the very basics of what it means to be a Wizard, for Wizards should seek good Magic, Xar…

"You have one last chance to be good," warned the Enchanter. "Be good, for any more disobedience and I will be forced to expel you and remove all your animals and sprites."

"YOU DON'T CARE ABOUT *ME*!" cried Xar at the top of his voice. "ALL YOU WANT IS A SON WHO IS *MAGIC*!!"

"SILENCE!!!" roared the Enchanter.

He moved his arms once more, and all around the hall, where columns and pillars and staircases had been shattered into thousands of tiny pieces by the blast of the spelling ring exploding, the tiny dusty fragments lifted up from the floor and danced in the air, like clouds of humming bees.

The Enchanter moved his arms as if he were conducting an invisible orchestra, and the dust responded to his instructions.

"It is easy to destroy," said the Enchanter. "But I am not like a Warrior, impressed by destruction. It is far harder to create, and creation is what we Wizards are all about. Play, fiddles, play!"

The fiddles shot up into the air and began to play themselves, and the millions of tiny fragments billowing through the gigantic hall in enormous drifts, like smoke from a forest fire, danced in time to the music, with such speeding energy that you could feel the heat coming off them and warming up the faces of the wondering Wizards looking up in awe.

It was a very effective demonstration of the power of the Enchanter, for invention was far more difficult Magic than demolition, and only HE could perform Magic as tremendous as this. He was doing it to make a point to his son and to remind Swivelli and the other Wizards gathered there of what Wizards should stand for.

And it worked. Even Swivelli reluctantly gasped in awe (while cursing under his breath, mind you).

"Create, Xar, create, and then you will impress me," finished the Enchanter, his arms whirling wildly and gloriously to the tune of the music he had inspired. "And in the meantime, you will stay in your room until I tell you to come out."

BAM!

With a final eardrum-bursting clap of thunderous Magic that lit up the hall like sheet lightning, the millions of tiny pieces of dust slammed together and formed whole columns once more. The crack in the floor closed, and Xar's clothes and the flying snake-chains carried Xar up, up to his room, where the door flew open, and the snake-chains swung him back and forth and then suddenly released him, depositing him on the floor.

The Enchanter made a sign to Xar's animals and sprites, and the animals leaped out of the hall and up the stairs, with the sprites following, and Caliburn too, with slow, reluctant wingbeats.

The door of Xar's room slammed shut behind them.

"It won't be enough," sniffed Looter, whose lips had at last come unstuck. "Ranter was right. You should have expelled him."

The Enchanter roared at Looter, unusually, for Looter was normally his favorite son. And when I say roared, I mean he opened up his mouth and a blast of furious Magic came out of it with such force that it actually blew Looter off his feet.

And then Encanzo stalked off and threw himself into his throne and put his head into his hands, thinking: *What is wrong with Xar? Why has his Magic not come in yet? I have given him the best giant in my land, the finest tree, the most brilliant advisor in Caliburn... But why can't I control him?*

Ah, being a father and a king is harder than it looks...

10. Fifteen Minutes Earlier, in Xar's Room

ow, the room Xar returned to was in a very different state than when he had left it only fifteen minutes earlier.

Bad things had been happening in Xar's room.

These bad things had been happening to Wish and to Bodkin, the sprites and the animals, who had all been locked in that room by Xar, if you remember.

Very, very bad things.

In order to explain them, I will have to go back in time, exactly fifteen minutes.

Of course, in real life, turning back time is impossible.

I think I've already mentioned that.

But contrariwise, *I* can do it, for I am the god of this story and thus have rather more Magic than perhaps is quite good for me.

Imagine Xar's room, fifteen minutes earlier.

The Spelling Competition was going on down below, and Wish and Bodkin were watching it through the floor.

You are in that very fifteen minutes, and even now, very now, through the drenching rain and wildness,

something is creeping up the fort walls with invisible, undetectable footsteps.

Something old and dark and very, very evil.

It could be a Rogrebreath, looking to get its blood back.

It could be a werewolf, wanting Xar to join its pack.

Or it could be...

Something else.

Normally Wizard camp would be entirely protected by an invisible barrier of Magic that hung around the forest grove.

But when Xar had taken the sword into the fort, the iron had tunneled a hole in the Magic. The path of the iron sword led up the tree trunk and into Xar's room. And such is the power of iron, that ANYONE or ANYTHING taking the path the iron had taken would be undetected by the Magic...

Too bad, because the two feathers that Xar had tucked into the jacket he left in his room were very gently, *ve-ry* minutely, beginning to glow at the edges with a sickly greenish light.

The snowcats and Squeezjoos and Tiffinstorm and the bear had fallen into the deep sleep of those who have spent a nice old-fashioned day out in the fresh air building Witch-traps and running through Badwoods.

But something in the change in atmosphere made Bodkin and Wish look up from where they were kneeling on the invisible floor of Xar's room and stare around themselves with shivers of sick alarm. The Enchanted Spoon was shaking with anxiety on Wish's head.

Below them, they could hear the sound of the Spelling Competition.

But outside in the forest, the rain, the thunder and the lightning, and the wind, which had been sending Xar's bedroom plunging this way and that as if a lunatic were rocking a baby's cradle, stopped with surprising suddenness.

The thunder ceased, to be replaced by an eerie quietness, a silence, as if the forest world surrounding them were leaning in to gaze at something unusual and frightening enclosed within its shut green fist.

The only sound was the water dripping from the edges of the invisible spell above them... *Drip... drip... drip...*

Wish could see right through the spell up into the starry, starry sky above, the branches of the trees strangely still as if painted against the dark sky.

There was a coldness in the air that Wish had felt when they were being chased in the wood earlier that evening, a coldness that seeped into her.

And to her horror, Wish could see that the black feathers hanging inside Xar's empty jacket were lighting up with a queasy, pallid yellow-green glow that pulsed steadily in and out as if in time with someone breathing.

Wish's breath was so thick in her throat she thought she might choke.

It was as if ants were crawling through her hair, sending each individual strand shooting upward in a thrill of horror.

Above them both, the spell was like a piece of glass, with the liquid of the rain already streaked across it.

But was that something else, some shadow moving like a dream beyond the glass, a nauseating, undulating, greasy movement that blotted out the stars as it moved?

Or was it just the bilious shadow of Wish's own imagination, the tired creation of her bloodshot eyes, after a long and weary and frightening day?

Wish was sure there was a dark shape moving glutinously behind the glass…

At least she *thought* she was sure…

What was it that they said about Witches? That they

were as invisible as ghosts but they had to turn visible when they attacked? Or else their hands passed through you as harmlessly as air?

And then with absolute terror, she knew it was no mirage.

Her painfully stretched ears definitely heard *whispering* in the invisibility above.

Drip... drip... drip... drip.

Whisper... whisper... whisper.

"Sti ereh...sti ereh...sti ereh..."*

"Wake up!" croaked Wish to the snowcats and Squeezjoos and Tiffinstorm in a strangled whisper. "Wake up *NOW*. We have to get out of here..."

The wind began to blow again, a couple of breaths that brought the hot, foul smell of WITCH down into the room, a pungent whiff of poisoned rat and adder's tongue as chock-full of death as a dose from an apothecary.

The snowcats, lying half smothered in leaves, woke to that smell. As one, they opened their sleepy eyes, and all of them knew instantly they needed to be silent, like deer that scent a fox.

Tiffinstorm opened her eyes, one, two, saw the glowing, pulsing feathers and turned as still as if stuffed.

Bodkin tried the door.

But Xar had locked it, of course.

---

*Witches speak the same language as we do, but each individual word is back to front. This means "It's here...it's here...it's here..."

"We're locked in!" said Bodkin in appalled horror.
"We can't get out of here!" before fainting dead away
with his fingers on the handle of the door.

"Bodkin!" shrieked Wish. "Wake up NOW!"

Bodkin woke up with a start, mumbling,
"Where? What? How?"

"Xar's room…" panted the princess. "Wizard
camp… We're being attacked by something really
spooky…"

"What isssss it??????" whispered Tiffinstorm,
staring upward and getting a good grip of her thorn of
a wand.

"The sword! O by the gods of the still
and standing waters… We need the Enchanted
Sword!!!!!!!!!!!!" yelled Wish.

Now, you see, there are no accidents.

There was a *reason* that the Enchanted Sword left
Xar's hand at that precise, very inconvenient moment
for Xar, down below in the Spelling Competition.

Let's face it, Wish needed the sword at that
moment for rather more serious reasons than Xar did.

SLLLLIIIIIIIIIIICCCCCCE!!!!!!

With a great piercing, ripping slice that made
Wish jump out of her skin and nearly die from the
shock of it, and woke up Bodkin, who had fainted
again and was still holding on to the handle of the

door, the Enchanted Sword sliced up through the ceiling of the main hall of the Spelling Competition and through the spell of Xar's floor.

The sword rose up, quivering, hanging in the air in the middle of Xar's room, pointing up at the glassy surface of the spell above, exactly an arm's length away from Wish.

All she had to do was reach out and take it.

Oh thank mistletoe and ivy and every single kind of standing water...

"*Once there were Witches...*" breathed Wish, reading the message on the blade.

"*...but I killed them.*"

She reached out her hand.

She took the sword.

There was a high, piercing, unearthly shriek from the air above her as whatever-it-was dived.

The undulating shape turned dark and very, very solid.

There was a confused rush...

Something of unbelievable force SMASHED into the invisible spell above...

There was another shriek like a curse...

...and through the glass above Wish, three talons pierced through the spell.

Three great shocks of talons, which were very, very

175

real, long, yellow-green, razor-sharp, and curved like swords.

Wish screamed.

If it were not for that spell, she would have been dead indeed, for whatever-it-was had been held up by the spell and crashed into it when it dived.

Zigzagging lines jigsawed across the spell, like ice before it shatters.

Wish thrust the sword upward, and that extraordinary sword leaped in her hands and dragged her with it, and there was another shriek as the iron of the sword sank through the spell into something soft...and—

Whatever-it-was, the huge dark shadow above her, shrieked again and was still.

Wish hauled out the sword, and it came out with a sickening, squelching noise.

Please...begged Wish. *Please let it be dead...*

There was silence for a moment.

Perhaps that thing, whatever-it-was, really was dead?

She had sunk the sword into it pretty deep...

All around, the snowcats were roaring, and Bodkin was repeating "Oh my goodness...my goodness...my goodness..." in a horrified way.

Wish could see
the dull, dark shape
slumped on the spell
above them. It wasn't
moving.

I've killed it,
thought Wish with
terrible sadness. *I've
really killed it...*

Tiffinstorm gazed at
the sword, her mouth open
in horror. "Don't touch the
sword..." whispered the sprite.

The end of the sword was
covered in a strange, milky green
substance, and it appeared to be smoking.

Be's careful, princess, be's careful!

A single drop
quivered on the
end, and as if in
slow motion it fell…
…down toward
Wish's hand.
But Squeezjoos rushed
forward, squeaking: "Be's careful, Princess,
be's careful!!"
…And in his determination to guard
the princess, he threw himself in between the
drop of falling green and Wish's hand, and he let out
a shriek as the green sizzled there, and the poor sprite
shook his own hand to throw off the smoking green
blood.

Squeezjoos leaped up in the air, screaming and
waving his hand in horror. Wish tried to catch him, to
soothe him, to calm him down, with
Tiffinstorm shrieking, "Don't touch!
Don't touch!" in a demented chalk-
screech.

More cracked lines appeared
all over the surface of the spell above
them, like lines on a frozen lake the
moment before it breaks.

178

"GET AWAY FROM THE BED!" yelled Wish, and the snowcats and the sprites flung themselves to the edge of the room—in the nick of time, for a moment later, the cracked, broken spell burst, sending bits of spell raining around the room, and the cold rainwater that had been lying on it came splashing down onto the bed, in a bucketing icy rush, and the dark shape crashed down too and took the bed down with it, down...down...down...burning a bright green hole in that floor, and sinking downward, ever downward, so that Xar's room had a great hole in the center of it like a sinkhole.

A sinkhole, seven feet deep with the corpse of a Witch at the bottom of it.

"I think it's dead," whispered Wish, shakily peering over the edge of the sinkhole. "It's not moving, anyway. Are you all right, Squeezjoos?"

"I's NOT fine..." whispered Squeezjoos, shaking his hand. "I's NOT fine...That is bad Magic...Very bad Magic..."

Even as he spoke, the green crept up his arm, to his heart and his head, turning him stiff as a tree twig, and he dropped, shaking and trembling, like a stone and fell down rigid to the floor. Wish picked him up gently.

It is as I said.

Bad things have been happening in Xar's room.

Very, very bad things.

And a lot can happen in fifteen minutes.

11. Xar Gets More Than He Wished For

Xar did not immediately notice anything different about his room when the Enchanter's Magic broke open the locked door and the flying chains slung him and the animals and sprites in there, with Caliburn flapping in just before the door was magically slammed behind them both.

Why would Xar think there would be anything different? He had only left that very same room about fifteen minutes earlier.

Anyway, he was too busy swearing loud and long and extremely creative curses at the shut door, and kicking it with his foot, to notice the strangely quiet, tense, and, quite frankly, *shell-shocked* atmosphere in the wrecked room behind him.

"Um...Xar..." said Caliburn. "I think we may have a problem..."

"I know we have a problem!" howled Xar. "My father and my brother don't realize how important I am! Nobody realizes!"

"No, I mean, a *real* problem, Xar."

Xar turned around.

His jaw dropped open.

Wish was standing, stricken, holding on to the Enchanted Sword.

"YOU took my sword!" spat Xar savagely. "It's all YOUR fault, you beastly burglar of a Warrior! I was beating Looter and then YOU interrupted! How did you do it, you treacherous daughter of Queen Sychorax?"

Xar made a grab for the sword and the sprites screeched simultaneously:

"Don't touch the ssssssword!!!!"

And that was when Xar realized that things had gone even more wrong than he'd thought.

His room was always messy, of course.

But now, right in the center where the bed once was, there was an enormous hole, seven feet deep, instead.

Wish and Bodkin were standing sadly on either side of it.

"WHAT HAVE YOU DONE TO MY ROOM???????" Xar gasped. "Oh my goodness, I only left you for fifteen minutes— what have you done to my room????"

WHAT HAVE YOU DONE TO MY ROOM

Bodkin pointed down the hole. "A Witch attacked us. We killed it."

"Oh by ivy and mistletoe and green things with long, hairy whiskers!" goggled Xar. "Are you quite sure it was a *Witch*? It wasn't just a Rogrebreath coming to get its blood back?"

"Take a look..." said Bodkin.

Xar peered down into the hole, and there, at the bottom, was something huge and dark and dead, with long, feathered wings for arms, and a nose like a beak, and even though it was not moving, a reek of dark Magic came off that crumpled feathered thing so strongly that it made Xar reel back.

Yup.

He'd never seen a Witch before, but that was a Witch, all right.

Oh by the nostril hairs of the Grim Grisly Gruntleogre...

What had his father just said about obtaining Magic from a dark source?

The reality of a situation is sometimes a little different from the imagining of it, and the recent scene with his father had made him realize that perhaps Encanzo wasn't going to be as open-minded about Witches and dark Magic as Xar had thought he would be.

And what was that threat about taking all of Xar's beloved animals and sprites away from him?

"Be good…" said Xar through white lips. "My father just said: Be good…I don't think this really counts as being good, do you?"

He gazed down at the hole in a sort of trance.

"I mean…a big hole the size of a beastly great monument right in the middle of my ROOM with a WITCH in it?"

Xar waved his arms around in agitation.

"How are we going to get RID of it??? We have to get it out of here! My father said one more disobedient thing and he was going to expel me! I think this counts as about FIFTY disobedient things, don't you?"

"You can't touch it!" screamed Tiffinstorm and Ariel. "Don't go near it!"

"How can we get rid of something we can't even touch??????" said Xar. "We'll have to cover it, but with what?" Xar started rather desperately kicking leaves down the hole, but it was like trying to cover a volcano with individual snowflakes.

"And that isn't the worst of it," said Wish, swallowing hard.

Carefully, Wish laid down the sword and opened a piece of cloth she was holding in the other hand. Inside lay Squeezjoos, shaking like he had the plague.

Okay, just when Xar thought that things couldn't get worse, they got worse.

"What on earth happened to Squeezjoos?" Xar gasped.

"He got Witchblood on him," said Wish sorrowfully. "I'm so sorry, Xar."

"Is that bad? What does that mean? What's wrong with him?"

Squeezjoos had turned jade green, and his wings had folded up like they had been crushed in an invisible fist. Every now and then the trembling would cease, and he turned absolutely rigid for a second as if he had been frozen, before breaking out into violent shaking once more.

"I's guarded the princess…" said Squeezjoos. "But I's fine. I's jussst fine…" But you could see from Squeezjoos's scared eyes that he was terribly frightened about what was happening.

Caliburn said sadly, "Sprites are much smaller creatures than you are, Xar. The Witchblood will affect them much harder. You have led this sprite into bad, bad trouble."

"I will take this sprite to my father," said Xar through numb white lips. "My father can do anything."

Caliburn said gently, "I think even your father will not be able to heal Squeezjoos, Xar."

It was time for some very hard truths.

"For very soon, this sprite will either die or fall into a coma," said Caliburn. "And when he wakes, he will have turned to the dark side. He will become a creature of the dark, and he will seek out Witches to be his master."

A horrible silence.

"And this means that the stain on your hand really IS Witchblood," said Caliburn. "I am so sorry, Xar. I tried to warn you. You wished to be Magic, and now you have the wrong kind of Magic..."

Xar turned over his hand.

There, right in the middle of the palm, was the bright green stain. There was no way of covering it, any more than he could cover the great big hole with the Witch in it in the middle of the room.

He tried to wipe it off on his cloak, but it did not move.

"I can't even make the Witchblood perform Magic..." said Xar sadly.

"If your father finds out that is Witchblood on your hand," said Caliburn, "he will send you to a Correctional Facility, and maybe the dark Magic will not yet have reached your brain, and you can be saved from turning to the dark side yourself. But your father would then be forced to expel you from the Wizards forever."

"No!" cried Xar. "No!"

"What would you have your father do, Xar?" said Caliburn. "The other Wizards were calling for you to be expelled just for TRYING to get dark Magic. But you have succeeded, Xar... You have been in the Badwoods, and that is forbidden. You have brought iron into the camp, and that is forbidden. You are using dark Magic, and that is forbidden. You have drawn a Witch to us, and that is forbidden."

"NO!" yelled Xar.

"Even your father cannot turn back time, Xar," said Caliburn. "Nobody can turn back time. That is impossible."

"That's the point of Magic, isn't it?" said Xar. "To do impossible things?"

There was a long silence.

"There are some things that are done that cannot be undone," said Caliburn.

Ah, "Do As You Would Be Done By, or You Will Be Well and Truly Done" is a harsh law indeed.

"You stupid Warriors!" raged Xar. "This is all your fault! This is your stupid sword and your stupid Witch, and I should never have left Squeezjoos with you when you can't look after him."

Wish and Bodkin looked away, for Xar, the boy-who-never-cried, was crying.

Xar knew in his heart of hearts he couldn't really blame Wish and Bodkin for this. He felt a sludgy, depressed weight of guilt. This was all his own fault. Squeezjoos had trusted him. If he couldn't save Squeezjoos, he would never forgive himself...

"I'm so sorry, Squeezjoos," said Xar wretchedly. "I never meant for this to happen...There must be some way I can make amends and put things back to the way they were?"

"I's trussst you, Master," said Squeezjoos through shaking green lips, looking up at Xar adoringly. "You iss my leader, and so you will ressscue me, because that is what a leader doess."

Xar carefully put Squeezjoos in the front pocket of his waistcoat, and then Xar put his arm in front of his face.

"I WISH I had never wished to be Magic," said Xar passionately. "I WISH I could give it all up so that

Squeezjoos could be fine again. I WISH I had never set that stupid Witch-trap in the first place, I WISH, I WISH, I WISH..."

But wish how he may, Xar could not turn back time.

They had all wanted Xar to learn a lesson, but this was a far, far worse lesson than anyone had ever dreamed of, and it was dreadful to see him crying and sitting there so small and silent and sad and un-Xar-like. Even his quiff of hair had drooped.

Xar cried, and Wish patted him on the back sympathetically, and the animals and the sprites pretended they hadn't noticed he was crying.

Every now and then Xar blurted out fiercely: "I am NOT crying, and I will KILL anyone who says I am!"

And the sprites pretended to be terrified of him to make him feel better.

Down in the hall below them, the sound of music stopped abruptly, to be replaced by voices.

Xar removed his arm from in front of his face, suddenly alert.

"Lissssten..." whispered Tiffinstorm. "Someone must have noticed the break in the Magic covering the fort—they will be telling the King Enchanter..."

The three children looked at one another, at the

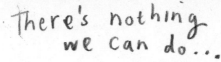

dying green sprite, at the sinkhole in the
center of the room with the corpse of a
Witch in it.

"They will know it issss something
to do with you, Xar... They will come up
here... into this room..."

This was bad.

There was no doubt about it.

This was really, really bad.

Wish looked at Xar's face, transformed from its
usual cheekiness into total misery and guilt at the plight
of his sprite.

She forgot Xar was an enemy who had stolen her
sword and kidnapped them.

She put out her hand and touched Xar on the
shoulder.

"Don't despair, Xar," said Wish. "It's not too
late... It's never too late. I have a plan for how we could
save Squeezjoos."

Bodkin felt the first stirrings of unease.

"*Yes?*" said Xar, lifting his drooping head.

"Do you remember I told you, earlier on, my
mother has this Stone-That-Takes-Away-Magic that she
keeps in her dungeons?" said Wish. "We *could* take you
back with us to Warrior fort, and then we can break
into my mother's dungeons and get Squeezjoos to touch

There's ALWAYS something we can do, Bodkin

the stone, and that will take away the bad Magic of the Witch and save his life," said Wish.

"Could that work?" said Xar, eagerly turning to Caliburn.

"Yes...no...I don't know!" said Caliburn. "I suppose in theory, that is what the stone does—it takes away Magic...but something tells me this is an extremely bad idea..."

"Well, generally it *would* be a bad idea to touch a Stone-That-Takes-Away-Magic," said Xar, with growing excitement, "but in this case we have a whole lot of Magic that we want to get rid of, don't we? Because at the same time I can touch the stone and get rid of this Witchblood on my hand, which my father wouldn't like and it doesn't even work..."

"I also wonder what happened to Crusher," said Wish thoughtfully. "He hasn't gotten back yet, has he? I'm a bit concerned that my mother's Warriors might have captured him."

"Do you think so?" said Xar, suddenly worried, for in his Xar-like fashion he had completely forgotten about Crusher. "Do you mean to say…I may have put Crusher in danger AS WELL? Wow…even for me, this has been a really bad day…"

Xar was looking crestfallen again, so Wish hurriedly pointed out that while they were in Sychorax's dungeons, if Crusher was in there too, they could release him.

"That's a brilliant plan, and it solves everything all in one go!" said Xar in relief. "For an enemy, and a weird one at that, you've come up with a great idea! What are we waiting for? Let's go!"

"Hang on a second!" boggled Bodkin. "This isn't brilliant at all, Princess! I am putting my foot down! You can't take this lunatic back to Warrior fort with us!"

"I have to agree with Bodkin," said Caliburn. "And if Queen Sychorax catches Xar, she'll put him in her dungeons forever, not to mention take away the Magic of all his other sprites…"

"My mother's not as bad as all that!" objected Wish. "She's lovely!"

"Well, I wouldn't say *lovely*, exactly," said Bodkin gloomily. "SCARY. That's what she is. SCARY. She is one scary mother."

"She's a queen and a mother and it's a mother's *job* to be scary," said Wish.

"Well, she's very successful at her job." Bodkin shivered.

"But we've got to go into the dungeons anyway to return my mother's sword, and we can't let poor Squeezjoos die, can we?" said Wish. "This is sort of our fault too, and he's flown by our side...Look at him!"

Xar sensed Bodkin weakening as he looked at the tragically rigid body of the little hairy fairy tucked into the front of Xar's waistcoat, shivering in pain and fear.

"Poor Squeezjoos..." Xar sighed. "He will be so unhappy trapped in a coma. He loved to dance, you know—to fly through the windy trees in autumn— and now his feet will be locked, his voice that sang to nightingales choked in his stony throat..."

"STOP IT!" said Bodkin, putting his hands over his ears.

"And even Xar..." said Wish. "He's conceited and full of himself and kind of annoying—"

"I am, aren't I?" said Xar proudly.

"But we can't let him get expelled from his tribe! Xar made a few mistakes...but doesn't he deserve a second chance? We *all* deserve a second chance," pleaded Wish.

Bodkin sighed. "All right," he said. "It's a mad idea…but all right, we'll help them. But you have to promise me, Wish, after all this is over, you really will start being a normal, ordinary Warrior princess…"

"I promise," said Wish.

The three of them shook hands on the plan.

"Who'd have thought it?" marveled Xar. "Wizards and Warriors, working together…"

The sounds of voices and running feet were getting nearer and nearer.

"Okay," said Xar briskly, picking up the Spelling Book and putting it in his pocket, "wolves, bear, you stay here. Caliburn, snowcats, sprites, you're coming with us. But we're going to need to be quick here, so we'll have to go by door…Tiffinstorm! Do the spell!"

"WhyisitalwaysMEwhohastodoeverything?" grumbled Tiffinstorm, getting out a number six from her wandbag, and lobbing one of her spells at the door of Xar's room.

"What do you mean, go by *door*?" asked Bodkin uneasily.

As if in answer to his question, with a mighty cre-e-e-eak, the door of Xar's room shrugged in its frame, and tore itself out of its hinges, and waddled into the center of the room, before tipping—SLAM!—flat on its face onto the floor, and then gently rising about a foot in the air, in a cloud of dust.

Xar picked up the sword and climbed on top of the door, shouting, "Come on, you guys! Quick! Quick!"

"Ohhh no…" said Bodkin, shaking his head hysterically. "The snowcats were bad enough, but are you really expecting me to ride on a DOOR, like a flying carpet in a story?"

"It's perfectly safe," said Xar, helping Wish up beside him. "Kind of…And the snowcats can run a lot faster when we're not on their backs…HURRY!"

"Come on, Bodkin!" said Wish excitedly.

The snowcats had already jumped out of Xar's window and climbed down the ladders and platforms, so it was too late to travel by snowcat.

Even the Enchanted Spoon had hopped on enthusiastically next to Xar and Wish, and seemed to be looking at Bodkin expectantly, as if he had faith that Bodkin could be the kind of person who would see flying on the back of a door as an exciting opportunity rather than an act of suicide.

Oh dear, I have to do this…I can't be less of a hero than a SPOON…But…

What am I doing???? thought Bodkin as he clambered onto the back of the door beside Wish and Xar. It wasn't even an entirely *complete* door, for the door of Xar's room had led a difficult life, so there were great cracks and splits all across it. "Held together by

Magic…held together by Magic…" Bodkin repeated to himself reassuringly as Xar jerked the key in the keyhole frantically to the right, and Bodkin grabbed onto the top of the door only just in time as, with a sickening lurch, it flew off, up through the nonexistent ceiling, and into the night.

For the first five minutes, Bodkin was so terrified he didn't even open his eyes—he just concentrated on not falling off and not fainting and not throwing up because of the wild swooping motion of the flying door. And when he did eventually open his eyes, he regretted it. They were slaloming madly through the trees of the forest and, through the crazy paving of the cracks in the door, below him he could see the running snowcats and the bright little blinks of the flying sprites.

Bodkin let out a moan of fear.

Wish's eyes were like stars, she was enjoying it so much. She and Xar were whooping with every swoop.

It had to be said: Xar was an excellent, if reckless, flying-door driver. The door swayed and soared like a peregrine falcon with Xar swiveling the key in the keyhole with exactly the right smoothness and dexterity to wing its way neatly through the forest.

"We're going to crash…We're going to crash…" moaned Bodkin.

"We're NOT going to crash," said Wish exultantly

as they swooped through the upper canopy. "We're flying like BIRDS! And we're going to get back before morning, and we're going to cure Squeezjoos, and free Crusher, and get rid of Xar's bad Magic..."

"We're going to crash, and if your scary mother catches us breaking into her scary dungeons, we'll be in such trouble it doesn't bear thinking about," chattered Bodkin through white lips.

"Don't think about, it then," advised Wish. "Maybe she *won't* catch us, Bodkin...and we haven't crashed YET, have we? Just relax and enjoy it—it's not every day you get to fly somewhere by door. Just go with it."

And as they soared gloriously and recklessly through the trees on the back of the broken flying door, the night wind blowing their hair back, Bodkin found to his astonishment that if he let himself relax and go with the motion of the door, he could whoop with joy along with the others.

Bodkin's father would have been amazed (and not very pleased) if he could have seen him now. This is the problem with adventures. They bring out parts of you that you never even knew were there.

The feathers fly on,
and we have to follow.
I told you
that these woods
were
dangerous...

PART Two
Making Amends

12. Iron Warrior Fort

ar and Caliburn and the sprites and the snowcats and Wish and Bodkin were lying in the undergrowth in front of iron Warrior fort. They had a problem.

Breaking OUT of a heavily armed Warrior fort with seven ditches and thirteen watchtowers is hard enough. But breaking IN is virtually impossible.

And it is made even harder if you are accompanied by a Wizard with a Witch-stain and a band of snowcats and sprites.

They could see the sentries on the battlements, pacing nervously up, down, up, down, constantly straining to see what was out there in the forest.

They had abandoned the door in the cover of the forest, for a flying door is rather conspicuous. And then Wish led them around to the stable entrance, which was where she had sneaked out in the first place. The doors there were always opening and closing, with hunting parties going out and returning.

Xar got the sprites to cover them with weather spells and invisibility spells so that they could sneak up on the entrance without being seen.

"Thisss will only work until we get inside the fort.

Tiffinstorm'sss Magic will not work in there," warned Tiffinstorm. "There isss too much iron…"

"Stop worrying, everyone," said Xar confidently. "I've broken into more forts than you've had hot dinners."

It took a while for the little party of snowcats, sprites, Xar, Bodkin, and Wish to maneuver themselves into position underneath the drawbridge.

And then the plan worked beautifully…at first.

Xar and Wish and Bodkin and the snowcats stole invisibly into the fort, under the cloak of Ariel's and Tiffinstorm's spells.

It wasn't until they were a good way into the stableyard that it was clear the spells were being affected by the sheer amount of iron surrounding them. To Xar's horror, he could see his feet below him, s-l-o-w-l-y becoming visible.

Wish and Bodkin were even more obviously there already, although Bodkin was materializing the other way around, and for a second he was just a ghoulishly floating torso.

But if we can just make it to the next building, thought Xar in a panic, *maybe we can hide in the shadows there…*

"Run!" he whispered. "Run!"

Too late.

A sentry had turned, to see the bottom half of a gradually-becoming-visible snowcat bounding across Queen Sychorax's stableyard.

"MAGIC!" roared the sentry.

They were discovered.

Wish had to make up an entirely new plan right there on the spot.

"HELP!" cried Wish, who was now entirely visible. "HELP! HELP! HELP!!!!! OVER HERE! WIZARD ATTACK!"

The Warrior guards turned.

And there was Sychorax's weird little daughter, pointing at a Wizard, with three furious snowcats and a cloud of buzzing sprites.

"WIZARD ATTACK!" cried the guards. "Sound the alarm!"

The Wizards don't often attack the Warriors, for obvious reasons.

But Warriors, nonetheless, are always ready for any kind of attack.

Ready in a manner that you could almost call overkill.

From all over came the thunderous sounds of clattering armor and clanking swords and stamping iron-clad feet as the soldiers of Queen Sychorax leaped into action.

"THE ATTACK IS IN THE THIRD
QUARTER! BACKUP IS NEEDED!" roared the
guards who had already surrounded them, swords
and spears at the ready. "CALL OUT THE
SPRITE-CATCHERS! READY THE SNOWCAT-
TRAPPERS! ALERT THE MAGIC POLICE!"

The shouting grew louder, and the Household
Defender Warriors poured from all directions into the
stableyard.

*Oh by the goggle eyes of the Greenbearded
Greentoothed goblin*, thought Xar. *There's masses of
them…I never thought there could be so many
Warriors IN THE WORLD.*

"Kingcat! Nighteye! Don't you dare move!" spat
Xar, for he knew that the snowcats were longing to
launch themselves at the enemy, and he could see from
the look in the Warriors' eyes that if the snowcats even
made *one* bound in their direction, the Warriors would
kill them instantly.

Xar put his hand to his belt to take out the
Enchanted Sword…

…but the sword was not there.

He looked up. Wish was ten yards away from him
now, and she had been swooped up into the arms of an
enormous Warrior.

"The princess has been secured and made safe!"

roared the Warrior, and one look into Wish's guilty eyes told Xar everything he needed to know.

Xar was furious.

Treachery! Betrayal!

Wish had *nicked* that sword off him.

He had fallen into the trap of trusting an enemy, and just when he had relaxed and let his guard down, thinking Wish was on his side, she had the sheer cheek to steal it off him when he wasn't looking.

(Xar conveniently forgot, of course, that he himself had done exactly the same thing only a couple of hours earlier.)

Wizards are very good at cursing.

It was a habit that they had caught from the Droods, who used it as a way of attacking the enemy.

So Xar cursed now, and he cursed loud and long.

"You treacherous, shrimpy BURGLAR of a Warrior!" yelled Xar. "My father was right about you guys! You're TRAITORS and LIARS and you, Wish, are as WICKED as your repellent, Magic-hating murderer of a she-devil-mother!"

"He insulted the queen and he's going for his weapon!" cried the Chief Guard. "Archers! Eliminate him!"

The archers at the back of the Warrior ranks raised their bows, all in time with one another, with exquisite precision. They were so well trained it would have been a pleasure to admire their timing—if they were not just about to kill you.

"NO!" shouted Wish from the arms of the Warrior who was carrying her. "HE'S NOT ARMED! DON'T YOU DARE KILL *ANY OF THEM* OR I WILL TELL MY MOTHER!"

Now, the Warriors were not above killing an unarmed Wizard. In fact, they did it quite a lot, when Sychorax wasn't looking. But they were, to a man and a woman, absolutely petrified of their queen, so reluctantly the archers' arms wavered in a disappointed sort of way, but they did not let go of their arrows. They lowered their bows.

"SECURE THE TARGETS!" shouted the Chief Guard. "CONTAIN THE REBELLION! LAUNCH THE SPRITE-CATCHERS! AND WHEN YOU'VE DONE THAT—"

The Chief Guard sighed, then swallowed hard. "Somebody had better go and inform Her Majesty."

The Chief Guard's Deputy stepped forward. "Er…do we have to?"

"Of course we have to!" barked the Chief Guard. "In fact, since you had the cheek to question my orders, I nominate *you* as the lucky person to go and tell her!"

Peeeeeooooowww!!!

208

The sprite-catcher Warriors fired bows that launched nets with little iron weights attached to them into the air toward the sprites.

Out in the open air of the forest, the sprites could fly fleet as arrows, dodging and feinting with such quicksilver swiftness that they were just a blur of energy and light.

But here, the iron surrounding them acted like a drug on their flying skills. They bumbled about, slow and confused, shrieking madly, poor little things, as they scrambled away, trying to get far from the scary iron, but instead plummeting to the ground, caught in the nets and gasping and straining for breath, like stranded fish.

All of them were caught except for the tiny hairy fairy, Bumbleboozle, who had crept into Wish's pocket as soon as disaster struck.

The guards leaped forward and Xar was bound with chains so tightly that only his head was poking out. The snowcats were chained up too.

"TURNIPS IN TIN CANS!" roared Xar, bright red with anger. And that was how Sychorax saw him when she swept into the stableyard a little time later and found a bundle of chains with a Wizard boy's head poking out of it, screaming insults at her troops.

Queen
Sychorax

13. The Questioning of Queens

At the entrance of Queen Sychorax, the Warriors bowed so low their foreheads nearly hit the floor.

Sychorax was scary.

But then she was a very great queen, and as Wish said, maybe great queens HAVE to be scary.

There were those who said that a woman was too weak to rule a tribe of invading iron Warriors—but they said it very, very quietly just in case Queen Sychorax should hear them.

She was lovely, all right—if by "lovely" you mean pretty.

Hair like a golden waterfall, slim as a candle, six feet tall and most of it muscle, all the sort of stuff that comes in handy if you're going to be a Warrior queen and you like to make an entrance.

Whether her *character* was lovely, well, that's an entirely different question, and we'll have to see about that.

She was dressed in white, with a single black pearl hanging from one ear.

Queen Sychorax talked very, very softly, in a golden pear-drop of a voice that was as mild as the bite of an adder. She did not have to speak loudly, that lovely Queen Sychorax, for everyone leaned in to listen, and you could hear a pin drop in the terrified silence that followed her around like a sweeping cloak.

Even Xar stopped his cursing for a moment.

"So…" said Queen Sychorax, in that quiet gentle voice, as sweetly pure as the stab of an icicle. "Where is this Wizard attack that has so rudely awoken me before daybreak?"

Petrified, the Chief Guard stepped forward and indicated Xar, the sprites, and the snowcats with a sweep of his armored hand.

"We have contained the attack, Your Majesty," said the Chief Guard.

"Yeesss," said Queen Sychorax, surveying the Wizard attack. "It's not a very *large* attack, is it, to warrant waking a queen so early in the morning? I thought I was supposed to have the finest Warrior sentries in the Warrior world, and yet one small Wizard boy can still enter my fort undetected?"

"STEP FORWARD THE SENTRIES WHO LET THE WIZARD ATTACK HAPPEN!" roared the Chief Guard.

The sentries stepped forward smartly.

"The sentries on watch should be locked in Dungeon 308, and as the officer in charge at the time, Chief Guard,

I hold you responsible, so you can lock yourself in too, and pass the keys back through the bars," said Queen Sychorax. "I have no need for failures in this fort."

"Yes, Your Majesty," bowed the Chief Guard, and he and the sentries marched off to lock themselves in Dungeon 308.

"Who captured the Wizard and his Magic companions in the first place?"

"Your daughter," said another guard, indicating Wish.

Queen Sychorax raised an eyebrow.

"Really?" said Queen Sychorax in surprise. "How...unusually Warrior-like of her."

Next she said, "Unchain the prisoner."

"But, Your Majesty, is that wise?" said the Deputy to the Chief Guard. "He *is* a Wizard, after all..."

Queen Sychorax gave him a look.

The Deputy undid Xar's chains.

The Warriors and the citizens of the fort, who had arrived on the scene, took a step back, for Wizards were known to be extremely dangerous.

Queen Sychorax glided around Xar, looking him over as if he were an unusual type of insect that she was seeing for the first time.

"Who are you, and what are you doing in my fort?"

"I am Xar, son of Encanzo, the Great King Enchanter," said Xar proudly. "And the wildwoods belong to US WIZARDS, not you stupid, Magic-less, heartless invaders!"

Queen Sychorax sighed. "The ignorance of these poor Wizards," she said. "We are civilization. We are progress. Look at us. Look at our weapons, our clothes, our tapestries, our furniture. You Wizards, in comparison, are barely better than animals..."

The fort was, indeed, very dazzlingly decked out, and Queen Sychorax had a thing about tidiness, so every piece of armor and sword was polished until it shone like silver. Even the giant heads hanging in the main hall, dead as doornails though they were, had their beards brushed daily. So the whole effect was pretty spectacular and Xar was secretly rather impressed by the sophistication of Warrior weaponry and the splendidness of their clothes and fort.

So this stopped him a moment.

Caliburn said warningly: "Warrior stuff is dangerous...It seduces you..."

"And why do you need these Warrior knickknacks?" hissed Ariel. "When you have the moon to dance under, and a violin to sing the tune? Are they worth your freedom, your wandering spirits?"

"That's right!" shouted Xar. "You Warriors have

come here and stolen our forest, and one day, when I grow up to be the leader of my tribe, I promise I am going to KILL THE LOT OF YOU!"

Queen Sychorax looked at him intently. "Will you now?" she said. "Wee-ee-ell...this is interesting. I *could* make sure that you never grow up, couldn't I? Or Encanzo might be willing to pay to have his son returned...or we could hold on to you in exchange for his good conduct..."

Xar looked the queen straight in the eye.

The thing about Xar was, he didn't scare easily.

"You, Queen Sychorax, are the SOFTEST pitiless Warrior queen I have ever seen!" said Xar.

Sychorax flinched.

The entire courtyard took an intake of breath.

Queen Sychorax's eyes sharpened to splinters.

"*What* did you say?"

"Evil destroyer of forest!" shouted Xar. "May you be ground by the teeth of a Rogrebreath into teeny little pieces of dust much smaller than the fleas of an Itch-sprite!"

"Be polite, Xar!" said Caliburn in an agonized fashion.

"Wickedness-on-legs! Pointy-ears! Hair-like-a-bear's-bottom! Nose-like-a-pointy-potato!"

Once Xar started cursing, he really put his

heart and soul into it. It had been a difficult day, what with being humiliated by Looter and told off by his father, and he put all the fear and the fury into a long, elaborate cursing of Sychorax, queen of the Warriors.

"Oh, Xar," moaned Caliburn, his wings over his eyes. "This time you're asking to get yourself killed—you really are..."

"You can curse all you like, Xar, son of Encanzo," whispered Queen Sychorax, her eyes like flinty arrows. "But it may not get you what you want. What *do* you want, by the way?"

Xar suddenly remembered what he wanted.

He wanted to save Squeezjoos.

He stopped midcurse, panting.

"I demand that you put my sprite and my hand on the Stone-That-Takes-Away-Magic as soon as you can!" said Xar.

Sychorax looked at him in astonishment.

She was used to prisoners who begged and prayed and beseeched and pleaded that they should never be taken to the terrible stone: "Please, please, please, Queen Sychorax, we will do whatever you want, but do not take us to the Stone-That-Takes-Away-Magic."

Not prisoners who demanded to be led there immediately, while at the same time insulting her.

This Wizard might be full of trickery.

But Sychorax was used to trickery.

She was tricky *herself*.

"Take me to the stone!" said Xar. "As quickly as your stupid, lumping great Warriors can move in those iron fool-suits of theirs. This is an emergency!"

And then he reached into his breast pocket, and his hands were shaking as he unwrapped Squeezjoos.

Oh, this was terrible. With a lurch of his heart, Xar saw that Squeezjoos was looking worse than ever. He was green as an emerald, trembling all over as if he had the flu, drifting in and out of consciousness, rigid one moment, fever-racked the next. For a second the hairy fairy's glazed, confused eyes focused as if he knew where he was, and he held up his feverish, shaking little arms in entreaty to Xar and the other Big People. "Help me..." whispered Squeezjoos. "Help me..."

Xar turned to Queen Sychorax.

"I want to save my sprite..." said Xar despairingly.

Queen Sychorax started as she looked at Squeezjoos.

"What happened," said Queen Sychorax grimly, "to your sprite?"

"He got Witchblood on him," said Xar.

The Warrior soldiers and citizens gave a great gasp of horror and stood back even farther from the Wizard boy.

Queen Sychorax was a very great Warrior queen, so she would never show fear. But her face turned to a diamond stiffness.

"A *Witch*, you say?" said Queen Sychorax.

"But Witches are extinct…" said the Deputy to the Chief Guard.

"Liar!" called a Warrior from the crowd. "All Wizards are liars!"

"I saw the Witch dead myself," said Xar. "It was definitely a Witch. And it gave me—this…"

Xar held up his palm to show the green stain in the middle of it.

"A Witch-stain!" cried the crowd, and they stepped back even farther.

"Cowards!" snapped Queen Sychorax. "According to legend, Witches' blood is only dangerous if it mixes with YOUR blood! Show me that hand of yours, boy!"

Xar put his hand out again.

Queen Sychorax stared at the green mark. She took a good look at Squeezjoos too, taking the little bundle he was wrapped in out of Xar's hands and looking at him from all angles.

And then she turned to the crowd.

"It is as I suspected," said Queen Sychorax, holding up the poor poisoned sprite so that everyone could see him, and then she lifted her gentle voice to one of ringing hardness. "WITCHES ARE NOT EXTINCT, AND THEY HAVE RETURNED TO THE FOREST!"

The crowd recoiled in horror.

"I HAVE BEEN RIGHT TO ARM US AS I HAVE DONE!" cried Sychorax. "Right to increase our sentries, add to our watchtowers."

To Xar, she said, "Now I see why you might want to visit the Stone-That-Takes-Away-Magic rather urgently, Xar, son of Encanzo. It is, as you say, an emergency, for unless your sprite touches the stone to remove the Witch Magic within the next twenty-four hours, I imagine the sprite will die."

Sychorax was a noticing sort of person and she certainly noticed the tears in Xar's eyes when she said those words and the shake of his head.

"No," whispered Xar, "no, he must not die! He will not! He must not! I will not let him! Don't worry, Squeezjoos, trust me, I won't let that happen..." for Squeezjoos, cowering and quaking in the queen's hands, and staring up at her stern, unrelenting profile, had let out a whimper as he heard these words.

Sychorax sighed sympathetically. "A queen of Warriors must be merciful as well as strong," she said. "And so I shall take you and your sprite to the stone, and I very much hope for both your sakes that it will not be too late."

Sychorax handed the bundle containing Squeezjoos to her Deputy, who held him out at arm's length, shaking, for he did not want to be holding a Witch-poisoned sprite.

"But before I take you there," said Sychorax sweetly, "I have a few questions to ask you..."

"Uh-oh..." whispered Caliburn. "Be careful, be very careful, Xar, of the questioning of queens..."

"You mentioned that you saw a *dead* Witch," said Queen Sychorax. "That interests me extraordinarily, for according to legend, Witches are hard to kill. So—who killed this Witch? And with what?"

There was a silence.

Standing some way behind Queen Sychorax, Wish was waving her arms about frantically to get Xar's attention, and staring at him in an agonized sort of way.

Xar could see the hilt of the Enchanted Sword poking out from beneath her cloak.

And Wish was mouthing something that looked a bit like: "I'm on your side..."

Was she really on his side? Or wasn't she? Xar didn't know.

But in that moment Xar realized that just possibly Wish might have stolen the sword, not because she was a treacherously tricksy traitor of a Warrior, but because she didn't want the sword to be captured along with Xar.

"*I* killed the Witch," said Xar eventually. "With a bow and arrow."

"Really?" said Queen Sychorax, raising an eyebrow. "For, by complete coincidence, only yesterday I lost a large, ancient Witch-killing sword from my dungeons. It disappeared, POOF! Just like that, and ever since, my Household Defenders have been turning the fort upside down looking for it. Do you know anything about that sword, Xar, son of Encanzo?"

"No," said Xar.

"A large, ancient sword with the words 'Once there were Witches...but I killed them' written on the blade?"

"I've never seen a sword like that in my life," said Xar.

"And do you know where it is now?" said Sychorax disbelievingly.

"No," said Xar. "How could I when I've never seen it in the first place?"

"You *lie!*" said Sychorax, swift as an adder.

"I'm not lying!" protested Xar.

"I am afraid that you are," said Queen Sychorax.

I said that Queen Sychorax was a noticing sort of person.

Her sharp, flinty eyes had spotted something sticking out of one of Xar's pockets—a half-full bottle of "Love-Never-Lies" potion.

"I know you are lying," said Queen Sychorax, "because that is one of your strange Wizard medicines, which changes color when a person lies."

She pointed at the bottle, and the liquid inside was a swirl of darkest indigo, the deep purple that indicated that the person who was touching it was telling a lie.

Bother it! thought Xar. *She's as bad as my father… That's the second time today I've been caught out by that beastly love potion. I really must remember not to carry one of the truth drugs around with me; it cramps my style.*

But how would a Warrior queen know about the "Love-Never-Lies" potion, and what it did?

"Study your enemy," said Queen Sychorax, as if Xar had spoken aloud. "It is extremely important to study your enemy very carefully. I know a great deal

about you Wizards and your curses and your Wort-
cunning and your troublemaking poisons, and this
knowledge often comes in useful."

Queen Sychorax reached forward, removed the
bottle of "Love-Never-Lies" potion from Xar's pocket,
and shook it, watching thoughtfully as the liquid
turned back to pale red again. "And the fact that you
were LYING tells me that you *have* seen my sword, you
do know where it is, and if you wanted to, you could
tell me its whereabouts right now...Search the
Wizard!"

Very reluctantly, the Warrior guards searched
Xar, for they did not really want to go anywhere near
a Wizard with a Witch-stain, but they were far too
frightened of Queen Sychorax to disobey her orders.

They found plenty of interesting things in Xar's
pockets. Curses and spells and potions and herbs
of all sorts.

But no sword.

"Hmm..." said Queen Sychorax. "I wonder what
you have done with it. Where is my sword, Xar, son of
Encanzo?"

"I refuse to answer!" said Xar, folding his arms.

"All right, then," said Queen Sychorax calmly. "I
will make a bargain with you. I HAD intended to hold
you for ransom. I WAS going to send a message to your

father saying that if he ever wanted to see his rude little burglar of a son alive again, he must give himself up to me. Taking away the Magic of the great Wizard Encanzo would be a blow the Wizards would find very hard to recover from."

Xar flinched in horror.

"But..." mused Queen Sychorax, "if Witches have returned to the forest once more, I really am going to need that Witch-killing sword.

"So," said Queen Sychorax briskly, "I will be very reasonable. If *you* give me back my sword, *I* will take you and your sprite to the Stone-That-Takes-Away-Magic, and then I will not hold you to ransom for your father after all. I will let you and your sprites and your animals go free. How is that for an offer?"

"Do you promise?" said Xar.

"Of course I promise!" snapped Queen Sychorax. "Are you questioning the word of a queen?"

It was a tempting offer.

Xar considered it.

He was trapped. He would never be able to overcome so many Warriors holding him at once, and this would at least get Squeezjoos cured and...

...and then he saw Wish's face again.

Wish was making anguished eye movements

toward the "Love-Never-Lies" potion in Queen Sychorax's hands.

The liquid had turned so indigo that it was very nearly black.

"You lie!" said Xar, pointing at the "Love-Never-Lies" potion. "You lie, and I refuse your offer!"

Queen Sychorax gave a start and looked down at the bottle. "Dear, *dear*," she said good-humoredly, "that *was* careless of me! And very clever of *you*, Xar, son of Encanzo. I like an intelligent enemy. It keeps me on my toes.

"You're quite right, I *am* lying," Queen Sychorax admitted.

"I have every intention of holding you to ransom for your father after I've taken you to the Stone-That-Takes-Away-Magic, whatever you do or say."

Wish was so horrified she could not help interrupting. "But...Rule Number Thirteen! A Warrior should never lie!"

Queen Sychorax looked at Wish as though she were a slug.

"Amendment to Rule Thirteen: A queen can break the rules," said Queen Sychorax, "in pursuit of a higher good."

Then what, thought Wish, *is the point of the rules in the first place?*

But she kept that thought to herself.

Queen Sychorax put the "Love-Never-Lies" potion back in Xar's pocket.

"You are a very disobedient boy, and you obviously have not been treated firmly enough," said Queen Sychorax. "But I think you will find that *I* am very firm indeed. You need to be given a lesson, Xar, son of Encanzo, and that is what a prison is for…"

Xar sighed.

Why did everyone want to teach him a lesson? Ranter, his father, Caliburn, and now this horrible queen.

It was very wearing.

"I shall lock you in my prison," said Queen Sychorax. "And I will not take you or your sprite to the stone," she continued in a hard voice, "until AFTER you have told me where the sword is. Give the sprite back to the boy!"

With relief, the Deputy handed Squeezjoos back to Xar.

"If you don't tell me where the sword is, you will have to watch your sprite die in front of you," said Queen Sychorax. "As soon as you tell me, I will take you and your sprite to the stone. And then I will hold you to ransom, and your father, if he is weak enough to love a rude, disobedient child like you, will come here to save you, and I will remove Encanzo's Magic too."

She smiled at Xar. It was a beautiful smile. Whenever she smiled at Wish, which wasn't often, Wish's whole world lit up with sunshine. But Xar didn't appreciate it.

"You and your father and your sprites are all going to lose your Magic, whatever happens," said Queen Sychorax in that voice as gently soft as a poisoned arrow. "But if you tell me where the sword is, you can at least save your sprite's life."

The queen continued, "And you love your sprite, don't you? Love is always a weakness. So I know you will make the right decision."

Xar was trapped. What could he do? Everything was getting out of hand. Squeezjoos might die, all through Xar's fault. His father might lose his Magic, all through Xar's fault.

"QUEEN OF EVIL! HEART OF ICE! COWARDLY IRON-CLAD LEADER OF THE RABBIT-HEARTS!"

shouted Xar, beside himself with anger and fear.

Queen Sychorax reddened with annoyance. Nothing much rattled her; she took threats, trickery, even violence in her stride. However nobody had ever dared to speak to her with Xar's sheer disrespectful cheek before.

The Warriors secretly admired the bravery of this one small Wizard, who was completely at the mercy of the most ruthless ruler in the forest but was still throwing insults at her with total abandon.

"Take this uncivil little Wizard and his sprites and his animals to cell number 445!" snapped Queen Sychorax.

Xar was putting on a brave and angry front, but inside he was feeling total despair and helplessness.

He fought and bit and struggled, but he was hopelessly outnumbered, and the guards dragged Xar and the snowcats and the sprites away, Xar still cursing Queen Sychorax at the top of his voice:

"YOU'RE SOFTER THAN BUNNY RABBITS! YOU'RE WEAKER THAN WATER! YOU'RE FLUFFIER THAN

THE FLUFFIEST LITTLE BABY
DORMOUSES, AND MY GRANNY
COULD BEAT YOU UP WITH ONE
HAND TIED BEHIND HER BACK!"

you're
the
softest
pitiless
warrior
Queen
I
have
EVER
seen!!

14. Queen Sychorax Is Disappointed by Her Daughter... Again

Queen Sychorax watched Xar being dragged away, bundled down into the darkness of her dungeons.

"What a rude boy," she sniffed disapprovingly. "Is it too much to expect Encanzo the Great Enchanter to bring up his son with slightly better manners?"

She turned to her daughter.

"I do hope that if YOU are ever captured by an enemy, Wish," said Queen Sychorax, "you will maintain your dignity and be civilly polite. Particularly if they are threatening to kill you. It is hardly going to put them off."

Wish was so confused she didn't know what to think or feel. On the one hand, she was dreadfully frightened for Squeezjoos; on the other, of course her brilliant, splendid, intelligent mother wouldn't ever do anything that was wrong...

Would she?

Surely her mother wasn't going to allow Squeezjoos to *die*?

"You're not going to let any harm come to Xar's sprite, are you, Mother?" said Wish. "You're going to take them to the stone in time, so he can be cured, aren't you?"

"That is none of your business," snapped Queen Sychorax.

"But it's not the sprite's fault that he got Witchblood on him...You saw how frightened he was, poor little thing," protested Wish.

"Sprites and Wizards are Magic, and Magic is *bad*, so it does not matter if the sprite was frightened and you should not be concerned about their fate anyway," said Queen Sychorax waspishly. "Why are you sympathizing with the enemy and how dare you question my decisions? I will do exactly what I think is right."

Wish hopped guiltily and anxiously from one leg to another. Queen Sychorax's eyes had narrowed with suspicion. Why was that stupid little Wish looking so conscience-stricken and so upset? Could she be hiding something? Was there more to her hopeless daughter than it seemed at first sight?

"The guards were saying that *you* captured this rude little Wizard, Wish?" said Queen Sychorax. "*You???*"

Queen Sychorax always made an effort to speak reasonably kindly to her irritatingly useless daughter, but something about the way she said the word "Wish" always suggested dissatisfaction, as if the word reminded the queen that she wished Wish was a completely different person than she was.

Which indeed she did.

For Wish was a great disappointment to Queen
Sychorax. The queen had hoped to have a daughter
who was tall and golden like herself, not someone small
and scruffy and weird with hair that wouldn't lie flat
and an eyepatch and a limp.

"So, Wish, did you fight this young Wizard and his
animal and sprite retinue, and overcome him with your
superior Warrior skills?" asked Queen Sychorax
skeptically.

Wish, looking up
adoringly into her mother's
golden face, *longed* to be
able to say that this was
what had happened. How
wonderful would it be to
see Sychorax's expression
change, so that she
looked back at Wish with
admiration, with respect,
with *love*!

But her clever
mother would never
believe her and it might
make her so suspicious
that she would

For Wish was a Great
Disappointment to
Queen Sychorax.

investigate further and then she might find the sword, and then all would be over for Xar...

"Well, no, Mother," admitted Wish. "I heard a noise, and I saw it was a Wizard and I was going to try to fight him, but then I fell over and shouted for help."

The suspicion faded from Queen Sychorax's eyes, and she now looked merely displeased. *That* was entirely believable.

"I wouldn't call that 'capturing' the Wizard, would you?" snapped Queen Sychorax. "You fell over and you shouted for help! *Falling over* is not considered to be one of the traditional Warrior skills, Wish..."

Queen Sychorax looked at Wish's eyepatch and her limpy leg as if she had lost the use of both of these body parts out of an act of willful disorganization.

"Why you can't be more like your stepsisters?"

Wish bit her lip to stop herself from crying. Crying was another of those things that Queen Sychorax considered to be a weakness that Warriors should not indulge in.

"You *could* choose to follow the example of your stepsister Drama, for instance," Sychorax continued. "*She* has made a quilt out of the beards of dwarves she shot down from a remarkably long distance. I deplore the violence, of course I do, but those sort of teenage high spirits are, after all, the Warrior way—when I was your age I had already hunted down and killed my first giant, all on my own...

"But *you* have willfully and inexplicably decided to go in an entirely different direction! I'm not sure why you think it's a good idea to look so ODD...so lopsided...so..."

The weight of Sychorax's disappointment was so depressing that Wish could feel herself drooping like her fingers were made of lead.

Be merciful... thought Sychorax as Wish wilted miserably in front of her. *I suppose the child can't HELP looking like a weird little twig that somebody accidentally trod on. I suppose she can't HELP bobbing about the place like an unbalanced bunny rabbit. A queen should be GRACIOUS as well as severely and incorruptibly just...A queen must be FORGIVING as well as unbendingly and unswervingly firm...*

Sychorax controlled herself with a strong effort.

"I *suppose...*" said Queen Sychorax, gritting her teeth, "you did your best, however inferior that best might be. How is your headache, thinking of physical and mental weakness?"

"My headache?" said Wish blankly, before remembering hurriedly that she had told her mother she was going to bed early with a headache so she could sneak out after the spoon. "Oh, er, the headache's much better, Mother, thank you," said Wish.

"And how are you finding learning how to be a Warrior?" asked her mother.

"It's quite difficult, Mother…"

Queen Sychorax sighed with exasperation. "Madam Dreadlock says that your spelling is going particularly badly—reading and writing is a sign of how superior and civilized us Warriors are, you know, Wish."

"Yes, but the thing with the spelling is, the letters won't stay still," explained Wish. "They keep wandering about in my head, and I forget what order they were in, in the first place.

"There are some people," Wish suggested bravely, "who think that spelling might not be as important as the things you are trying to spell…"

"Well, those people are CRAZY," said Queen Sychorax. "You'll just have to try a bit harder, won't you? Starting with your appearance…"

Wish was looking even more than usually bedraggled. Cloak on inside out and back to front. Ripped clothes, twigs all over the place, hair whipped up into frenzied knots from when Squeezjoos had made a nest out of it earlier.

"Even a substandard Warrior like you should always be well put together, Wish," said Queen Sychorax, sweeping away. "Every hair in place. Every weapon sharpened. Every fingernail shining. Remember that."

And just as Queen Sychorax was sailing off, in a rustle of long, gracious white skirts, a certain knot that attached a little iron key to the belt she wore around her waist undid itself, like a small snake uncoiling, and the key dropped to the floor.

It was a very tiny key, so when it dropped onto the flagstones, it made a very tiny noise that the queen did not hear. She disappeared around the corner, not knowing she had lost it.

Ting!

Wish, looking after her mother dejectedly, heard the noise.

She picked up the key.

She opened her mouth to say, "Mother, you've dropped your key!"

And then she shut it again.

The key was small and black and cold.

The hair stood up on the back of Wish's neck as she realized it was the key, not only to every room in Warrior fort, but *to her mother's dungeons.*

How strange that Queen Sychorax should lose it at that precise, particular moment.

Did it drop, or did it jump?

If you were a fanciful person, you might have said

that it was almost as if the key were *looking* for Wish and wanted her to use it.

But we are not fanciful people, and that would be ridiculous.

It was the key
to her mother's
dungeons.

15. Breaking into Queen Sychorax's Dungeon

W ish and Bodkin and Bumbleboozle tried to sneak down into Sychorax's dungeons in the daytime, but it was impossible. There were too many people around.

"We'll have to wait until everyone goes to bed," said Wish. "But how are we going to get past the sentry guarding the entrance to my mother's dungeons?"

"I has a great sleeping spell—let me put him to sleep!" squeaked Bumbleboozle.

"Your spells won't work here, I'm afraid, Bumbleboozle," said Wish.

Bodkin looked guilty. "I still think this is a terrible idea," he said. "But just in case you wanted to go through with it, I put a small sleeping draught in the sentry's serving of wild boar stew when I was serving him dinner. Magic people aren't the only ones who know something about herb-work..."

"Oh, Bodkin, THANK YOU!" said Wish in delight.

"Don't thank me," said Bodkin gloomily. "My father would be very disappointed in me. I just felt sorry for that poor little Squeezjoos, but I should be able to overcome mere personal weakness and do the right thing...I don't know what's come over me."

So, late that night, Wish and Bodkin crept down to the great door that was the entrance to Queen Sychorax's dungeons.

The sentry who was supposed to be guarding it had indeed fallen fast asleep, so they tiptoed past him, unlocked the door with Sychorax's key, and slipped in, soft as shadows, closing the door behind them.

As the door shut, Bodkin had a suffocating feeling of panic.

Sychorax's dungeons tended to have that effect on people.

"You stay here, Bumbleboozle," said Wish. "So you can come and warn us if my mother or anyone else comes down after us."

"Okay!" squeaked Bumbleboozle. The smaller hairy fairies were always extremely pleased to be given a role. And she was delighted not to have to go any farther.

For in the center of the room they were standing in was the true entrance to the dungeons. A great pit, with a movable platform hanging above it.

Bodkin stared into the pit. "We're going to have to go down there, aren't we?" he said, pathetically hoping somehow Wish might say no.

"Yup," said Wish, climbing onto the platform.

"Good-bye..."

whispered

Bumbleboozle. "Good luck...It
was niccce knowing you...For Big People
you were kind of lessss ssssmelly than mossst..."

"Thank you," said Bodkin. Shakily, he
climbed onto the platform, and Wish untied
the rope and gradually let it out and...

DOWN...

DOWN...

DOWN...

...they went, the temperature dropping like a
stone, as did Bodkin's heart, as the platform lowered
deeper, ever deeper into the underground prison.

Wish's heart was sinking too, for coming down here felt like not only a betrayal, but also a trespass.

Sychorax would have secrets here...

Because...

A queen must have her secrets...

And Sychorax DID have secrets...

All of Sychorax's secrets were hidden underground.

Wish knew that, and she also knew that she really, really did not want to find out what those secrets were.

But she had no choice.

DOWN...

DOWN...

DOWN...

They went deeper, ever deeper.

When the platform finally came to a soft landing, what seemed like a horribly long time later, they landed in the secret midnight world of the prisons of Queen Sychorax, buried in a hundred yards of stone and earth, deep below the Warrior hill-fort.

Wish and Bodkin stepped off the platform into a grim little chamber, with a steady *drip, drip* of water coming from the ceiling, and lit by dim and guttering torchlight.

There were no fewer than seven corridors leading off the chamber.

Sychorax's dungeons were on the site of what in

ancient times had been a mine, so they were haunted not only by the prisoners of the present but also the giant and dwarf and human miners of the past. Mine had turned to prison, and the dungeons were now a great spreading maze like a gigantic long-legged spider's web, with corridors meandering and crossing over one another in trickily confusing fashion, just like the torturous maze of tricky Queen Sychorax's mind.

Off these corridors were endless little chambers, some with prisoners in them, some with...other things...But how were Bodkin and Wish to know which way to go?

"And what's that NOISE?" whispered Bodkin.

Sychorax's dungeons, as I mentioned earlier, were always filled with noise.

An iron music of despair and sweetness all mixed together, for longing does have its own sweetness, and beautiful things can come out of pain.

The Once-Magic-People imprisoned in those underground regions could no longer perform Magic. They could not work their spells, the sprites could not fly, the giants were ve-ry slowly shrinking.

For in one of the secret cells, in the lowest, deepest chamber of all, was Sychorax's Stone-That-Takes-Away-Magic, and they had all been taken there, and they had touched the stone and lost the Magic that made them what they were.

They were then led back to their cells and kept there, until they readjusted and got used to life without their Magic.

No one had quite gotten used to it yet, and so the Once-Magic-People who were living there filled the dungeons with noise. Melancholy noise, angry noise, regretful noise. The sound of the stamping feet of ogres, treading in sad, slow circles. The howling of werewolves, the song of sprites, singing in high, eerie voices about the bright old days.

It was the one thing they could do now. They had lost their wings, their spells, their hope. They had lost their sight, their light, for when the Magic went from sprites, their colors faded, the inner light that burned so bright flickered and died.

But they still made noise.

They were brought iron spoons and iron dinner plates to eat from, and they clasped the iron in their no-longer-Magic fists or paws, and they tapped out a melancholy beat that drummed through the prison like the ache of a long-lost love.

When Wish and Bodkin entered the dungeons, they could hear the song of a sprite called the Once-sprite, who was standing on the shoulder of Crusher the giant, locked in one of Sychorax's cells. For Wish had been right. Crusher had indeed been captured by Queen Sychorax's Warriors when Xar had left him behind in the clearing of the forest.

And here Crusher the giant was now, hidden somewhere in Queen Sychorax's dungeons, his eyes closed, thinking great thoughts and hoping against hope that Xar would come and save him.

Meanwhile, on his shoulder, the Once-sprite was singing of one particular bright blue of a summer's day when he flew up, up and slept on the wing like a swift, allowing the air currents of the atmosphere to be his bed, so high that the last thing he saw as he fell asleep was the many islands of Albion spread out below him, the forests reaching from sea to sea.

And he sang it so beautifully that all the inhabitants of that underground chamber thought that they could see it too, and joined in the "Song of Lost Magic," stamping, beating an iron beat in time with the giant's great beating heart as if they were up there in the skies, not down buried deep, lost, and forgotten, landlocked forever. Poor Squeezjoos. Was this to be his fate too?

Once you have heard the "Song of Lost Magic," you never forget it.

The confusion of emotions in that song—the despair, the hope, the regret—coupled with the exquisite re-creation of the Magic world and the powers that the Once-Magic-People realized in the moment of losing they had lost, and the way they echoed down the corridors repeating and mirroring and bouncing off the warren of walls, created a maze of noise and emotions and moral choices at least as disorientating and overwhelming as the physical maze itself.

"Have we done right? Have we done wrong?" sang the songs. "What have we lost? But had we no choice?" And this song ran into other songs, about the beauty of the wildwoods at midnight, where only the eyes of Magic could see in the dark, the formation of hair-ice on the elder-tree twigs as the first deep frost of winter came to the forest, and cyclamen buds, deep violet and leafless, pushing their way through the earth and the discarded autumn leaf clutter from the trees above, too quiet for dull human eyes to see their slow growing but clear as daylight for the eyes of Magic.

And it wasn't even certain which were the songs of living people and which were the songs of long-dead ghosts of the Once-Magic-People imprisoned in these warrens long ago, whose voices had sunk and frozen

into the walls, only to be ricocheted back to life again
by the slicing blow of a present sound-wave, as if the
spirits of the long-dead goblin and hob-elf and she-
dwarf miners were still there, picking the sounds out
of the walls with their enchanted axes and sending the
songs off on their way again so that they were alive
once more in the ears of Bodkin and Wish.

Ah yes, it was a strange haunted place, that
underground prison, where Magic and iron and past
and present and good and evil were being held together
in a much more complicated and contradictory manner
than you might expect from Sychorax's confident iron
hill-fort standing so proudly above them.

"We have no map," said Bodkin, covering his
ears, for the noise was so muddling it made it difficult
to *think*, let alone make any clear choices. He had
already explored down one of the corridors and found
it split in two other directions at the end of it. "How
are we going to find where she's imprisoned Xar?
We're never going to locate him in a maze as big as
this one."

A maze can be as effective as locks and keys if you
are trying to hide something.

Wish and Bodkin walked around the chamber
in despair for a while, before the Enchanted Spoon
noticed something, down at the bottom of one of the

unlit deep black corridors. A tiny sprinkle of light, blinking on and off like a remote star.

The spoon rapped Wish gently on the head to get her attention and then tip-tapped his way along the corridor to draw her attention to the little pool of light.

Wish felt her way after the spoon, with Bodkin saying, "Where are you going?" and following her reluctantly.

And when she had reached the bright little particles, she could see another patch, way in the distance, beckoning her like werelight. "Sprite dust! Xar must have sprinkled sprite dust along the way so we could follow him! That's clever!" said Wish admiringly.

So on they went, feeling their way toward the distant sprinkles of light, deeper and deeper, losing themselves in the twisting corridors of Sychorax's dungeons.

"It must be somewhere around here," said Bodkin as they came to a long corridor with at least twenty-five rooms coming off it. "We'll just have to check every room."

"Do we have to?" said Wish. "It's all very well for you—it's not YOUR mother—but I feel really weird finding things out about my mother that I REALLY DO NOT WANT TO KNOW."

Reluctantly, Wish took out the key and unlocked the nearest door, which swung open with an ominous creak.

"You look, Bodkin," said Wish, putting her hand over her eye.

Bodkin peered around the edge of the door…

…and fainted.

Wish very hurriedly shut the door.

"*What was in there????*" said Wish when Bodkin came around again.

"You REALLY, REALLY don't want to know," said Bodkin.

After that, Wish decided that it was kind of worse, the not-knowing, because then it left it up to her imagination as to what it might be in there, so she made up her mind she was going to look this time.

Bodkin opened the next door and immediately shut it again with an "EEEEEWWWW!!!" of disgust.

"What was in there??" cried Wish.

"Heads," said Bodkin.

"Oh, come on, I've had enough of this," said Wish, pushing him out of the way. "It can't possibly be heads. You're just completely determined that my mother should be this bad person…"

And she shoved Bodkin out of the way and went into the room.

It was heads.

"EEEEWWW!!!" said Wish.

Wish shut the door again, very, very quickly.

"I'm sure there's a reasonable explanation for that," she said. "My mother is very interested in anatomy."

"Really?" said Bodkin skeptically.

Other rooms contained less gruesome things.

A whole collection of Spelling Books, for example. A library, with everything carefully lined up in rows and labeled, for Sychorax was a very neat person.

A potion room.

Many, many collections of banned Magic objects.

But even after a long time searching, they still hadn't found Xar.

BEWARE,
highly dangerous
fairy stories.
READ WITH CARE
(these books can explode)

← key in case of emergencies

Meanwhile, down in cell number 445, as hour after hour passed with no sign of Wish and Bodkin and the sword coming to rescue him, Xar's spirits were sinking, and he was very close to despair. Of course, Sychorax's dungeons were designed with spirit-sinking in mind. That's part of the POINT of a dungeon, after all. You don't design them to be cheerful, airy spaces with a nice view and comfy seating.

Every now and then during the day, Sychorax would visit, and ask whether he had changed his mind about telling her where the sword was, and the sprites and Xar got the opportunity to shout and hiss rude remarks about her nose, and that cheered them up a little. But then she went away again, and the dank and miserable dark prison air would sink into their bones and the "Song of Lost Magic" would depress them even further.

"Sssshee'ssss not coming, that Wissssh..." hissed Tiffinstorm, whose light was fading fast. "Stupid Warrior of a girl—why would you trussst her?"

"She took the sword...she warned me about the 'Love-Never-Lies' potion..." said Xar moodily, for he was worrying about the same thing himself.

"They're too stupid to follow the sprite dust... They're too cowardly to come here anyway...They hate you...They won't be able to unlock the doors..."

The miserable sprites kept up a steady flow of discouraging comments, for they were desperately unhappy.

"You've kidnapped them, you stole their sword, you tricked them," said Ariel. "Why would they rissssk their lives for you, the enemy, the turnipsss in tin canssss?"

"Ariel has got a point," said Caliburn gloomily.

Had Xar been stupid to put his life in the hands of two enemy Warriors?

"They liked Squeezjoos," said Xar. "I know they did."

He looked down at Squeezjoos. Squeezjoos was so dark now he was nearly black, and his little heart was barely beating.

He was racked with seizure after seizure, where he was overcome with such shaking and delirium that he was not himself, but now he came to his senses for a second.

"What's happening to me?" whispered Squeezjoos, and you could see the fear in his eyes. "Am I going to the dark side?"

"Of course not," said Xar, and just as Squeezjoos fell back into a coma again he whispered so faintly Xar could barely hear it: "Xar will save me…" and put one tiny clawlike hand trustingly against Xar's chest.

Xar would have to give Sychorax what she wanted…

At least Squeezjoos would live…

But then his father's Magic would be in danger…

Xar was not a despairing person, but even *he* was beginning to run out of hope, when he heard footsteps and whispering in the corridor.

"You look in this one, Bodkin, I just can't bear to…" said the voice of Wish.

"They're here!" cried Bodkin's voice as Bodkin's face appeared in the grille.

There was a *click, click, click*ing noise, and CREEEAK—the heavy door of cell number 445 swung open.

Xar could never have imagined that he would be so astonishingly grateful and thankful to see two Warriors, one tall, skinny one and one little, limpy one. Even the sprites were delighted, somehow finding the energy to buzz excitedly, although they barely had the strength to fly now, and were lower and lower in the air, as if they had lead in their shoes.

"You came!" said Xar to Bodkin and Wish, so excited he even hugged them—who would ever have thought that Xar would hug a Warrior?

"Of course we came," said Wish stoutly. "I said I would, didn't I? I wouldn't leave a friend in trouble like that…"

Xar agreed that she was an excellent friend, who had shown unexpected initiative, for a Warrior.

"How did you get in and how are you opening the doors?" asked Xar.

"Bodkin gave the sentry a sleeping draught," said Wish. "And my mother dropped her key to the dungeons. How is Squeezjoos?"

She could see the little sprite shaking inside Xar's waistcoat.

"He's not doing well, I'm afraid..." said Xar as Wish unchained the snowcats with Queen Sychorax's key, and the snowcats burst out excitedly. "We need to get him to the stone as fast as we can."

But just as they were preparing to leave, Bumbleboozle zoomed like a little speedy midge streak of lightning in through the grille of the door in a state of the greatest alarm. She was thoroughly out of breath, for she had flown all the way from where she had been on lookout up at the entrance to the dungeons.

"Queen Sychorax!!!!!" she shrieked. *"She's coming!!!!"*

"Queen Sychorax is coming!!"

16. A Really Bad Moment for Queen Sychorax to Turn Up

Queen Sychorax is coming?" said Bodkin, just about managing not to faint again.

"She mustn't find me here!!" squealed Wish, absolutely petrified.

It was one thing to secretly decide that she wanted to be friends with a Wizard. It was quite another to be found by her mother in the act of not just *sympathizing* with the enemy, but also actively unlocking their cell and helping them escape.

"Don't worry," said Xar. "Hide, and I'll deal with her...I'll be polite this time, I promise. Give me the sword and lock the door behind you..."

"Be nice to her, Xar!" warned Wish, throwing Xar the Enchanted Sword.

"Trust me," grinned Xar.

Bodkin and Wish ran out of the room and hid around the corner in desperate haste, for from the sound of her footsteps, Queen Sychorax was approaching at quite a speed.

She was coming to offer Xar one last chance to see sense and get his sprite to the Stone-That-Takes-Away-Magic in time to save his life. Surely even a Wizard boy with no conscience at all would not want his sprite to die? But Xar was proving to be unexpectedly obstinate.

She was alarmed to find that she had lost her key (luckily she had a spare) and furious to see her sentry fast asleep, and as soon as she set foot in the dungeon, she sensed something had gone wrong.

Queen Sychorax knew every noise that went on in her underground home. Every drip of water, every muffled moan from her prisoners, every tap of the guard, every flicker of candle, every line of song—ghost or sprite—was familiar to Queen Sychorax.

There was something awry, she knew it. She moved up from her normal glide to a most unaccustomed, actual RUN, so that her footsteps made quite a racket in those echoing corridors.

If Bumbleboozle had not warned them, Sychorax would have caught her daughter in the act of aiding and abetting the enemy.

But Bodkin and Wish had whisked around the corner in the nick of time, locking the door again behind them.

So when Queen Sychorax unlocked the door of cell number 445 and swept in with a regal swish of her rich red cloak, Xar was standing in the middle of the room, as if nothing had happened, the Enchanted Sword behind his back.

"What is going on?" panted Queen Sychorax.

"Nothing," said Xar innocently.

"Hmmm," wondered Queen Sychorax disbelievingly, her eyes ranging suspiciously all over Xar, for she did not trust him for one second.

"This is your last chance, Xar, son of Encanzo," snapped Queen Sychorax. "I will not come back again tonight, and your sprite will be dead by morning. Where is my sword?"

"Would this be the sword that you are talking about?" said Xar thoughtfully, taking the sword out from behind his back.

Queen Sychorax went absolutely rigid with shock.

A low growling sounded behind her, and three enormous snowcats with teeth like kitchen knives were slowly, menacingly creeping out of the shadows.

"How were they unchained from the wall?" breathed Sychorax, as white as her dress. "Who brought you my key? And where did you get my sword?"

"Never you mind. But don't move, Queen Sychorax," said Xar, "or I will kill you with this sword!"

That beastly boy!

She should have brought guards with her...but the guards had thoroughly searched him, so she thought she was perfectly safe visiting an unarmed little boy and a few sprites, all safely locked up in her most secure cell.

Sychorax's hand crept toward her waistband, where her own sword was hanging.

"I said, don't move," said Xar, and there was a gleam in his eye that made Queen Sychorax halt. Wizards were generally a peaceable people, but Xar was not like most Wizards the queen had ever met.

"So, Xar, son of Encanzo," spat Queen Sychorax, infuriated to find the tables had been turned on her. "What are you going to do now that you've burgled my sword?"

"I'm going to take my sprite to the Stone-That-Takes-Away-Magic," said Xar, "and then I'm going to release the giants and other Magic prisoners that you have wickedly locked up here, and we can all escape from this fort of dullness and iron turnip-heads and go back to Wizard camp, where we belong."

"You will be arrested as soon as you leave these dungeons," said Queen Sychorax. "Giants are rather visible, and this fort is swarming with guards."

"But you're a tricky wicked queen with a lot of secrets," said Xar, "so I bet you have a secret exit from these dungeons, and a secret password too."

"Perhaps I do," said Queen Sychorax drily, "but it is highly unlikely I would tell you about either, in the circumstances."

"How about if I strike *you* a bargain, just like you

offered *me* one," said Xar craftily. "If you tell me the way to the chamber of Magic-removal and the way to the secret exit, and also the secret password, I will leave you this sword."

Queen Sychorax was delighted, although she didn't show it. She really, really wanted that sword, especially now that Witches had returned to the forest. The boy thought he was so clever, but he obviously didn't realize the importance of that particular Enchanted Sword to offer it up so easily...

"I accept your bargain," said Queen Sychorax smoothly. "The way to the chamber of Magic-removal is—"

"Ohhh no..." interrupted Xar. "No, no, *no*, please stop right there, Queen Sychorax."

He reached into his waistcoat and withdrew a small bottle. "Apparently, queens can tell lies—in pursuit of a higher good, of course. So I'm afraid you're going to have to tell me the answer while holding the 'Love-Never-Lies' potion, so I know you are telling me the truth."

Queen Sychorax gave him a look of the purest dislike.

Xar handed her the "Love-Never-Lies" potion.

"The way to the chamber of Magic-removal is to turn right and go down the corridor, and it's the seventh door in the great cavern. And from there you can reach the secret exit by turning LEFT at every second turning, and the secret password is CONTROL," said Queen Sychorax.

Xar made her say it twice, to check the love potion wasn't changing color.

But it remained red, so she must be telling him the truth.

He took the "Love-Never-Lies" potion from her.

"And now I'll leave you the sword," said Xar, holding up the "Love-Never-Lies" potion, so that Queen Sychorax could see it clearly.

And as soon as he said those words, the liquid inside turned blacker than soot.

"*Whoops*," said Xar happily. "Dear oh dear! How confusing!

"It appears that *I* was lying!" Xar grinned. "It's so difficult to keep up, isn't it?"

TRICKED!

The horrible little Wizard boy had tricked Sychorax into giving him the secret password and he was going to take the sword anyway!

It is always annoying for a very tricky person like Queen Sychorax to finally meet someone even trickier than herself.

So Queen Sychorax lost her temper. It was most unlike her, but it had been a trying day.

"You rude, lying, disobedient trickster of a boy!" shouted Queen Sychorax.

"Now, now," tutted Xar. "Be polite, Queen Sychorax. Insults will get you nowhere. Please, could you very kindly lend me your keys, and your cloak as well? I think it will be helpful for me to disguise myself as you so that your guards let us leave without a fuss. Thank you so much."

With gritted teeth, Queen Sychorax handed him her keys to all the cells and her very distinctive bright red cloak, lined snugly with royal black-and-white fur.

"You have to admit," continued Xar, putting Queen Sychorax's magnificent cloak around his shoulders, "a boy of destiny like me does need a really cool weapon that is Magic-mixed-with-iron...I'm not surprised you're so keen on this sword—it's something quite out of the ordinary."

Sychorax gave a smile made out of icicles.

"I'm afraid I'm going to have to lock you in your own cell," said Xar apologetically. "It's not exactly suitable for royalty. But you are a very wicked queen to have taken away the Magic of my people, and kept us prisoners, and threatened to kill my sprite. You need to be taught a lesson, and that is what a prison is for."

"Can I do her hair, Xar?" begged Bumbleboozle.

"Please can I do her hair? She's been so mean to poor Squeezjoos…"

"Oh, all right," said Xar. "But do it *gently*."

Bumbleboozle flew into the queen's hair, and in two snaps of a ladybird's wing, she had whipped it up into a creatively complicated rats' nest of tangles. Sychorax was standing absolutely still, and white and bone-deadly with anger.

Bumbleboozle buzzed backward to survey her handiwork with satisfaction.

Above Sychorax's pointed-with-freezing-rage face, so dignified, so regal, so tidy, so *furious*, her beautiful pure waterfall of controlled golden tresses was now shooting upward in a vertical mess of scrambled electricity, like a furball having a fit.

"Oohhhh…that's good, very good," hissed Tiffinstorm in malicious delight, and the sprites nearly fell out of the air, they were laughing so hard. "Those elf-locks will take weeks to brush out."

"And while you are brushing them, it will help you remember," cautioned Xar, "to leave us Magic people alone in the future."

"And I warn you," spat Queen
Sychorax, every word a cold white
arrow, "never to set foot in my
territory ever again. Or by the gods
of the trees and water, I swear I shall
make you regret it…"

"You'll have to catch me
first," grinned Xar. Then he said,
"Good-bye, Queen Sychorax,"
giving her a very low bow, and he
and Caliburn and the snowcats and
the sprites swept toward the door,
Xar with a very satisfactory royal
swish of Sychorax's own cloak.

Just as Xar was about to
leave the chamber, he had
a thought, and he turned.

"Er...by the way...I didn't really mean it about being soft," said Xar. "You are just as tough as a Warrior queen ought to be."

He ran out the door, and Bodkin, waiting hidden by the doorway, locked the door of the chamber behind him.

Leaving Sychorax all alone in cell number 445, thoughtfully adjusting her armor.

She had a lot to think about.

"You were very mean to my mother!" scolded Wish, once they were out of earshot.

"I was very *polite*!" protested Xar. "I said nice things about how tough she was!"

"You said she was a very wicked queen! And Bumbleboozle really messed up her HAIR!" said Wish in awed horror. "She's going to be absolutely hopping mad, isn't she, Bodkin?"

"Absolutely hopping," said Bodkin gloomily.

"I was very merciful..." said Xar. "If she wasn't your mother, I'd have killed her. Now, what did she say again about the way to the chamber of Magic-removal?"

"Right down this corridor, and then it's the seventh door in the great cavern," said Bodkin promptly.

They were riding on the backs of the snowcats, down through corridors that led them deeper, ever deeper underground, so low that the air was shiveringly cold, and a trembling Wish lay down farther and farther into Forestheart's thick fur coat.

Xar could feel that Squeezjoos had gone rigid inside the package above his heart. If they didn't get him to this stone quickly, they would lose him entirely.

The corridor eventually opened up into a great cavern, lit by flickering torchlight.

Tiffinstorm gave a horrified hiss and ducked behind Xar.

"It'sssss over there…" she hissed.

There were seven doors leading off the cavern, and the seventh door had a faded sign above it saying: CHAMBER OF MAGIC–REMOVAL.

The doorway was crooked and not as large as they might have expected. If a giant wanted its Magic removed, it would have to lie down in the cavern and stretch its arm through the door.

A strange magnetic force seemed to want to pull Xar toward that crooked door, like an ice-cold wind tugging him, and then he realized it was the sword hanging beside him twisting around and pointing at the door as if it were an iron finger.

Every single instinct in Xar's bones was telling him: "Run away…Go no farther…Stop here…"

Nighteye and Forestheart and Kingcat paced in anxious circles, growling and spitting and howling.

"Don'tgoINthere, don'tgoINthere, don'tgoINthere, don'tgoINthere," hissed the sprites.

"But we have to go in," said Wish, getting down off Forestheart's back.

"For the sake of the sprite," said Xar, springing off Kingcat.

Wish put the key in the keyhole, and the door to Sychorax's chamber of Magic-removal swung open.

Will it be
in time to
save Squeezjoos?

17. Queen Sychorax's Chamber of Magic-Removal

The chamber of Magic-removal had a very high ceiling and it was perfectly round.

The only thing in it was a stone.

The stone was a dark gray.

It was just an ordinary but unbelievably large stone.

Rough around the edges, like solidified lava.

"Is THAT the Stone-That-Takes-Away-Magic?" asked Xar in disbelief, for there didn't seem anything particularly scary about it.

But the sprites and the animals were more sensitive to the strange atmosphere in the room, and they hissed like hornets in their anxiety, and the snowcats restlessly padded around the circular room, their hair all on end.

Xar reached into his breast pocket and took out Squeezjoos, rigid as a dark green jewel, his breath like tiny green icicles rattling stiffly in his paralyzed body. His light was dying, dying, and barely there, growing fainter and fainter like his breathing.

"Now you have to put him on the stone," said Wish.

"You sssshould not do this, Xar," hissed Ariel, holding up his skinny arms and spitting out a warning.

"You have to lisssssten to the stories of the fairies, sssssstories from our ancient past—the fairy talesss have wisdom in them…"

Mustardthought finished Ariel's sentence: "…and all the fairy tales say: DO NOT TOUCH THE SSSSTONE."

"My father's father's father told me in a story, NEVER to touch this stone, Xar…" said Tiffinstorm. And the other sprites echoed: *"And mine, and mine, and mine…"*

And the walls of the chamber echoed back the words that might have been the words of *these* sprites, or they could have been the ghost-words of sprites who had been here once and faced the same choices in the past: *"And mine, and mine, and mine…"*

"The sprites are right," said Caliburn nervously. "You do have to listen to the stories, for stories always mean something. The question that worries *me* is: WHAT exactly *do* they mean?"

Now that they were there, in front of the stone, confronted with the reality of actually touching it, Xar found he was terribly torn about what to do next.

The voice of the Once-sprite was singing bright and pure as a nightingale somewhere in the darkness above them—of his regret at the loss of his Magic, of how his wings that used to brush the very stars on a windy winter's night were now paralyzed—and the yearning ache of that song reminded them all exactly how big a decision this was.

Xar always knew what to do.

But for once in his life…he wasn't sure.

"What shall I do?" said Xar, in an agony of indecision. "Maybe Squeezjoos would actually *prefer* to go to the dark side, rather than give up his Magic entirely. Perhaps he'd think it would be better to die, if it will mean he cannot fly!"

"This is our only chance to save Squeezjoos's life," said Wish. "What if you put him on the stone for just a second or two, to take away the Witchblood Magic, but take him off very quickly again to leave him with enough Magic to fly with?"

"Might that work?" Xar asked Caliburn.

"Well, I can't guarantee it," said Caliburn. "I've never come across Witchblood before."

"But we have to be hopeful," said Wish. "We can't just let him die. We have to hope that this will work, and we can make something good happen even in this dark place."

"Help me," said Xar to Wish. "I can't do it on my own."

The five sprites and the hairy fairies formed a glowing halo above Xar's and Wish's head, alarmed and suspicious, Ariel spitting out words of protection like "CCVRBXTLT" and "DJERKLTITOCOLX," and the spiky glowing letters quivered with fear and anxiety as they hovered in the air before melting away.

Xar and Wish took deep breaths, and knelt by the stone, gently holding up Squeezjoos, tipping him so that only the Witch-stain on his chest touched the surface of the rock.

Xar turned his face away.

And then...

Nothing happened.

The poor little hairy fairy jerked a little, and was still.

"Do you think it's too late?" whispered Xar, for Squeezjoos's light had gone out entirely and for one second he was like a stiff little piece of ivy lying there against the stone.

And then, just when Xar had thought he had lost him, a very faint twinkling of light flickered from Squeezjoos's chest and grew brighter...and brighter...

The green slowly faded from the little sprite's legs...from his arms...and finally from his chest, so that with a sudden *whoosh!* he took in air, and his eyes opened, and feebly he beat his wings...

"He's alive..." breathed Wish in passionate relief, as Squeezjoos buzzed gently to life.

"Quick, take him off the stone!" said Xar.

Wish and Xar peeled Squeezjoos off, gently but firmly, and the little hairy fairy sat in Xar's palm, blinking, dazed, as if awaking from a coma.

"He's alive!" cried Xar, punching the air as the little sprite breathed very, very quietly and whispered, "I's alive! I's alive! I's alive!"

"He's ALIVE!" smiled Xar. "Do you think he can still fly?"

"It's a little early to tell, Xar," said Caliburn. "He's going to need some time to recover."

Fairies are not like humans—the wildwoods are so dangerous they would have died out years ago if they did not recover quickly from illness. Bravely, Squeezjoos raised his head, unfurled his shaking wings, and launched himself unsteadily into the air.

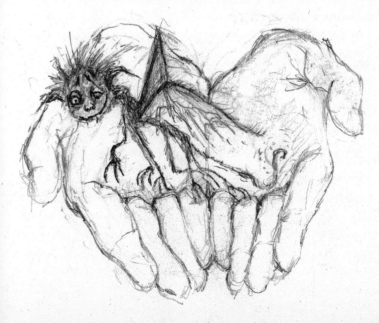

"He can still fly!" cried Xar. "I'VE MADE AMENDS! IT'S ALL GOING TO BE FINE!

"You see, Caliburn, for all your gloomy, what-is-done-cannot-be-undone stuff, it is just like I said—*nothing* is impossible! And that was perfect timing! I am SO CLEVER, oh the brilliance of *me*. It was such a great idea of mine to leave him enough Magic so that he could fly..."

"Quick, Xar!" said Bodkin. "Put your own hand on the stone now to get rid of the Witch-stain...and then we can leave this horrible place."

Xar sighed.

"Come on, Xar," urged Caliburn. "You know this is the second part of our mission. And you must have learned something from this night. All of these bad things have happened because you tried to get bad Magic from a Witch..."

"I know, I know," said Xar sadly. "But you have no idea how hard it is, growing up in a world of Magic, when you have no Magic of your own."

"It *is* difficult, but you have seen what the Witchblood did to Squeezjoos. That is bad Magic you have in your hand, and bad Magic *will* go wrong."

"Okay, okay," sighed Xar. "I'll do it."

Miracle of miracles, it seemed that Xar really had learned something over the course of the day.

Xar knelt down and put his hand with the Witch-stain on it against the stone.

It was a bizarre feeling, but it didn't take long.

There was an electric quivering sensation in his palm, and it stuck to the stone as if magnetically attracted to it. For the next minute, he could feel something being pulled out of him, and then the force went away, and when he lifted his hand off, there was no green stain anymore.

Xar could not help sighing as he looked at it. For a moment he had been special, even if it was special in the wrong way. Now he was just ordinary plain old Xar again, way too old for his Magic not to have come in.

Caliburn landed on his shoulder and said sympathetically, "You did the right thing, Xar. I'm proud of you. That was the wise, grown-up thing to do. I know it is difficult, but you have to wait patiently for your own Magic to come in, and not just leap in and try to fix things immediately."

"Yes, I know, but it's so hard to do that. At least Squeezjoos is cured," he said, to cheer himself up.

"I IS!" whispered Squeezjoos, peering sleepily over the edge of Xar's pocket. "But why is we still all here in thisssss creepy dungeon?"

"Good point," said Xar. "Let's get out of here!"

Wish was kneeling right beside the stone, in Xar's way, and trying not to panic.

"Wish? I said come on!"

Wish did not answer him immediately. She swallowed.

"I can't get my hands off the stone."

18. Oh Dear... The Story Turns in an Unexpected Direction.

There was a nasty silence.

"What do you mean, you can't get your hands off the stone?" said Xar.

"I mean they're stuck...my hands are stuck to the stone..."

"*How is that possible???!*" exclaimed Bodkin in horror.

What had happened was this.

Wish had been kneeling down, helping Xar hold Squeezjoos against the stone. And as she got to her feet, she stumbled clumsily, as she often did. She put both hands out, with flat palms, against the stone to steady herself.

And she could not get them off again.

Puzzled, she tried to pull away, but the harder she pulled, the more stuck they were.

Now she was kneeling down once more, both hands on the stone, her forehead pressed against the cold gray surface. Her hands were stuck to the stone like glue. She tried to move her little finger, but it would not budge. A not-unpleasant, warm feeling was in her hands now, and she was beginning to feel a little sick. She was getting the oddest sensation—it was as if some compelling force from within the stone was dragging her inside out, emptying her like it was draining a bottle of wine.

"What's happening?" demanded Bodkin. "Why can't she get her hands off the stone? Has something gone wrong? What does this mean?"

"This is strange…ever so strange…" said Caliburn, extremely puzzled.

Xar and Bodkin tried to help Wish pull her hands away, but they were stuck fast.

All that pulling and scraping at Wish's fingers did was make her fingers bleed, and she cried out for them to stop. The sprites could not use spelling, of course, in Sychorax's iron dungeons. So they just buzzed around, wailing, "You have to lissten to the sstoriesss…Listen to the fairy talessss…Don't touch the sssstone…"

Which wasn't very helpful, frankly, since Wish already HAD touched the stone, so it was rather late to warn her not to.

"Oh dear, oh dear, oh dear…What's going on?" wondered Bodkin uneasily. "There's something weird happening, I know there is…I wish we'd never come here. Are you all right, Wish? It's not painful, is it?"

"No," said Wish, "it's not painful. I feel a bit sick, but it doesn't hurt."

Wish was feeling nauseated, and confused, and scared.

It was very claustrophobic to be stuck in a horrible cavern in a dungeon a hundred yards underground, with your hands stuck to an enormous gray stone. Wish's imagination started playing tricks on her.

What if she was stuck there forever? This was the problem with Magic objects, and why you had to be very careful about touching them. You never quite knew what the rules were.

What if *that* was the moral of the fairy tales, that if you put your hands on the stone and you were the wrong kind of person, like a Warrior rather than a Magic person, you *could never get them off again*?

Seven minutes passed.

Eight minutes passed.

"What is happening?" Wish kept repeating.

"Nine minutes…ten minutes…What is going on?" said Caliburn, very bewildered.

It was so hot in the room that sweat was rolling down Xar's face in great wet tears and his shirt was soaking wet.

Stranger still, the heat seemed to be affecting the Enchanted Spoon. He drooped on the princess's shoulder, trying to comfort her, but almost bent double, poor spoon, as if, in sympathy with her predicament— the life was being sucked out of him as well.

The snowcats and the sprites sensed danger, and

formed a defensive circle around Xar, the sprites holding up their arms, trying, and failing, to spell and curse with such intensity that the air bristled with frustrated Magic.

Wish was limp now, and frantic with trying not to panic. "I'm not going to be stuck here forever, am I, Caliburn?"

"No, no," said Caliburn, trying hard to be reassuring, "no, no, not *forever*... 'Forever' is a long word... I'm sure it's just a little hiccup... Some small misunderstanding, and any moment now you'll be able to get your hands off..."

Wish's forehead was very near the stone.

Was it her imagination, or did the rock in front of her seem to be getting lighter? Lighter and lighter, and somehow more transparent, as if the surface of the stone was just a membrane, and she could see right into the stone itself?

Oh by mistletoe and oak and all things sweet and poisonous.

As Wish looked, fascinated, mesmerized, she thought she saw an eye open somewhere in the heart of the stone...

...and a horrible little creaking voice whispered: "Hellooooo... I've been waiting for you..."

Xar stared openmouthed. "The stone seems to be talking now."

"It's not the stone!" Wish gasped. "There's something *in* there..."

There was a moment of blinding, dazzling color, and as Wish's eye adjusted...

She was looking straight into the eye of an enormous Witch, all curled up inside the stone, legs folded up underneath itself like a large dark grasshopper.

19. Magic Can Never Be Destroyed; It Can Only Be Hidden

Encanzo the Enchanter had a saying that Sychorax would have done well to remember: "Magic can never be destroyed; it can only be hidden."

How very true that saying was.

For this was the secret of the Stone-That-Takes-Away-Magic.

It was taking away Magic for a *reason*.

"What...is...*that*?" whispered Wish in absolute horror.

"I," said the horrible, terrifying, creaking voice, "am the Kingwitch..."

"Oh eye of newt and toe of beastly frittering frog!" cursed Caliburn in horror. "Destiny has led us up the garden path! It's the wrong kind of star-cross! It's the universe in one of its trickiest moods! It's fate having a VERY BAD DAY INDEED!"

It was, indeed, the Kingwitch.

And it looked like fate had been playing a mischievous game with them.

You see, Wizards used to have a tradition of never writing anything down.

The problem with *that* is, when the truth gets passed from mouth to ear over the course of a number of centuries, it can get deformed and fragmented along the way.

It seemed like the sprites were right to be saying: "DO NOT TOUCH THE STONE."

It appeared like the fairy tales might have had a point.

As Caliburn said, the trouble with stories is: *You have to know what they mean.*

For now at last the *real* secret of the stone was discovered.

Here was the truth of it.

Many centuries ago, the Kingwitch had been defeated in the last Witch War and cast inside this stone. For hundreds of years he had been soaking up the Magic from outside, waiting, and waiting.

Queen Sychorax thought she was bringing the Once-Magic-People to the stone of her own free will. How could she dream that she was responding to the will of the Witch-Inside-The-Stone? That inside the very heart of the iron fort, quiet inside the gray rock, there was another heart, another will, that was pulling, scheming, wishing, and wanting with such dreadful invisible force, like a long-legged spinner in the center of a great gray web?

"It'sssawitchit'sssawitchit'ssssawitchit'ssssawitch!"
shrieked the sprites and the hairy fairies, climbing up
the air in their fear, sending out little clouds of black
terror-smoke.

"*Give me your Magic…*" whispered the Kingwitch.
"Give me your Magic…GIVE ME YOUR MAGIC…"

"There must be some mistake," pleaded Wish,
forcing herself to look at the horror inside the stone.
"I'm afraid I don't have any Magic to give you…I'm not
a Wizard…I'm just a very ordinary Warrior princess.
Please let me go…"

"Oh, but you *do* have Magic," replied the voice of
the Kingwitch. "Trust me, I know Magic when I feel
it. And the Magic that you have isn't ordinary at all. It's
a very special kind of Magic, a Magic that I have been
waiting for, for a long, long time.

"The kind of Magic-that-works-on-iron…"

Oh.

My.

Goodness.

"GET ME OFF THIS STONE!" yelled Wish at
the top of her voice.

Pandemonium in the chamber of Magic-removal.

Bodkin and Xar hauled at Wish's fingers, but her
hands would not budge.

"It can't be true, can it?" wept Wish. "I'm a Warrior! Warriors can't be Magic! It's impossible!"

But there's no such thing as im*possible*. Only im*probable*.

And the moment that the Kingwitch had said those words, every single person in the room knew it must be true.

It explained everything.

It explained why Wish had been feeling a little different and peculiar lately. For the last couple of months, plenty of odd things had been happening to her. Needles wriggling to life in her hands, rugs inexplicably moving beneath her feet or curling up at the edges when she stepped on them.

Objects she touched, slipping through her hands like water or tingling with electricity when she put her fingers on them...things that she thought she had put in one place, turning up unexpectedly in another...her hair lifting up when she met particular people or entered certain rooms, and softly wriggling itself into a bird's nest of tangles...clothes ripping...shoes coming loose...keys going missing...

She'd thought it was just her being forgetful, and clumsy, and absentminded, even more useless than she generally was. But...

Wish was thirteen years old, and that was the time when a person's Magic first came in.

"The spoon..." whispered Bodkin to himself.

A Warrior who was Magic!

Inconceivable.

But could it possibly be that the iron spoon had come alive because Wish's weird Magic-that-works-on-iron was enchanting it?

The character of the spoon, drooping on Wish's shoulder—now Bodkin came to think of it—was very Wish-like.

Kind and loyal.

A little reckless.

A little odd.

How could Wish enchant something without even knowing that she was doing it?

Because Magic is hard to control, particularly when you're not even aware you have it.

And that was typical too. Of course, if Wish was going to be Magic, it would be very Wish-like of her to have a Magic that was so different from other people's.

"Oh dear, oh dear, oh dear..." flapped Caliburn. "I knew we weren't asking the right questions! The questions we should have been asking are: Why are the Witches waking NOW? Why here? Why us? And the answer is, they are waking because Wish's Magic has just come in..."

Caliburn was right. There are no coincidences...
For centuries those Witches had lain asleep. But they
had indeed chosen this particular moment to wake from
hibernation because they sensed that Wish had come
into her Magic and it was something that they needed.

"Give me the Magic..." chanted the Kingwitch
inside the stone in that same dreadful creaking, croaking
voice. "Give me the Magic-that-works-on-iron..."

"Why does he WANT it?" wept Wish, already
knowing it was a question to which she didn't want to
hear the answer.

Caliburn had worked out why.

"*He's trying to get enough Magic to break out of the
stone!!!!*" screamed Caliburn. "*We HAVE to get her off it!*"

"GET ME OFF THIS STONE RIGHT
NOW!!!!" yelled Wish again.

"Tiffinstorm, try to spell her off the stone!"
ordered Xar. "I'll have a go at pulling her again."

Tiffinstorm hissed furiously, spitting with anger
and irritation. "SSSSSSSsssss!!!! Great galumphings,
smelly human girl!! You's gone mad, Master! What we
need to do NOW is get out of here!!!!! Things are about
to get nasty..."

"Obey me," said Xar sternly.

The sprites desperately riffled through their spell
bags. Invisibility, love potions, cursing spells, flying—all

small-time Magic, useful for things in everyday life, but not for facing a great dark evil like a Witch. They tried every wand in their quivers, the drivers, the number fours, the number fives...but of course their Magic could not work anyway in a prison full of iron.

The Kingwitch's horrible creaking voice got louder and louder, filling the room with horror.

"GIVE ME YOUR MAGIC GIVE ME YOUR MAGIC GIVE ME YOUR MAGIC..." chanted the Witch, and the louder he chanted, the more panicky Wish became.

"How do I use this Magic to get *away*?" shouted Wish.

"GIVE ME YOUR MAGIC GIVE ME YOUR MAGIC GIVE ME YOUR MAGIC..."

"You have to WANT something really, really bad...WISH for it! SPELL IT!..." Xar replied. "And then POINT it out with your hands!"

"I can't!" panted Wish, who was feeling so sick she wanted to give up and die right there. "My hands are stuck to the stone! Why can't I get them off? It was so easy to take Squeezjoos away!"

"The Witch will have *let* you take Squeezjoos away!" said Caliburn, hovering in terror over the stone. "Whereas it won't want to let *you* go at all..."

With her hands stuck to the stone, she couldn't

perform Magic independently of the Witch, even if she had known how to perform Magic in the first place. Any separate thought was being sucked out of her through those hands. She could feel the numbing effect of the Witch's thoughts entwining with her own, as if she were being eaten by a large animal and was coming around to its point of view in the digestion process.

After all, the Warriors have sworn to destroy Magic, so it is perfectly reasonable for Witches to fight back... said her thoughts, and she did not know whether they were her own or the Witch's.

"GIVE ME YOUR MAGIC GIVE ME YOUR MAGIC GIVE ME YOUR MAGIC..."

Wish could see right into the Kingwitch's body where his two black hearts were beating, and every little artery was lit up like a tiny green network of roads or the veins on a leaf. But there were other roads too: roads of Magic crisscrossing the Kingwitch's bright green arteries, tiny little paths winding through a white forest.

Both the Kingwitch's palms were pressing right up against the stone, on the inside, exactly opposite where Wish's hands were stuck on the outside, and she could feel the Magic flowing out of her fingers and into the hands of the Kingwitch in steady, rhythmic pulses in time to the beating of her heart.

I wish to get away…I wish…I wish…I wish… wished Wish.

Chaos in the chamber of Magic-removal as the hypnotic chanting of the Witch grew deafeningly stronger, and the sprites let off their spells randomly, and the snowcats howled and roared.

"FIGHT IT!" cried Caliburn. "TRY WITH EVERYTHING YOU HAVE TO BREAK AWAY! BE DISOBEDIENT! Think of Xar, defying his father! Get angry, Wish, and fight back! Curse the Witch! Don't give up your Magic because you think that's what a Warrior ought to do!"

Wish thought of Xar, earlier in the camp, yelling at his father, and as she did so, she could see the flow of Magic going from her to the Witch slowing.

"It's too late…" said Bodkin. "The stone is moving…"

The stone had begun to rock, gently at first, and then wilder, *faster*, wilder, *faster*.

Oh Witches' whiskers and murmuring mistletoe and yellow toenails of the barmiest bog-ogres in bogdom, thought Bodkin.

The Witch might have finally soaked up enough Magic to break out of the stone!

"Leave! Leave! Leave!" shrieked the sprites and the hairy fairies, burning bright as meteors.

But they couldn't leave Wish there on her own. Not Bodkin, not Xar, not Caliburn, not the snowcats, not even the sprites.

Sprites have a bad name for themselves. People say they are treacherous, flighty creatures who do not know the meaning of love, or loyalty.

But all I can say is: *These* sprites, despite their terror at the rocking stone, at the Witch about to emerge, at the fear of death itself, stayed by their master's side. They were hissing and spitting like bonfires, but nonetheless they stayed.

Without thinking, Xar drew the Enchanted Sword.

The light shone on the blade.

Once there were Witches...

...but I killed them.

He held the sword up over his head, gave a great big yell, and plunged it right into the stone with all his strength.

Of course, that ought to be impossible. A sword made of iron...to enter a stone?

But that Magic sword sank into the stone right up to the hilt, as if Xar were plunging it into the earth.

BOOOOOOMMMMM!

Every single strand of Wish's hair sprang up and shone like fire. A smell of burning hair added to the

smoke of the room. The door of the
chamber exploded out of its hinges and
slammed into the opposite wall. Lightning
shot off the surface of the stone, and Wish was
catapulted off it. She shot backward through the
air and landed with a horrible thud at the back
of the room.

Little lines shot all over the surface of the
stone, just like the lines that appear on an egg
before a chick is born.

"The stone is cracking!" screamed Tiffinstorm.
"The stone is cracking!"

The stone cracked from side to side.

A great jagged split an inch wide zigzagged across
the stone with the sword stuck in the center of it.

And out of that split, *something* slithered.

20. The Story Gets Even Twistier

At first the something looked like a little slick of black oil, leaking out of the stone, like the yolk leaking out of a broken shell.

It couldn't be the Kingwitch, could it, for how could that thing they had seen inside there creep out of a split only an inch wide?

Surely the Witch must be dead, when a great big Witch-killing sword had been driven right into the stone enclosing it?

That must be the dead Witch's blood, leaking out of the broken stone.

But in front of their eyes, the pool of liquid grew larger and larger.

And then the black water solidified, turned in front of their eyes into something flesh and blood that moved, a real and living body.

A feathery, soggy scarecrow of a something, feathers soaking wet.

Sometimes people like to reassure themselves that Witches can't possibly ever have been as bad as the fairy stories said they were. One look at the Kingwitch told you that they were every bit as bad, and maybe even somewhat worse.

Just *looking* at a Witch has been known to scare a person to death. They can, of course, assume many forms, some of them quite pleasant, but mostly they find it helpful to look as scary as possible.

The *thing* had a nose like a knife, so razor-sharp and pointy at the end that it looked like you could cut onions with it. There were just two black holes instead of eyes on either side, like deep wells with something flinty and slimy as mercury glinting queasily at the bottom of them. The mouth dripping that revolting black saliva from the fangs. Jaws that could unhinge to swallow a deer in one gulp. A body like a human mixed with a panther and those black feathery wings.

All in all, the Kingwitch was not a pretty sight.

Power reeked from that slithering thing, as slowly, slowly he unfurled his wet black wings to their full extent, and they dripped onto the dungeon floor, black smoking drips, as he lifted his beak and looked straight at Xar and Bodkin.

And then he vanished.

"Where is it...Where is it?" said Xar, whirling around.

The animals howled in horror, the sprites opened up their fang-filled mouths and shrieked in fear, for there are few things more scary than an enemy you cannot see.

Wish, over on the other side of the room, picked herself up, shaking.

"Nobody panic…" said Caliburn, panicking like crazy. "Where is it? Can anyone see it?"

The three of them whirled around and around, trying to see the invisible Witch.

But there was nothing there.

"It's going to attack Wish!" said Xar. He knew this, but he wasn't sure why.

Sure enough, the air above Wish seemed to thicken and darken.

Bravely, the Enchanted Spoon, standing on Wish's head, turned to face that darkness.

But an Enchanted Spoon is the sort of thing you might want on your side if you were making *dessert*, not if you are facing one of the most terrifying life-forms who has ever walked this planet.

Xar tried to drag the sword out of the stone, but it was stuck fast, as if it had been rooted there all along. However hard he pulled, it would not budge.

So with another bloodcurdling yell, completely unarmed, Xar, the boy who cared for nobody but himself, launched himself at the diving Witch.

As the Witch screeched downward, diving at Wish, he was turning himself visible as he plunged, and turning yourself visible is not as easy or painless

as lighting a candle. It looked, indeed, as if the
atmosphere itself were being ripped apart like a curtain,
as first the head appeared, half melting at the edges
with black sparks and smoke, and then, with a terrible
smell of burning feathers, the Witch himself, screaming
like a falcon.

Wish ducked automatically.

The Witch had been aiming straight for her head,
intending to tear it off. (Dear little creatures, these
Witches, aren't they?)

But Xar and the snowcats leaped the mightiest
leaps they had ever leaped, and they caught the diving
Witch by his tail.

So instead the Witch's talons scraped across Wish's
face, ripping off her eyepatch as the Witch soared up
into the air, and Wish yelled and put her hands over her
head as she fell to the floor.

With a furious scream, the Witch shook off
Xar and the snowcats, swirling around viciously, and
turned to attack the insignificant and irritating human
boy who had shoved the sword into the stone, and
frustrated his pursuit of Wish.

The Witch smiled, and oh by mistletoe and all
things sweet and juicy and poisonous, a Witch's grin is
a terrible thing. He unhinged his jaws, so that he could
swallow Xar in one gulp.

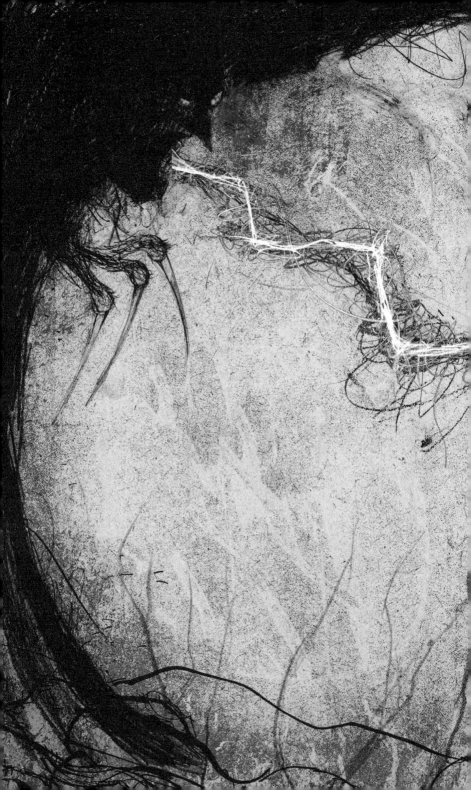

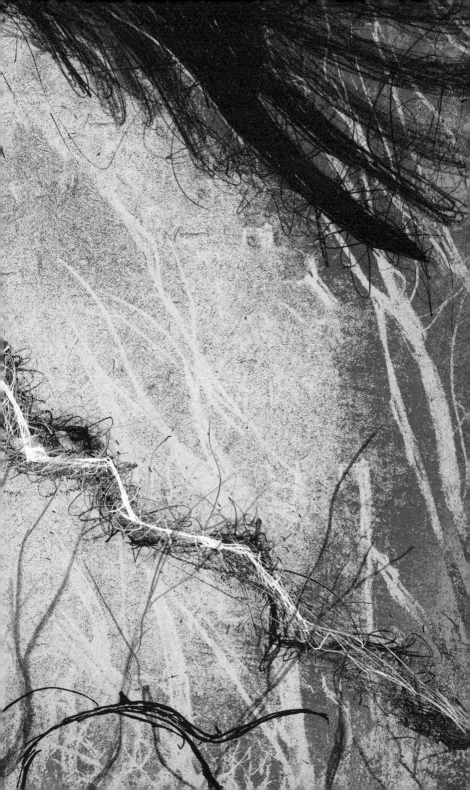

The hot Witch's breath reeked so revoltingly of rotten eggs and death that Xar nearly passed out from the stink of it.

At least I'm going to die gloriously, thought Xar through his terror, *not some kind of non-entity. I'll be the first person to be killed by a Witch in hundreds and hundreds of years...*

How like Xar to be thinking of fame and glory even at the point of death.

The Witch swooped. This time he would not miss.

21. Wishing

odkin shouted, "No!"

Over in the other corner of the room, Bodkin saw Wish uncurl her hands from over her face.

She lifted her head, and she too shouted, "NO!!"

The Witch had torn off her eyepatch, and it had fallen to the floor.

Wish's eye that was normally hidden underneath the eyepatch was closed and there was a deep scratch over it. It was ever so slightly larger than the other eye, and all around the edge was a deep purple bruise, as if the poor human skin found the burning force of it difficult to bear.

As Wish shouted, she opened her eyelid just a tiny, tiny crack, and the color of the eye underneath was very odd indeed. It was a color that no one had ever seen before, a hitherto-unimagined color. I can't describe it, apart from comparing it to other things. It was a color that managed to be both warm and cold at the same time, a color that reminded you of volcanoes, of thunderstorms, of electricity, of POWER.

Wish could feel the power within her, and it was truly terrifying, a rage and a riot, a thunderstorm in her head, so violent it made her head ache as if goblins were

303

hammering it from the inside. The individual hairs on her head twitched upward vertically in the air.

A confused sickening wind ricocheted around the room, sending the sprites and the feathers and the dust bowling through the air, and the floor bent and shivered like it was a nauseated sea.

In the depths of that extraordinary eye, strange clouds formed, like the beginning and the churning and the building of ideas, and there was a tiny snapping noise and...

...the Magic screamed out of Wish's eye so forcefully you could see the impossible color of it, in the shape of a bent and twisted star, hitting the Witch at exactly the same moment that the Witch pointed his taloned finger to shoot one piercing blast of white-hot Magic back at Wish.

...And then...

BANG!!!!!

The Witch exploded into a mass of charcoal and black feathers.

Bodkin and Xar and the snowcats were blown off their feet.

The dust and feathers of the Witch fell through the air like dark rain.

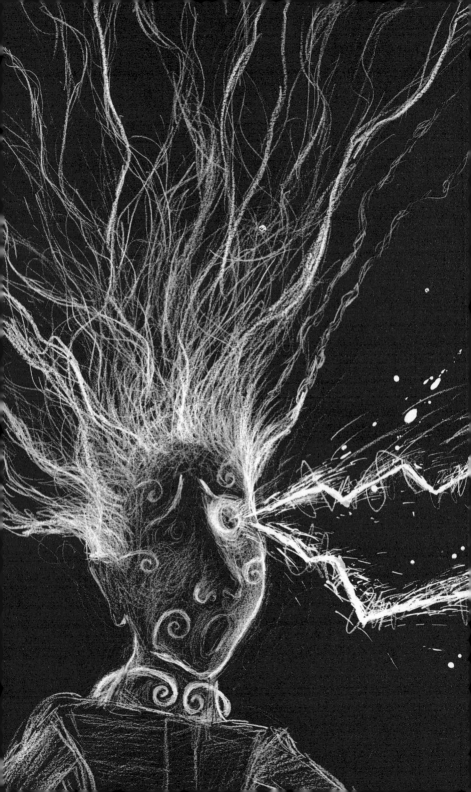

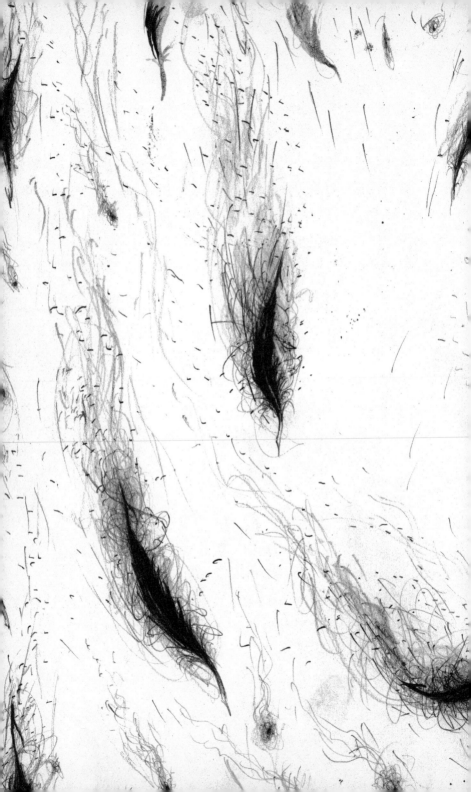

22. Making Amends and Paying the Price

The walls and the floor ceased their wild shaking and came to a shuddering halt with such violent abruptness that a few large stones fell out of the doorway.

"Oh my goodness…I don't believe it…*I did it!*" Xar gasped in astonishment, raising himself onto one elbow, coughing and spluttering, and then staggering to his feet in the dust clouds, trying to catch the dropping feathers in his joy. "I killed the Witch!

"Wake up, Assistant Bodyguard, wake up!" Xar gently prodded the prone body of Bodkin with his foot, for Bodkin had fainted once again with the shock of it. "I'VE KILLED THE WITCH! I DID IT!"

"The Witch iss dead! The Witch isss dead!" sang the sprites, joyfully turning somersaults in the air.

Groggily, Bodkin came to, rubbing his head. "What happened?"

"He EXPLODED!" marveled Xar excitedly, for Xar was a boy who loved an explosion. "He actually EXPLODED! It was magnificent! The loudest explosion I have ever heard! I can't believe you missed it!"

Xar whooped
joyfully as he held out his
hand to help Bodkin to
his feet.

"He exploded?" said
Bodkin in a dazed way,
reaching out a hand
to catch one of the
feathers still dropping
through the wreck of
the room.

"Look!" said
Xar, pointing at the
feathers lying all
around them. "That's
all that's left of the
Witch...Wish's Magic
exploded it...but it was
MY brilliant sword-
thrust that made him weak
enough for the explosion
to work."

He raised his fists in
the air: "I AM THE BOY
OF DESTINY! FEEL MY
POWER!!!"

FEEL MY POWER

"Oh my goodness, we *did* it!" shouted Bodkin
as he realized the enormity of what they had achieved.
"We've killed the Kingwitch! Wizards and Warriors
working together!"

Xar and Bodkin hugged each other as the snowcats
capered joyfully around them on the churned-up floor,
howling with happiness.

"Yes, I have to admit, Wish, you were a bit of a
help with that weird thing you did with your eye. What
WAS that?"

Xar turned to congratulate Wish…

…but Wish was not there.

It was only then that they realized how silent
it was.

The walls were not shaking; the churned-up floor
was perfectly still beneath their feet.

And it wasn't only feathers that were falling
quietly through the chamber and landing on the floor
beneath them.

There were also flakes like
snowflakes, and each individual
flake was a very unusual
color.

Silence, apart from the gentle falling of black feathers, snow-of-an-unusual-color, and dust.

"But where IS Wish?" said Bodkin in a bewildered way, looking around the room, at the open doorway with the door blasted out of it. "Did you see where she went?"

"Look! The door has come off its hinges!" said Xar. "So maybe she ran out to fetch help or something…"

And then he noticed the spoon, lying motionless in the center of the floor.

Xar knelt and picked up the spoon.

It was hard and cold now that all enchantment had gone from it.

A perfectly ordinary iron dinner spoon.

Carefully, Xar laid it back down on the floor again.

Silence in the chamber of Magic-removal.

Move, spoon, move!

Caliburn flew to Xar's shoulder with long, slow, reluctant wingbeats and perched there in misery.

"I am so sorry, Xar..." said Caliburn. "But in the confusion I think you did not notice a second explosion nearly at the same time as the first. Wish was taken by surprise... She was shocked into letting down her guard... The Kingwitch let off a final burst of Magic, and it hit her directly..."

"*She* exploded as well as the Kingwitch?" said Xar, unable to believe it because he hadn't seen it with his own eyes.

Impossible.

Inconceivable.

Come back, Wish! thought Xar fiercely... *COME BACK!*

"I WISH! I WISH! I WISH YOU WOULD COME BACK!"

But he couldn't breathe life back into those fragments, however much he longed to.

"BREATHE! BE ALIVE AGAIN! MOVE OF YOUR OWN ACCORD!"

But the strange-colored dust that was
once Wish lay cold and still, and not any of
Xar's wishing could make it move again. Even
the very greatest conjurer in the world could
not do that.

Actions have consequences. You must pay
the price of making amends, and some things
happen that cannot *un*happen.

Xar cried.

He and Bodkin knelt down in the
room, and they cried together, their
heads bowed, while the black feathers
and the weird-colored dust lay
quiet and unmoving in a circle all
around them.

Even the sprites wept, and fairies do not cry.

It is one of the things about them. They never ever cry.

But their tears dropped down onto the feathers and the snow.

And then…

And then…

And *then*, through streaming eyes, Xar thought he saw the edge of the spoon twitch.

He blinked.

Maybe it was an illusion.

But no, there it was again, a definite wriggle of the outline of the spoon.

"What's happening?" whispered Bodkin with round wondering eyes.

"Whatt'sssss going on…" whispered the sprites, gripping tight to their pin-sharp needles of wands. Their hair shot out electrically. The room bristled once again with Magic.

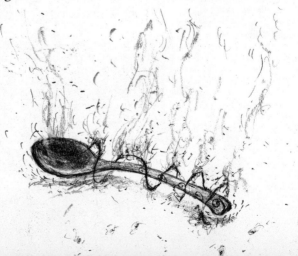

The strangely colored little flakes of Wish lifted themselves up from the floor, a great cloud of little fragments that sang like birdsong as they flurried around in the air, shuffling and rearranging themselves as if they had some internal memory of exactly where in the infinitely complicated jigsaw puzzle that makes up a human being their tiny individual piece was supposed to be.

They never bumped into one another, those millions and millions of tiny, dusty, ashy pieces, flying around in a whirling flurry of animation, until they settled gradually onto the floor, forming the nose, eyes, ears, mouth, legs of Wish, like they were creating a sculpture out of thin air, building LIFE itself in front of Xar's and Bodkin's very eyes.

For a second, the perfect sculpture was still, dead, perfect but inert, the robotic outline of what once had been Wish.

But above Xar's and Bodkin's heads, the last fragments of Wish were forming themselves into the shape of a human heart, suspended in the air.

"Look!" breathed Tiffinstorm, pointing above them, and Xar caught his breath.

That's impossible… thought Xar. *I can't be seeing that… a flying heart…*

The small brown heart descended from above,

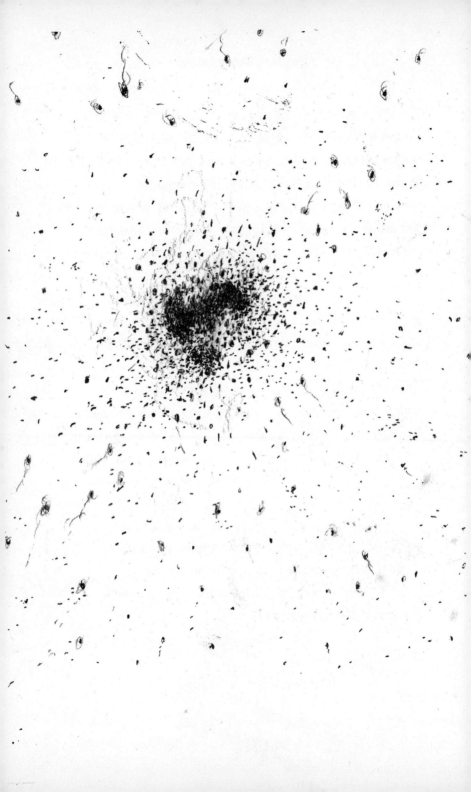

rather fast, in a hurry, and plunged softly through the chest of Wish lying on the floor…

And Wish sat straight up like a wooden automaton and took a huge gulp of air, gasped it, like she was drinking in life itself, and went from death to life in a shaking, spluttering, ugly-with-spittle-and-phlegm moment.

"What…what happened?"

"SHE'S ALIVE!!!"

23. When the Adventure Is Over the Problems Begin

SHE'S ALIVE! SHE'S ALIVE! SHE'S ALIVE!"
Around the room they danced now,
with even greater jubilation than before,
the Enchanted Spoon doing mad
pirouetting circles.

"Oh my feathers and beak and tail..." breathed
Caliburn. "Thank goodness for that. For one horrible
moment I thought it was all going to go dreadfully
wrong, and fate and the universe had given us the worst
bad hair day of all...but she's alive!"

Wish staggered to her feet, in the clouds of dust.

"I'm fine," said Wish shakily. "I'm fine..."

With her hair up in all directions, in an enormous
electric ruff, she looked like a piratical sea urchin.

"Quick! Put your eyepatch back on!" said Bodkin,
bending down, picking up the eyepatch from the dusty
floor, and hurriedly handing it to her, for the uncovered
Magic Eye was making the walls shake again.

As soon as Wish put the eyepatch back on, the
floor stopped heaving, the walls straightened.

"What...happened...there?" asked Wish, finding it
difficult to keep her balance.

"It was incredible!" shouted Xar.

Unbelievable.

Impossible.

Inconceivable.

"What we have just witnessed," said Caliburn in impressive tones, "is one of the most extraordinary sights in the entire universe: that of a Great Enchanter regenerating themselves."

"What on earth are you talking about?" Wish blinked.

"You're alive," shouted Bodkin. "You died, but you're a Great Enchanter, so you have more than one life…"

What happened?

"That's the stupidest thing I've ever heard," said Wish. "I wasn't DEAD…I just fell over for a second there."

"You were in PIECES!" said Xar joyfully. "Tiny, little pieces all over the room…and then you came back together again! It was the most amazing thing I've ever seen!"

"Nonsense," said Wish, a little more uncertainly, for what with one thing and another, she was feeling a little untogether, as *you* would be, if you had just been taken apart and put back together again rather rapidly.

"That's impossible…What are you saying? You're saying that I can die and come back to life?" said Wish.

"Yes, but there's a catch," said Caliburn. "Even Great Enchanters are made of flesh and blood, and that wears out after a while. So you have to be careful of your lives, Wish. For you do not know how many you will have."

"Okay…" said Wish, finding all this a little difficult to take in. "And what about my eye?"

"It must be a Magic Eye," said Caliburn. "Extremely rare. Very powerful. I've only ever seen that twice before, in all my lifetimes. And never that color. That must be the color of Magic-that-works-on-iron."

"Hang on a second," said Xar crossly. "The person

The spelling Book

The Magic Eye

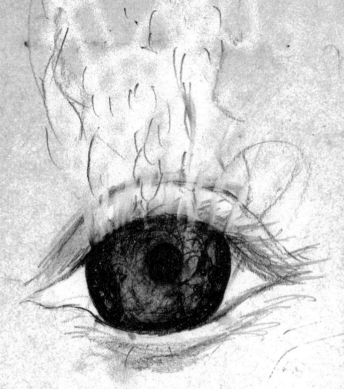

Very, very rarely, a Wizard is born with a Magic
Eye. This is a very powerful Magic that can be
difficult to control. It is often associated with
Enchanters who have more than one life.

PagE 5, 3 2 1, 9 4 2

who has Magic-that-works-on-iron is the boy of destiny. *Wish* can't be the boy of destiny! She's a *girl*, for starters!"

"Nobody says the person of destiny has to be a boy, Xar," said Caliburn. "This isn't the Dark Ages, you know..." (Well, it *was*, actually, but nobody ever thinks they are living in the Dark Ages.)

"But I don't understand," said Wish. "I've taken my eyepatch off loads of times, and trust me, nothing like *that* has ever happened before."

"Yes, well, you've only just turned thirteen, so the Magic will only have just come in, won't it?" said Caliburn.

"So not only am I Magic," said Wish, very, very upset, "but it's a really weird kind of Magic, and it's all my fault that these Witches are waking?"

"Well, not your *fault*, exactly," said Caliburn. "However, if the Witches could get hold of the Magic-that-works-on-iron, then they might have a hope of rising once again. They know from centuries of bloody wars that without that power, they cannot defeat the Warriors. That is what they have been waiting for, all these years."

SHOOOOOOOOOOOT.

This was bad, really bad.

It's not a pleasant thought to think that the most

terrifying creatures on earth want to target YOU in particular.

Wish was feeling very conflicted about all this.

On the one hand, it was, of course, a disaster for a Warrior to suddenly discover she was Magic.

But on the other...

In the past she had always been *Wish*, a word that when spoken was accompanied by a sigh of disappointment; Sychorax's very ordinary seventh daughter, a little bit clumsy and a little bit blind, who was trying and failing to be a Warrior like her stepsisters. But now she had discovered she was **WISH**, quite a different sort of word, a word that was another name for Magic itself, and this new **WISH** was an individual of some considerable specialness, who might look ordinary on the outside, but on the inside had a glorious (if rather dangerous) secret.

"We can think about all this stuff later. In the meantime, it's all worked out!" said Xar joyously. "We've saved Squeezjoos! Wish is alive! We killed the Kingwitch! I've broken that horrible stone and made amends! Everything ends happily! I knew it would all turn out right in the end."

He turned triumphantly to Caliburn. "You see? That wasn't so hard, was it?"

"Oh, Xar..." said Caliburn, shaking his head.

"You're going to be the death of me. These adventures of yours are very, very bad for my heart."

Bodkin stared at them all in awe. In the last five minutes, he had rocketed so violently from terror to despair to rapturous joy that he felt as if a Great Gray ogre had been rattling him in a bucket.

"You mean," he whispered in awe, "you have experiences like this *on a regular basis?*"

"All the time," sighed Caliburn. "This was a particularly bad one, admittedly..."

Bodkin looked around the devastated room.

Sychorax's precious chamber of Magic-removal was ruined, the floor a mess of rubble, the stone exploded, the door blown off its hinges, the scrape of a Witch's talons on the door frame.

An ancient peril, the Witches, dead for hundreds of years, woken up and come out into the world once more...

"What do you mean, 'worked out'?" said Bodkin. "I don't call this 'worked out'! It's a mess! A total mess! The Witches are *out there,*" said Bodkin. "And it's all our fault! I should never have let the princess out of the fort...I should have told the grown-ups..."

Wish gently patted him on the shoulder. "Now, now, Bodkin. You're being too hard on yourself. It's not all our fault. The Witches were out there anyway...They were always there; we just couldn't see them. We have to look on the hopeful side. And look how much we learned from this adventure!"

Wish continued, "Warriors and Wizard fought a Kingwitch side by side, and defeated him! That has to be a good sign for the future."

They left the sword in the stone, for it would not budge, even when Wish pulled at it.

Fate didn't seem to think that either of them was ready to wield that sword.

"I don't understand," said Xar, bewildered. "We need that sword, more than ever, now that Witches have returned to the forest."

"But the sword is a bit...*wayward*, isn't it?" said Caliburn. "And we don't really understand its secrets yet. So maybe this is the right place for it, at the moment."

Caliburn might be right, for goodness knows where you could safely conceal and imprison an Enchanted Sword that seemed to have a mind of its own, and wanted to kill Witches, and could slice through floors and ceilings, and if even Queen Sychorax, who was a prison *expert*, couldn't work out a solution of how to contain it, well, the stone was probably as safe a place for it as any, for the moment.

They left a note for Sychorax by the sword in the stone. Wish wrote it, so the spelling was a little erratic.

Dere Quean Sykorax,

I have returned yor Sord. DO NOT TUCH THE BLADE, if you are ever ABle to take it out. It may be staned with witchblud. Sorry.

Best wishes,
Xar, Son-of-Encanzo,
GRAND WIZZard of forever

It wasn't hard to find the Once-Magic-People who Sychorax had imprisoned. You just had to follow the noise, and as soon as they entered their dungeon, the singing ceased, and the Once-Magics stared at them, unable to believe they were there.

The giant Crusher raised his shaggy head.

"Xar!" he roared. "You've come to save me! I knew you would!"

"Of course I have!" said Xar, conveniently forgetting that if Wish hadn't pointed it out, he wouldn't even have noticed Crusher was missing. "Because I am a leader and that is what a leader does!"

One look at that giant's kindly, innocent face

crinkling up in delight as Xar hugged his ankle made everything worthwhile for Wish.

This imprisonment of the Once-Magic-People was wrong; she could tell it was wrong.

Her mother was mistaken.

Not *wicked* like Xar said she was, of course not, but mistaken nonetheless.

"Let's get out of here!" roared Xar, punching the air.

But to Xar's surprise, the Once-Magic-People were not so keen to escape as he expected. They stood there, even the loudest of the hobs rather silent and depressed, as if the air had leaked from a balloon, and the poor sprites who had lost their ability to fly were so mortified they ran away, scuttling like mice across the prison floor.

"They're ashamed, Xar," explained Caliburn. "For what is a giant without his size? What is a sprite without her wings?"

They were like Warriors returning from battle, terribly wounded, these poor people, and they no longer knew how they would fit into the world of the Magic.

But Xar coaxed them out.

He jumped up onto a rock in the center of the dungeon.

"Don't be embarrassed, everybody!" cried Xar. "I

am Xar, boy of destiny, and at present it seems, because of some weird divine oversight that I don't understand, even *I* have no Magic yet! I have come to rescue you, and I will take you back to my father, Encanzo, the Greatest Enchanter who has ever lived, and I am sure he will be able to restore your Magic."

"I don't think you should be promising them that, Xar," said Caliburn. "I'm not sure that's possible..."

But the promise offered hope to these people. The thought of Magic being returned to them brought a shine even to the dullest and most crestfallen boggit or will-o'-the-wisp's eye.

Crusher the giant scooped up the little sprites who could no longer fly and kindly offered them a lift in his pockets, or they perched like little nits in his hair, and the gradually-growing-larger party galloped and sprang and ran through the corridors, back to the chamber of Magic-removal, because that was where they could pick up the path to the secret exit.

At the chamber of Magic-removal, the little party stopped.

"This is where we part," said Bodkin.

"Come with us, Wish," said Xar. "Come back to our camp. You can be Magic there..."

Xar and Wish had met in a crossing of paths and stars in the forest only twenty-four hours earlier.

Here, deep in the underground prison, was another crossing of the ways, and Wish had to decide which way to go.

One way, the sprite-dust trail of light led back through the dungeon maze and up to Sychorax's hill-fort.

The other way, a tall dark corridor led toward the secret exit and out into the forest, and that was where Xar and the Magic creatures were going.

It was extremely tempting to take *that* path, for it seemed like the path of excitement and wildness and Magic and snowcats.

But...

"I can't leave home," said Wish. "I'm only thirteen. *This* is my home...and my mother isn't as bad as you think she is."

"Your mother is a very dangerous person!" said Xar.

Even though Bodkin wanted Wish to come back up to the fort with him, in all honesty, he had to agree with Xar. "Remember those heads in that chamber, those Spelling Books piled high in the cells...Sychorax is trying to be a sorceress, Wish."

"Murmuring mistletoe, do you think that's true?" Wish gasped. "But how can she, when she's the one who always goes on about how bad Magic is, and how we should fight against it?"

Yes, Sychorax had plenty of secrets, and Wish had learned rather more about her mother than she wanted to know.

"But she's trying to do the right thing, I know she is, and my mother deserves a second chance," said Wish stubbornly. "We *all* deserve a second chance, don't we?"

"Wish is right; she should stay here," said Caliburn, thinking not so much of giving Sychorax a second chance, but of the many evil people, Wizards and worse, who might like to get their hands on Magic-that-works-on-iron. "Wish's Magic is so powerful it will be better off for the moment in the protection of Warrior fort. In fact, now that I come to think of it, the Warriors have to keep Xar's Spelling Book, just in case."

"Oh that's so kind of you, Caliburn," said Wish. "But I won't be needing it." She gave a little shiver. "I'm not going to be doing any more Magic for the moment, not till I can convince everyone in the Warrior tribe that Magic isn't as bad as they think it is."

"No," whispered Bodkin urgently, even though he was absolutely longing to look again at the pictures, at the stories, the recipes, the spells, the whole wonderful world of Magic in that book, which Caliburn had now taken from Xar's pocket.

"No, Wish shouldn't have Magic things anymore...Look at all the trouble that beastly spoon

and the Enchanted Sword has got us into! Wish is a
Warrior princess, and she needs to give all this Magic
stuff up..."

Caliburn gave him an affectionate look. "Ah...
Magic can be concealed...Magic can be hidden, but
giving Magic up...that is very hard indeed. Look what just
happened here in this fort!

"However, the kind of Magic *Wish* has," admitted
Caliburn, "is so dangerous and so special, that it is
probably better for you to conceal it. Nobody must
ever find out, or Wish will be in terrible danger. There
is a lot to be said for the nice, quiet, ordinary life of a
Warrior princess. She is very lucky to have *you*, Bodkin,
as her guardian angel."

Bodkin blushed. "I don't know what you're talking about. What is an angel? Is it something like a sprite?"

"A little," said Caliburn. "Remember, I cannot stress this more strongly, *no one must ever find out about this.* That's why you need this book. There are many, many useful chapters in there about concealing and hiding your Magic from others…and if, by some unlucky chance, dangerous people start going after you, people with wicked hearts and deep spells and strong Magic of their own, why, then this book may save your life."

Wish took the book from the bird. It was in a terrible state, burned and stained, with pages dropping out like confetti.

"You can write in it too," said Caliburn. "Write your own story, and that always helps if you're trying to keep a secret. Take a feather from my back—there's one that's about to fall out—and keep it with you all the time."

Wish drew the falling-out feather from Caliburn's back and placed it carefully inside the Spelling Book, and put the book in a pocket in her cloak.

"Good-bye, Squeezjoos," said Wish as the sprite hovered crossly in front of her. "I hope you get well soon…and you fly just as well as you ever did…"

"I don't know why you's don't want to come back to Wizard camp with usssss…but I don't care…" grumped

Squeezjoos, crossly tweaking Wish's hair and pinching her nose and giving her little bites like stinging nettles. "You's have a face like a warthog...and you are stinkier than a cow pie..."

"Oh, you're cursing me, that's wonderful, Squeezjoos! You must be feeling better!" said Wish delightedly.

Squeezjoos looked dolefully into her eyes. "But why are you staying? *Come with us*...Don't make me SAD..."

"I'm so sorry, Squeezjoos..."

"Never mind..." hissed Ariel, his eyes spitting with malice. "We'll miss you but we'll get over it, won't we, Mustardthought? They can stay here in their lumping great fort of dullness FOREVER."

Ariel waved his thorny arms and spat out a few words that sounded like "XPCTELRBURTIBUT" and "CCRVMLBCXTT." They did not sound friendly.

"Good-bye, Xar," said Wish.

"Good-bye," said Xar, whistling carelessly, his hands in his pockets, for he did not want anyone to think he was upset.

And then they parted ways.

Xar and his Magic creatures ran and flew down the corridor, the sprites trailing beautiful little snakes of light that spelled words like "good-bye" and "don't come back" and "beware" and "good riddance." Wish and Bodkin watched them until they vanished into the darkness, singing songs that were eventually too far away to hear.

And then, sadly, Wish and Bodkin went in the other direction, up to where the guard was still sleeping at the dungeon entrance, and then back through the fort they tiptoed, carefully avoiding the sentries.

Meanwhile, Xar and his Once-Magic-People took every second left-hand turn till they got to Queen Sychorax's secret exit, an enormous door, which must have been constructed by the quick clever hands of hob-elves, for it was not only huge but also slanting inward from the slope of the hillside outside.

It was a wonder, really, that it could be a secret,

for the door was large enough for a giant to get in and out, if they merely bent their head a little.

Once they got there, it was far easier to break *out* of the fort than it had been to break *in*.

Xar did an impression of Queen Sychorax, shouting, "OPEN UP, AND BE QUICK ABOUT IT! The password is 'CONTROL'!"

And CRREEEAAAKKKKKKK!

A guard standing on the other side opened the door, which was wood on one side and turfed like grass on the other, and they all trooped out. Xar was wearing that very distinctive red royal cloak, so the guard assumed that what looked like Queen Sychorax on the *outside* was Queen Sychorax on the *inside* as well.

The guard did not seem surprised to see his queen going out of the fort in the company of a giant and a whole load of Once-Magic-People. He merely sent a hand signal up to the sentries at the battlements to let them know not to shoot.

"Nobody run…" whispered Xar, for he could feel the snowcats quivering by his side. "We mustn't look frightened—if we look scared and start running away, then they'll suspect something is wrong."

All the sentries saw was someone wearing Sychorax's red cloak in the middle of the party, as the soft tread of the snowcats made paw prints in the snow, and Xar and his Magic creatures strolled quietly away from the fort and into the forest, the sprites blinking out like snuffed candles as soon as they hit the sky.

Xar only relaxed once he and the snowcats had reached the safety of the cover of the trees. He looked back at the fort. The door had been shut, and no one would guess there was a door there, unless they knew it already.

And the little antlike figures of the sentries on the battlements did not look even remotely alarmed or agitated.

It was almost as if Queen Sychorax made a *habit* of surreptitiously coming in and out of that secret entrance, with all sorts of strange Magic people and things, without the citizens of the fort knowing anything about it.

Despite the fact that Magic was very strictly banned, by order of herself.

Ah, she was an interesting woman, that Queen Sychorax.

But tricky.

Ve-ry tricky.

24. What They Didn't See

I t wasn't only Xar and the Magic creatures who escaped into the midnight of the forest.

As soon as Xar and Wish and Bodkin had left the chamber of Magic-removal, there was silence for a second.

And then a strange wind crept up inside the room, although it is impossible for a wind to blow inside.

The black feathers and the dusty fragments of the Kingwitch lying all around began to blow about restlessly.

For you see, every light has its dark.

Day only exists with night.

Wish died and came back to life, did she not? For it turned out she was a Great Enchanter, and Great Enchanters have more than one life.

But there was more than one Great Enchanter in the room.

If Wish could come alive again...

So too could the Kingwitch.

Slowly, slowly, slowly, the millions and millions of Kingwitch fragments rose up into the air, making a strange, sweet humming noise, and the tiny individual bits whizzed around at tremendous speed, like a swarm of bees, shuffling and reshuffling themselves, just like they had with Wish, as if they had some internal memory of where they were supposed to be...

And a strange singing filled the room, sweet and evil all at the same time.

How many times this Witch's life...?
How many times must it be killed...?
How many lives must yet be left...?
Risk it all...
Risk it all...
Risk it all...

Not even a Great Enchanter knows exactly how many lives they have, so it is always chancy to risk one, in case that was the last one you had.

But it appeared that the Kingwitch had one more life left to him, at least.

Up, up, and up the feathers and fragments rose, and as they rose, they joined back together again in the dark and dangerous form of the Kingwitch.

One of his wings was fractured and hanging limply, but he was very much alive.

"...semitemoS uoy evah ot esol a elttab ni redro ot niw eht raw..." croaked the Kingwitch.

Which means: "Sometimes you have to lose a battle in order to win the war..."

The Witch gave an unintelligible shriek, and then he made himself invisible again, melting into the air like smoke.

He flew back through the broken doorway.

He was weak, so weak, after the fight, and the being-trapped-in-a-stone-for-centuries, and the wounding from the Witch-killing sword. He needed to get away, to rest, before he could attack again. So he lurked, like an invisible bat, flying above everyone's heads as Xar and his Magic creatures ran along the corridors. When they escaped through Sychorax's secret door, the invisible Witch escaped too.

And out into the world the Kingwitch flew, slowly turning visible as he reached the trees.

25. Mother and Daughter

odkin and Wish parted ways at the door of Wish's house, in the middle of the fort. (Wish lived in a house all on her own, for princesses were so grand they had houses all to themselves, which was a little lonely but showed their status.)

Bodkin was feeling surprisingly gloomy, for now that it was all over, he was a hero no more, just an ordinary Assistant Bodyguard. It had been one stolen day, one glorious twenty-four hours, where he could ride and fight beside a princess, just as if he were her equal, and a proper Warrior himself.

"Now," Bodkin said to Wish, trying to sound more cheerful than he felt, "we can all get back to normal, Princess. You give me the spoon, and I'll take him back to the kitchen, where he can return to life being an ordinary dinner spoon...It's time to give up Magic things, just like you promised me..."

"Ye-e-es," said Wish thoughtfully. "But then I HAVE still got the Spelling Book, haven't I? Maybe I'll give up the spoon *tomorrow*..."

"All right, then," agreed Bodkin. "You promise you will tomorrow?"

"I promise," said Wish.

"Good night, Wish," said Bodkin. "Good night, spoon."

"Good night," said Wish, shyly shaking Bodkin's hand.

"Um, Princess," said Bodkin, for something had been bothering him, "that—fainting thing that happened a little bit tonight...you don't think that's going to be a problem, do you, with my future in bodyguarding?"

"Is there any other profession you would be interested in?" asked Wish tactfully.

"Well, yes, as it happens, I've always wanted to be a Fool, and I'm quite good at the whole storytelling thing, and—*but that's not the point!*" said Bodkin. "The point is, all of my family have been bodyguards, so I have to be one—and am I going to be any good at it, with the slight fainting issue?"

"I'm sure you'll grow out of that," said Wish. "*Tomorrow*, maybe...but in the meantime, look what brilliant bodyguarding you just did! You are a hero, and a very good friend."

"I am not a hero; I am an Assistant Bodyguard," said Bodkin, very relieved, "and that is what an Assistant Bodyguard is *for*. To assist."

But he didn't deny that he was the princess's friend.

And then they both went to bed.

The princess to her royal bed of goose-down feathers.

The Assistant Bodyguard to his bed of straw underneath the kitchen table.

They both slept soundly, for it had been a tiring night, what with one thing and another.

But everything cannot be the same as it always was, of course.

Once an Assistant Bodyguard has been on an adventure like that one, he is changed forever.

Like the Enchanted Spoon, he had been burned at the edges by Witch's fire and scorched by the breath of sprites. He had opened his eyes in Wizard camp, he had listened to the speech of ravens, and they had made him see things from their point of view.

I may have said this before, but...

This can be the problem with adventures, which is why Bodkin's father was so very, very against them.

Meanwhile, Sychorax had a long, long night, all alone in that darkness, and she had plenty of time for thinking.

Who knows? She may have even learned a lesson or two.

That is, after all, what a dungeon is *for*.

And when, eventually, the guard woke up and unlocked the prison cell where she was trapped, Queen Sychorax ran out the door and straight to the chamber of Magic-removal, for she had heard the commotion of the night before, and she had imagined all sorts of terrible possibilities about what might be happening.

She saw the stone, the sword; she read the note, and that chilly queen turned colder still.

Queen Sychorax was no fool. The note said it was from Xar, but the handwriting on the note—the spelling—made the queen immediately think of Wish.

She ran (not even gliding this time) to the platform, up to the surface, through the streets of the hill-fort, passing the staring eyes of her citizens, her beautiful golden hair an absolute bird's nest shock of electric horror that would take her a week to brush out (and she was lucky to be able to brush it out at all—sometimes sprites can mess up your hair with such intricate Magic that the only solution is to cut it off entirely).

She ran straight to the house where Wish lived. Queen Sychorax did not often go there, for queens are very busy, and they do not always have time to visit their children, like normal people.

Bursting into Wish's room, Sychorax found her daughter fast asleep, snoring on the bed, and the queen let out a sigh of relief.

Relief quickly turned to anger, as so often it will.

She gave her daughter a gentle shake to wake her up.

Wish opened a sleepy eye and was instantly, electrically awake when she saw her mother standing over her like an enraged iceberg.

Oh dear.

"Good morning, Mother," gulped Wish warily.

"The Wizard boy has gone," said Queen Sychorax in a white-cold fury, taking in the scratches on Wish's face, the wildness of Wish's hair, which like Queen Sychorax's own hair was still whipped up into a frenzy of tangles by the sprites using it as a nest. "Escaping with all the other Magic creatures. Chaos! Disorder! Anarchy! The Stone-That-Takes-Away-Magic is broken!

"And I've lost the sword, as well!" stormed Sychorax. "It's trapped in the stone, at a time when it is needed most, when Witches have returned to the forest. It's an all-around disaster.

"*Someone* must have stolen my key... *Someone* must have helped that wretched Wizard boy escape...

Someone must have taken him the sword—the *Someone* who has done this is a TRAITOR to their mother, their family, their entire tribe of Warriors..."

Wish avoided her mother's angry gaze and looked thoughtfully into the distance.

"I just had this very strange dream," said Wish. "I dreamed there was a Witch inside the Stone-That-Takes-Away-Magic who called himself the Kingwitch."

Sychorax started in astonishment.

Her anger evaporated and turned to uneasy alarm.

"A Kingwitch *inside the stone*?" gasped the queen. "What nonsense are you talking? Impossible...surely that's impossible..."

But...

If Witches were not extinct, that meant the legends about the Kingwitch might be correct as well. In all the old fairy tales, the Kingwitch was the leader of Witches, the mastermind who controlled them all.

"In my dream, the Kingwitch had been inside the stone for a very long time indeed. Who knows? Maybe someone long ago imprisoned him in there, to make the world a safer place," said Wish.

"The fairy stories about the stone always say not to touch it, don't they? But the meaning of WHY we are not supposed to touch it has been lost. Centuries and centuries, that Kingwitch must have been willing people to come to the stone so he could take away their Magic and break out of the stone. And he will have been working his will on you too, Mother, on me, on Xar, on all of us.

"In my dream, the Kingwitch broke out of the stone."

"Nooooo..." whispered Sychorax, with fierce, bright eyes.

But she was thinking, hard.

Wish could sense her mother weakening, so she carried on, speaking thoughtfully and innocently, looking dreamily into the distance.

"Another odd thing in the dream," continued Wish, "was that in the dungeons below us, there was this room full of *heads*. But they weren't just any old heads. They were heads that I recognized, of people who came to court and argued on your behalf, Mother, or said nice things about you when you were away...

"I'm not sure we would want the citizens of Warrior fort to know about those heads, Mother," said Wish.

"Dreams are odd things," said Sychorax, staring at her daughter very, very closely indeed.

Mother and daughter looked at each other, their faces identical masks.

Behind both those masks they were thinking: *What do you know?*

For the first time,
mother and daughter
looked surprisingly alike.

For the first time they looked surprisingly alike: hair in ridiculous upward waterfalls, faces carefully arranged to give nothing away, wary eyes.

"It's complicated," said Queen Sychorax at last.

"Yes, it is," said Wish.

She put out her hand and closed it over Queen Sychorax's icy one. "It must be difficult being a queen," said Wish.

Queen Sychorax returned the pressure.

"Yes, it is," said Queen Sychorax.

"What happened to the Witch-Inside-The-Stone? Where is it now?" asked Queen Sychorax.

"We killed it with the sword," said Wish. "In the dream, of course."

"Hmmmmmmmmmmmmmmmm," said Queen Sychorax. "You were lucky to survive."

She touched her daughter's face, with the scratches on it.

Queen Sychorax looked down at Wish, and for one split second her mask dropped and there was no disappointment in her eyes, but a wary respect, suspicion, and fear.

Queen Sychorax would never underestimate her daughter again.

Her frosty cliff of a face melted into a glint of a smile, like the sun appearing through clouds over a glacier.

"Well done, Wish," said Queen Sychorax. "That must have been a very frightening dream, a nightmare, in fact, and it sounds like you have dealt with it in a very...Warrior-like fashion."

Wish was so relieved she beamed right back at her.

My mother smiled at me!

Queen Sychorax's smile disappeared, and she was her brisk, composed self once more.

She adjusted Wish's eyepatch, which had gone a little askew.

"I may have made a mistake about that stone," admitted Queen Sychorax. "Even queens make mistakes sometimes. So in these *very special* circumstances, I am prepared to overlook whatever happened this past night."

Queen Sychorax's voice turned diamond-hard. "But in the future, you do need to do as I tell you. I want you to have no contact with anything Magic whatsoever, no Wizards, no Magic creatures, not even the smallest Itch-sprite. Do you understand me, Wish?"

"Yes, Mother," said Wish.

"And if you see that wretched, tricksome Xar, son of Encanzo," said the queen, "you must tell me at once, you hear me?"

"Yes, Mother," said Wish.

My mother SMILED at me!

But underneath the blankets, I am afraid to say, I happen to know that Wish was crossing her fingers.

"From now on, Wish, you must work hard at being a normal Warrior princess. You can start by keeping this eyepatch on at all times, nice and straight. Remember," said Queen Sychorax sternly as she got to her feet. "We are Warriors."

She held up her finger. "And a Warrior should always be well put together," said Queen Sychorax. "Every hair in place. Every weapon sharpened. Every fingernail shining. Remember that."

And then she swept out Wish's front door, where a crowd had gathered, watching in staggered silence as Sychorax—her long white gown raked ragged, her hair a fright—swept through the courtyard, with as much dignity and gravitas as if she were at her own coronation. Guards scurried up to her to offer them her cloaks, and in one superb gesture she waved them away.

Every inch a queen.

Someone started applauding nervously—they weren't quite sure why—and the other Warriors joined in, even though they did not know what they were clapping for. What had happened? Who had dared attack her? *What on earth, for the green gods' sake, was going on with that hair?*

And then she turned, at the entrance to her own quarters.

The crowd grew silent.

They leaned in to hear what she would say, expecting her to tell them the story of exactly what had happened, down there in her dungeons.

"I never," said Queen Sychorax in her quiet, mild voice, "want anyone to mention this EVER again."

And they didn't.

26. Father and Son

Meanwhile, Encanzo the Enchanter was pacing the main hall, distraught with fear, for although he had sent out search party after search party looking for Xar, the boy had not yet been found.

The day before, when Encanzo the Enchanter and his Wizards burst into Xar's room, they found it empty, and a great hole in the middle of it.

And as Encanzo knelt down by the side of the hole and saw the dead Witch lying at the bottom, and his son vanished, well...

"*What have I done?*" the Enchanter asked himself, imagining, for one terrible moment, that the Witch might have killed his son, before realizing to his infinite relief that, *no*, quite incredibly, it was the other way around.

Looter peered over his father's shoulder and turned a little white. "What is that, Father?"

"That," said Encanzo grimly, "was a Witch."

By mistletoe and leafmold and the ginger sideburns of the Great Grim ogre.

Witches weren't extinct after all!

And the proof was right there, in the middle of Xar's bedroom.

It took a while for the Wizards, crowding into the wrecked ruins of this room, to take all this in.

"You see!" said Ranter triumphantly, for even when something really dreadful has happened, there is always a satisfaction in being right all along. "I told you that the boy would do something truly appalling in time! And he has! Witches are not extinct, and after hundreds of years of peace, Xar has brought a Witch right here into Wizard camp!"

It *was* somehow typical that it would be Xar who found one.

"How could Xar have killed this Witch?" asked the Enchanter with a sort of reluctant admiration. "Witches are virtually impossible to kill..."

"Well," admitted Looter slowly, "he did cheat in that Spelling Competition by bringing in this whopping great big iron sword thing-y that he said he had stolen from the Warriors..."

"Was it a sword of power?" gasped the Enchanter.

"It looked pretty ancient," said Looter. "And I think he did mention something about it being a Witch-killing sword...but you know what Xar's like: He lies his head off all the time."

"*Why didn't you tell me about that?*" raged the Enchanter, turning on Looter, as the lightning of his fury crackled around the devastation of Xar's room.

So now, a little over twenty-four hours later, the Enchanter was pacing, up, down, up, down, hoping against all hope that Xar might yet be found.

Looter was not particularly enjoying how distressed everybody seemed to be at the loss of Xar. Even Ranter was sighing and saying things like: "He was a good boy, really…lively, of course, mischievous…but he meant well…"

"This is all Xar's fault," said Looter sulkily. "He brought the Witch here. It serves him right."

But the Enchanter was blaming himself.

What did the boy say to me, just before I banished him to his room? thought Encanzo.

"YOU DON'T CARE ABOUT *ME*! ALL YOU WANT IS A SON WHO IS *MAGIC*!!"

Encanzo wanted to be able to tell his son that was not true.

But it was too late.

His son was not there.

Encanzo had been up all night, in the form of a peregrine falcon, and had flown low over the treetops, mile after weary mile, searching for his son. But Xar was an expert at covering his tracks, so even the bright red eyes of the falcon, peering deep down into the leafy blackness, could spot no sign of the boy, however hard they looked.

Encanzo had consulted his star maps so scorchingly long that his eye beams burned holes in them, but Xar was hidden in a fort of iron, so peer how the Enchanter might, there was no sign of the boy there either.

It was as if he had vanished off the face of the earth.

And then the Enchanter began to think the unthinkable.

Nobody knew much about Witches.

What if, just before it died, the Witch had dispatched the boy and made Xar's corpse disappear, in some manner unknown to Encanzo?

The Enchanter had sent Xar to his room to teach him a lesson.

But as so often seems to happen, the lesson being taught was to the Enchanter *himself*.

I WISH I had not shouted at the boy! I WISH I had listened to him, not threatened to expel him! I WISH he may not have died without knowing that I love him! thought Encanzo the Great Enchanter.

But even a *very* Great Enchanter cannot turn back time.

There was a shout at the doorway.

The pacing Enchanter turned eagerly.

It was him! It was Xar!

There he was, climbing off Nighteye, his snowcat, looking a little guilty, a little unsure of his reception, but still as cheeky and irrepressible and full of himself as ever.

Maybe even more so.

All-powerful Enchanters are, at heart, still parents like the rest of us.

Encanzo the Great Enchanter ran to his son on trembling legs, and with pathetic eagerness and relief, he scooped Xar up into his arms.

"XAR! YOU'RE ALIVE! AND YOU'VE COME HOME!" cried Encanzo the Great Enchanter.

"I have," said Xar, grinning with surprise from ear to ear, for he had been expecting expulsion at the worst and at the best a few awkward questions, which was what normally happened when he made it back from an adventure. "Er...sorry about the dead Witch, Father...and my room...and I've lost my Spelling Book again...but look!"

Xar beckoned to the giants, the Wizards, the dwarves, and sprites who he had rescued from Sychorax's dungeons to come forward.

The crowd gathered in Wizard camp gasped as they recognized family members, friends, and colleagues who they thought they would never see again.

They rushed to embrace their lost relatives with cries of joy.

Even
All-powerful Enchanters are
still parents, like the rest of us...

"I wanted to make amends," said Xar proudly. "I tried to take Magic from a Witch, and I stole a sword that brought the Witch to us, so I returned the sword to Sychorax's dungeons, and while I was there, I realized she was keeping our people prisoners, so I rescued them."

Well, for astonishingly mad but brave acts like that one, they would all be prepared to forgive Xar even if he had led TROOPS of Witches into the camp. (As long as he killed them all, of course.)

Encanzo was very rarely pleased with his son.

But here was his son doing something right for a change!

The most important "right thing" of all being:

He had returned home ALIVE.

For the first time, Encanzo the King Enchanter shook his son by the hand as if he were an equal.

Xar thought he had never been so happy in his life.

To see his father looking at *him*, Xar, with such pride, such love, such admiration.

To see everyone else in the camp cheering and applauding him.

The Enchanter turned to the crowd.

"Perhaps there needs to be room in the Wizard world for those who have no Magic!" cried the

Enchanter. "For look! These brave Wizards, giants, and sprites are returning to us with their Magic removed. We need to find a place for these people, do we not, in our society?"

And the crowd cried back, "We do, we do!"

"I would like to propose three cheers for my son Xar!" said the Enchanter. "Who braved the terrors of Sychorax's dungeons to bring these old friends back to us, at great danger to himself and his sprites and animals."

"Xar! Xar! Xar!" cheered the Wizards.

"Why is Xar *SO ANNOYING*?" raged Looter, clenching his fist.

"My son has returned to me, and he returns a better person. Xar has learned a lesson," smiled the Enchanter, "that it is far, far wiser to wait for your Magic to come in, than to try to obtain it from a dark source..."

He turned to his son.

"And Xar has taught ME a lesson too. It is far, far better to have a son who has no Magic than to have no son at all...

"Welcome home, Xar."

The Enchanter hugged his son.

And then the Enchanter turned once more to the cheering crowd.

"So I declare this a day of thanks and celebrations... Let's see, what shall we call it?" said the Enchanter, and, if he hadn't been such a very Great Enchanter, that might have been a twinkle in the grim gray of his eye. "We shall call it...the CELEBRATION OF XAR NOT COMING INTO HIS MAGIC! *Let the festivities begin!*"

Now, Wizards never need much excuse to have a party.

The hall went mad, with fiddles magically playing themselves, the zigzagging glow of sprites zooming everywhere, and Wizards and snowcats and giants and dwarves and animals of all shapes and sizes dancing and singing and howling to the dark winter sky.

"Are we free now, Master?" Ariel asked, flying up to the Enchanter, wanting to get him while he was in a rare good mood. "Don't forget that you promisssed us, Caliburn and me...our freedom when the boy grows up and no longer needs us...We are spirits too brave for a boy like Xar..."

"I haven't forgotten," snapped the Enchanter, his benevolence disappearing, "but let's face it, Xar will need you for a little while longer. I will not release you and Caliburn until the boy grows up into a wise and thoughtful adult."

"That may never happen," said the raven.

"In which case you will never be free," said the Enchanter grimly. "And by the way—Caliburn?"

"Er…yes, Enchanter?" said Caliburn, starting guiltily.

"At some point I will want a full report of exactly what went on over the last twenty-four hours. Now is the time for celebration, but later you must tell me the whole truth, and nothing but the truth, Caliburn."

And off the Enchanter swept, with a rather unnerving thunderclap sweep of his cloak, to join in the merrymaking.

"I'd rather you didn't tell him the WHOLE truth." Xar grinned.

"Ye-e-e-es," said Caliburn. "I think I might leave out the bit about the sword being iron and Magic mixed together. And the sprite being poisoned. And the Witch-Inside-The-Stone. And Wish being the girl of destiny—in fact, now that I come to think of it, there's not a great deal of the story I can tell, is there?"

"Definitely don't tell him THIS, then," said Xar, a mischievous glint in his eye as he opened up his hand.

There, right in the center of the palm, was the very faint pale green mark of a washed-out Witch-stain.

Caliburn gave a squawk of absolute horror. "The Witch-stain! What happened? I thought you'd gotten rid of it!"

"So did I," grinned Xar, closing his fist around it again. "But I must have come off the stone too quickly. And you know the best thing about it?"

Now Xar could not repress his excitement. *"I think it's beginning to work!"*

"But...but...but...Xar!" gabbled poor Caliburn. "It's bad Magic! From a dark source! We've just GONE through all this and I thought you'd learned your lesson and returned a better person, just like your father said! What has the whole moral of this entire adventure all been about?"

I will not release you
until Xar becomes a wise
and thoughtful adult

But Xar had already hurried off, worried he was going to miss some of the Xar-Not-Coming-Into-His-Magic-Celebrations.

The sprites joined enthusiastically into the festivities and were zooming around, getting into their usual mischief, such as:

Tiffinstorm had a wonderful time aiming spells at people's food, so that when they picked it up, it was something yummy like a nice slice of apple pie, but by the time it reached their mouths, it had turned into something disgusting, like a giant slug.

Squeezjoos set off a stink spell (though typically he got it wrong, and instead of smelling of bad eggs, it smelled rather deliciously of lemons).

And Xar showed off to all the prettiest girls, without a care in the world...

Meanwhile, poor old Caliburn was sitting on a tree branch, worrying and trying to comfort himself.

"Maybe because the Kingwitch is dead," the bird said to himself, "the Witches will go back to sleep again. Maybe even if they wake again in our lifetime, they will not find the girl, because she will not be so silly as to venture out of the iron fort again, because *maybe* she is one of those rare humans who learn from their mistakes.

"Maybe."

Then, as is the way of worriers, having made

himself feel better about *one* worry, he immediately started to worry about something else.

"Xar wished for Magic, and he got it, and it is bad Magic indeed…and if his father ever finds out about it, then Xar will be in bigger trouble than ever…" worried Caliburn.

"And although they are happy with him NOW, it will not take them long to remember his past disobediences: give a weredog a bad name, and all that…"

The old raven cocked his head to the other side, as if to consider the alternatives.

"But then maybe Xar will learn to *control* that Magic of his before his father finds out. There is good in Xar, and this adventure has brought that out too. The *good* in Xar will control the *bad* in the blood…

"Maybe…

"*Maybe.*"

"Caliburn!" yelled Xar from below. "Stop sitting up there being all gloomy and worrying!"

Xar looked around him to check no one was looking.

And then he pointed his hand with the Witch-stain on it up at the tree branch.

Xar must have tried to perform Magic a thousand times before, and it had never worked.

But this time was different.

This time he felt this extraordinary tingling feeling, a kind of pins and needles in his entire right arm. It was as if some weird muscle that he had never felt before was stretching out and unfurling.

And to Xar's delight he could feel the Magic curving out of his fingertips.

BAM!

It exploded the tree branch that Caliburn was sitting on, and with a disgruntled shriek, the old bird fell out of the sky in a flurry of feathers and flapped protestingly in front of Xar's grinning face.

"IT WORKED!" cried Xar, looking at his hand in total delight. "EVERYTHING HAS BEEN WORTH IT! I DID GET MAGIC IN THE END AFTER ALL!"

Caliburn sighed a very, very deep sigh.

The moral of the adventure had gone all wrong somehow.

And Xar learning to be good was going to take a little *time*.

But in the meantime…

"Worry *tomorrow*, old bird!" Xar smiled. "Tonight we DANCE!"

And the Wizard boy took the raven by the wings,
and the old bird forgot to worry and he became like
a chick again as Xar whirled him around and around,
dancing with him, under the cold of the midnight stars.

Epilogue

o, that was the story of Xar and Wish, and how their stars crossed on a midnight deep, long, long ago in the ancient past.

Before the British Isles knew they were the British Isles yet, and the Magic lived in the dark forests.

And, a little like Caliburn, I am still trying to figure out the moral of it.

You have to listen to the stories, for stories always mean something.

But what worries me is...what exactly DO they mean?

It's the story of how Xar got himself some Magic, and how Wish found out she was special, and how the Kingwitch escaped from the stone.

So everyone got their wishes, but not *quite* in the way they expected.

Because—and I think I have mentioned this once or thrice before—you have to be careful what you wish for, guys.

It may come true.

Right at the beginning of this story, I said it was being told by one of the characters.

Did you guess which one?

I could be any of them, couldn't I?

371

Xar or Wish or Bodkin the Assistant Bodyguard with the dream of being a hero, Sychorax or Encanzo or one of the sprites or that dusty old bird, Caliburn, the raven-who-has-lived-many-lifetimes.

I could be any of these characters, good or bad or a mixture of both.

I am not going to tell you the answer to who I am yet.

You will have to keep on guessing.

For we have not reached the end of the story, not by a long shot.

The Kingwitch is out of the stone, like a genie out of the bottle.

He will be looking for Wish, for she has the Magic-that-works-on-iron.

And Xar has bad Magic, and we do not yet know how that will turn out.

Under Wish's pillow, the Spelling Book is sleeping. But it could wake any moment. Let us hope that Caliburn is right, and it will help her fight back against wicked people with strong Magic and evil hearts who might want to get hold of the Magic she possesses...

FOR WHERE THERE IS ONE WITCH, THERE WILL BE OTHERS...

Keep hoping.

Keep guessing.

Keep dreaming…

Signed: *The Unknown Narrator*

Once there Was Magic...

Once there was Magic
Wandering free
In roads of sky and paths of sea
And in that timeless long-gone hour
Words of nonsense still had power
Doors still flew and birds still talked
Witches grinned and giants walked
We had Magic wands and Magic wings
And we lost our hearts to impossible things
Unbelievable thoughts! Unsensible ends!
For Wizards and Warriors might be friends.

In a world where impossible things are true
I don't know why we forgot the spell
When we lost the way, how the forest fell.
But now we are old, we can vanish too.

And I see once more the invisible track
That will lead us home and take us back...
So find your wands and spread your wings
I'll sing our love of impossible things
And when you take my vanished hand
We'll both go back to that Magic land
Where we lost our hearts...
Several lifetimes ago...
When we were Wizards
Once.

ACKNOWLEDGMENTS

A whole team of people have helped
me write this book.

Thank you to my wonderful editor, Anne McNeil,
and my magnificent agent, Caroline Walsh.

A special big thanks to Jennifer Stephenson,
Polly Lyall Grant, and Rebecca Logan.

And to everyone else at Hachette Children's Group,
Hilary Murray Hill, Andrew Sharp,
Valentina Fazio, Lucy Upton, Louise Grieve,
Kelly Llewellyn, Katherine Fox, Alison Padley,
Naomi Greenwood, Rebecca Livingstone.

Thanks to all at Little, Brown,
Megan Tingley, Jackie Engel, Lisa Yoskowitz,
Kristina Pisciotta, Jessica Shoffel.

And most important of all, Maisie, Clemmie, Xanny.

And SIMON for his excellent advice
on absolutely everything.

I couldn't do it without you.

Turn the page for a sneak peek at Wish and

Xar's next action-packed adventure!

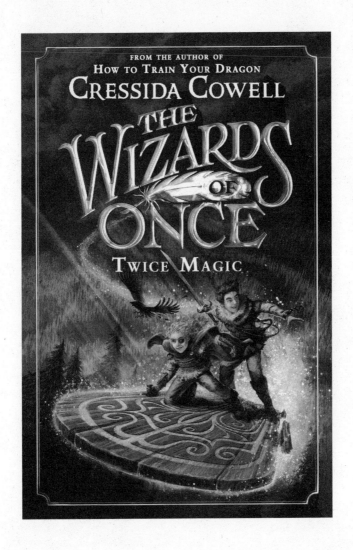

NOBODY gets out of the terrible prison of GORMINCRAG

Sea of
↙ Skulls

1. Escape from Gormincrag Is Impossible

It was a quarter past midnight, four weeks before Midwinter's End Eve, and a thirteen-year-old boy was dangling precariously from a disintegrating homemade rope hanging from outside the darkest tower of Gormincrag, the Rehabilitation Center for the Re-Education of Dark Magic and Wicked Wizards.

(That, by the way, is a long and fancy name for a jail, and not just any old jail, the most secure and impregnable jail in the wildwoods.)

The boy's name was Xar (which is pronounced "Zar"—I don't know why, spelling is weird) and he really, really, *really* should not have been there.

He was supposed to be INSIDE the prison, not OUTSIDE it, dangling fifty feet above sea level from one of the windows. That's one of the most important rules about prisons, and Xar really should have known that.

But Xar was not the kind of boy who followed the rules.

Xar *acted* first and *thought* later, and this was exactly what had led him to be put in the Gormincrag Rehabilitation Center in the first place, and given him

the reputation of being the
naughtiest, wildest boy born into
the Wizard kingdom in about
four generations.

See if you think that reputation
is justified...

In the past week, for example, Xar
had:

*Put what was supposed to be sleeping potion
into the Rogrebreath guards' wine, but it
turned out to be cursing potion instead...glued the
bottoms of the entire Drood High Command to their chairs in
the hope that it would give him time for a quick getaway—but
forgot to glue the chairs to the floor, so the Droods just ran
after him with chairs stuck to their bottoms...treated*

himself to some stolen invisibility potion, but unfortunately
it had only made his HEAD disappear, giving the Drood in
charge of Reprogramming a terrible shock because he imagined
on visiting Xar's cell that the prison had been invaded by
headless GHOSTS…

None of these disobedient things had been
intentional, exactly. They had all just happened by
accident, in the course of him trying to escape, for
even though Xar was a happy-go-lucky cheerful sort of
person, two months of imprisonment had given even *his*
high spirits a bit of a battering, and his quiff of hair had
drooped a little under the pressure, and he had
been feeling, at times, a little desperate.

Gormincrag was well known to be
impossible to escape from, but Xar never
let a little thing like impossibility put him
off. So although to an outsider his present
predicament might have looked pretty bad,
Xar was remarkably pleased with himself for
a person who was hanging on to a crumbling rope
swaying violently above seas known to be infested with
such dreadful monsters as Blunderbouths, Daggerfins,
and Bloody Barbeards.

His wide-awake eyes were bright with excitement
and hope.

"You see!" Xar whispered triumphantly to his

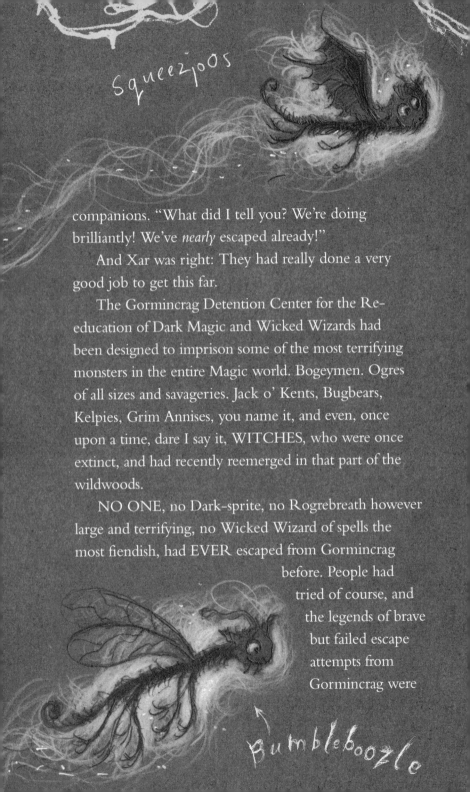

squeezjoos

companions. "What did I tell you? We're doing brilliantly! We've *nearly* escaped already!"

And Xar was right: They had really done a very good job to get this far.

The Gormincrag Detention Center for the Re-education of Dark Magic and Wicked Wizards had been designed to imprison some of the most terrifying monsters in the entire Magic world. Bogeymen. Ogres of all sizes and savageries. Jack o' Kents, Bugbears, Kelpies, Grim Annises, you name it, and even, once upon a time, dare I say it, WITCHES, who were once extinct, and had recently reemerged in that part of the wildwoods.

NO ONE, no Dark-sprite, no Rogrebreath however large and terrifying, no Wicked Wizard of spells the most fiendish, had EVER escaped from Gormincrag before. People had tried of course, and the legends of brave but failed escape attempts from Gormincrag were

Bumbleboozle

told from sprite to sprite across the years. But no one had ever successfully made it out of there alive.

Even if, by some extraordinary chance, you made it beyond the prison perimeter without the skulls screaming, the grim towers of Gormincrag were built on seven islands set in a sea called prettily "the Sea of Skulls," and the treacherous waves would get you, or those vicious merfolk, the Bloody Barbeards, would swim out of their holes in the Drowned Forest on the seafloor and get you, and bring you back.

As the son of a King Enchanter, and a boy with a great deal of personal charisma, Xar had quite a few followers.

At the moment he was accompanied by five sprites (Tiffinstorm, Timeloss, Hinkypunk, Ariel, and Mustardthought)—and these were beautiful, fierce-looking creatures, resembling a cross between a very small human and an angry insect, and three hairy fairies, (Squeezjoos, Bumbleboozle, and the baby), smaller, more beelike animals, who were too young to have climbed into their cocoons and metamorphosed into proper adult sprites yet.

The Baby

Sprites can light up like stars in the night-time, but these ones did not want to be detected at the moment, so they had subdued the light of their little bodies to the very dimmest of glows.

These sprites all belonged to Xar, and loyally, quietly, invisibly, they had sneaked in to Gormincrag to try and help him escape.

"Yous right, Master!" Squeezjoos, one of the hairy fairies, whispered back. Squeezjoos was a tiny little six-legged creature, larger than a bumblebee but still so small he could fit into your hand, and he was buzzing excitedly around Xar's head. "Yous ALWAYS right! That'ss why youss the leader and you never leads uss into any trouble! Oo! What's this fasscintressting cave?"

This "fasscintressting cave" was in fact a large skull with its mouth open. Squeezjoos buzzed in to investigate and the mouth snapped shut with an ominous clang and the eyeholes squeezed tight closed as if they still had lids on them. "Helloooo?" buzzed Squeezjoos in anxious echoes from within. "Helloooo? I think I iss stuck!" The sprites nearly fell out of the air they were laughing so much, but Xar intervened in quick alarm, hissing, "Don't go over the boundary of the battlements anybody! There's a Magic force field around this castle, and it's fine getting IN, but you can't get across it to get OUT!"

At some considerable danger to himself, because the skull was just out of reach, and he had to tie the end of the rope to his ankle and dangle upside down to get his

I can't look...

hands on it, Xar then
very, very carefully
and delicately released
the mouth bone of the
skull so that Squeezjoos
could buzz out triumphantly
squeaking, "I is fine! Don't worry
everyone! I is FINE!"

And then Xar swung
himself back onto a
safer ledge again and
explained to his interested
companions that those
skulls were the screaming
kind, and they were one
of the final defenses
of Gormincrag.

I is FINE!

If you put one finger tip beyond the perimeter of the prison, the skulls would open up their mouths and scream bloodcurdling yells, which would wake the guards of Gormincrag and bring them down upon you.

This was typical of Xar. Although he had spent his entire young life leading his followers into considerable trouble, to do him justice, he always tried his hardest to get them OUT of it, even if it put him personally in great peril.

Xar was also accompanied by a talking raven—who had his wings over his eyes, such was his horror at the whole dangling-upside-down-and-rescuing-hairy-fairies-from-screaming-skulls episode—and a seven-and-a-half-foot Loner Raving Fangmouth werewolf called Lonesome, who made anxious grunting noises when Xar mentioned the Gormincrag guards.

Xar had met Lonesome in the prison, and while it is not really advisable to make friends with Loner Raving Fangmouth werewolves, neither Xar nor the werewolf had a lot of choice in the matter. They both wanted to escape.

The werewolf gave a smothered howl of discontent.

"What is the werewolf saying?" asked the raven.

The talking raven was called Caliburn, and he would have been a handsome bird, but unfortunately it was his job to keep Xar out of trouble, and the worry and general impossibility of this hopeless mission meant his feathers kept falling out.

"I think he's saying, why are we heading in *this* direction?" said Xar.

Xar was the only one of them who had been taught werewolf language, but Xar wasn't great at concentrating in class, and the problem with werewolves is they do mumble their words, so sometimes you could mistake a grunt for a gurgle, or an *oooarrghh* for an *eerrggagh*, and completely misunderstand what they were talking about.

"We're going *this* way," explained Xar, "because we're just going to drop into the Drood Commander's Room…It's an important step in our escape…"

The werewolf gave a smothered howl of horror and waved his shaggy paws around with such alarm that he nearly fell off the rope.

"You shouldn't be escaping! And we shouldn't be helping you!" said Caliburn in a flurry of anxiety. "But surely if we *are* helping you to escape, the idea would be to do it *quietly*? Crusher and the animals are waiting for us down at the bottom of the western battlements…"

(Crusher was a Longstepper High-Walker giant, and he and the wolves, the snowcats, and the bear were also Xar's companions.)

"We should be joining Crusher and the others!"

Caliburn pointed out. "Hopping over the back of the wall, without telling anyone, not presenting ourselves to the head of the prison for a nice little chat and a cup of herbal tea!"

"Yes, well, that's why no one has ever gotten out of this armpit of a jail before," said Xar. "How many times have YOU tried to escape from here, Lonesome?"

The werewolf mumbled something that might have been "twenty-three"...

"You see?" said Xar. "Trust me, everyone! I have a plan that could just be the cunning-est, most brilliant, and daring escape plan in the entire *history* of the wildwoods..."

Xar had a lot of good qualities, but modesty wasn't one of them.

Inch by inch, the little party crept down the ropes, landed on the windowsill outside the Drood Commander's room, and peered inside.

The room might have been the shape of a star, or a circle, or a pentagon, who knew? For the walls had a habit of moving around while you were looking at them, and the floor looked like the sea, and the ceiling might have been the sky. It was enough to make you feel a little bit sick just to look at it.

The only still point in the room was a gigantic desk.

Three Wizards were sitting around the desk, talking.

One of the Wizards was the Drood Commander of Gormincrag, and Xar pointed to the spelling staff the Drood Commander was holding.

"That's the reason we're here..." whispered Xar. *"Because the Drood Commander's spelling staff controls everything in this castle."*

"Ohhh no...oh noo..." whispered Caliburn the raven, in a frenzy of alarm. "Don't tell me that your plan is to steal the Staff-That-Commands-the-Castle?"

Xar nodded. That was indeed his plan.

"It'sss brilliant! Is brilliant!" squeaked Squeezjoos, buzzing around in such an overexcited fashion that he was very nearly sick.

"Sssshhhhhhhh..." everyone else whispered back.

The werewolf gave a small grunt that might have been approval. It was quite a good plan actually. At least, it was something the werewolf had never tried before.

But as Xar peered into the room, the shaggy weight of the werewolf's fur on his shoulder, he started so violently he nearly fell off the windowsill.

For he suddenly recognized the other Wizards who were talking to the Drood Commander of Gormincrag.

Debra Hurford Brown

Cressida Cowell is the #1 internationally bestselling author and illustrator of *The Wizards of Once* and the How to Train Your Dragon series. She grew up in London and on a small, uninhabited island off the west coast of Scotland, where she spent her time writing stories, fishing for things to eat, and exploring the island. She now lives in Hammersmith, England, with her husband, three children, and a dog named Pigeon.

Find out more about
the wonderful world of

CRESSIDA COWELL

www.cressidacowell.com

Where you can find out all about
her books, events, games…
and lots more!